Mrs. Odboddy
Undercover Courier

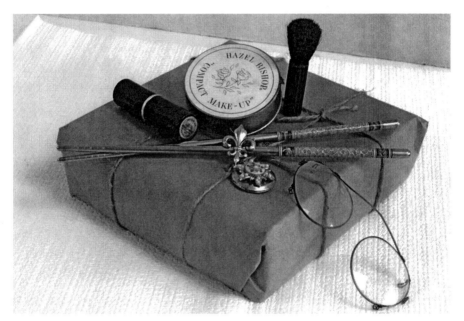

A WWII tale of mystery, mischief, and mishaps.

An Elaine Faber Mystery

To Sheny
Elaine Faber
2021

Elk Grove Publications

Mrs. Odboddy: Undercover Courier

Published by Elk Grove Publications

© 2017 by Elaine Faber

ISBN-13: 978-1-940781-16-7

This novel is a work of fiction. Though based on actual WWII historical events, involvement of the novel's characters are purely fiction and the product of the author's imagination. Any resemblance to actual events, locales, organizations,or persons, living or dead, is entirely coincidental and beyond the intent of either the author or publisher.

Cover photos: *Can we talk?* © Everett Collection, Shutterstock.com ID:227271556; *Train with Carriages* © Graeme Knox, Shutterstock. com ID: 73650349; *Signpost* © sicbak, iStock.com ID: 183047976

Scene Break Train © Nikola Roglic, 123rf.com ID: 24703458

Cover layout and book formatting: Julie Williams, juliewilliams.us
Printed in the United States of America

Dedication

This book is dedicated to the following very special people.

Elk Grove Publications for always being willing to drop everything important and provide instant assistance with my publishing needs.

To Julie Williams, my mentor, editor and friend for assistance with everything from editing to cover design, but mostly for encouraging me to 'dig deeper' and discover what's really going on in Mrs. Odboddy's head.

To my kids, Michael and Londa, for non-stop cheerleading and advice through the dreary process of bringing another story to life.

To my beta readers, Sandy Lassa, Lois Parrish, Sherri Bergmann, and Ellen Cardwell, for their suggestions and insight into punctuation and other such boring but important nonsense.

To my critique group, Sandy, Ellen, Erin, Dee, and Suzi who have traveled on this journey with Mrs. Odboddy, exuding enthusiasm and good cheer along the way.

A special thank you to Lee, my long-suffering husband. Every day, he lends a sympathetic ear when I whine, and shares his technical advice regarding handguns, vintage automobiles, explosives and various other things that go bump in the night.

Lastly to my fans, who may be small in number, but large in loyalty, without whom I'd have given up writing a long time ago. Your requests for another book keep me looking forward to the next story.

This book is dedicated to each of you with the hope you enjoy another Agnes adventure, always a hometown patriot, and now, an undercover courier.

Thanks to every one of you.

Elaine

Chapter One

People don't usually murder people they like.

ightning flashed and thunder rattled the windows of Wilkey's Market where Agnes pushed a little metal cart through the crowded aisle. *If we didn't need coffee, I wouldn't have come out in this weather.*

With coffee rationed to one pound per person every six weeks since the attack on Pearl Harbor, her one daily pot was a cherished delicacy. *So, here I am, wet to the skin, risking catching my death for my coffee.*

Another clap of thunder rumbled in the distance. Rain spattered against the windows. Agnes greeted the butcher, cutting thick slices of liverwurst on his slicer. "Morning, Joe. Do you think the building is apt to blow down in this storm?" She giggled.

Joe grinned. "Store's been standing since before WWI. Doubt another storm is likely to blow 'er down this time around." He glanced out the window. "Though, it looks like maybe the rain is letting up a bit."

Agnes peered into the glass case where the bins were only half filled with cuts of liver, kidneys, ham hocks, ox tails and other internal organ meat. "There's not much choice again today, is there?"

Joe shrugged. "It's the best I can offer this summer." His face brightened. "We have a bit of ground turkey available, if you've got a meat coupon. My wife found a recipe in the *Saturday Evening Post* for a ground turkey and pasta casserole."

Agnes thumbed through her ration book. "I think I have one. Yes. I'll take a pound. I suppose it's our Christian duty to send all the good cuts to the troops overseas. We must all be prepared to make sacrifices for the war effort."

Joe nodded, weighed the ground meat, and wrapped it in white butcher paper. "You got plans for the afternoon?"

"I'm making zucchini bread with the last zucchini from my victory garden. It's my granddaughter, Katherine's, favorite."

"Nothing like a good slice of zucchini bread slathered with apple butter on a chilly morning." Joe handed the meat packet across the counter.

Like so many American housewives, Agnes fought the war right in her own backyard, by growing vegetables in her victory garden, canning fruit and vegetables and volunteering to help the war effort.

Agnes tossed the meat packet in her basket and headed for the checkout stand. "Have a good day, Joe."

Agnes dodged puddles across Wilkey's Market parking lot, struggling to balance her purse on her wrist, her umbrella and a bag of groceries under each arm. She lowered her head and aimed for her yellow and brown 1930 Model A Ford, parked two rows over and three puddles down. Why hadn't she let Mrs. Wilkey's son, George, carry out her bags when he offered? Maybe Katherine was right. She tried to be too independent No harm in accepting a little help from time to time. Let the kid experience the joy of helping others.

As she approached her car, a black Hudson slowed and stopped alongside her. The passenger door opened and a man stepped out.

"You Mrs. Odboddy?" He ran his hand over his bald head. A scar zig zagged across the back of his hand.

Agnes's stomach twisted. "Depends. Who's asking?" She took two steps closer to her Ford. "What do you want?" Her gaze roamed the parking lot. Not a man in sight, except the thug blocking her path toward her car.

The man reached out and grabbed her arm. "You're coming with me!"

Blood surged into Agnes's cheeks. She caught her breath. Wouldn't you know it? Kidnapped in broad daylight and not a gol-darned cop in sight! No wonder, with every able-bodied man off fighting the war, leaving defenseless women and children victims of rapists and murderers. In less time than it took to come up with a plan, she dropped her grocery bags, wielded her umbrella and smacked it across the man's shoulders.

"Hey! What's the big idea? Smitty! Give me a hand. The old broad's putting up a fuss." Scar-Hand snatched the umbrella from Agnes and shoved her toward his car.

Oh, good grief. What shall I do?

Smitty ran around from the driver's side.

Despite her struggles and a few well-aimed kicks, the two scoundrels shoved Agnes into the back seat and tossed her umbrella onto the floorboards. "Don't give us any trouble, Mrs. Odboddy," Smitty growled, rubbing his shins. "Like it or not, you're coming with us."

Agnes scooted across the mohair seat, huddled into the corner as far as she could get from Smitty's leering grin. "What do you want with me?"

Smitty and Scar-Hand jumped into the front seat. Smitty gunned the engine and the car lurched through the parking lot toward the street. He glanced over his shoulder. "Don't try any funny business, lady. The chief asked us to bring you to him, and that's where you're going."

"If you're holding me for ransom, you're out of luck. I don't have any money." Agnes's heart pounded against her chest. How much was one old lady worth? With her son and husband both gone since WWI, Katherine was about the only person who might give a rat's patootie about her life. Unfortunately, Katherine was just a working girl and together they probably didn't have two hundred bucks between them. No, the townsfolk of Newbury wouldn't care much if she disappeared from the face of the earth. The thought made her stomach roil.

Was she about to vomit? It would serve Smitty right if she puked all over his fancy Hudson. The car headed down Main Street and out of town. She turned and waved frantically out the rear window at a car following behind them. Maybe, if she could get his attention…

The man in the car smiled and waved back. No use.

No! Can't you understand? I need help. I'm being kidnapped! She grabbed Scar-Hand's shoulder. "Where are you taking me?"

He shrugged and stared straight ahead. No answer.

Agnes ran her hand over her cheeks, cold to her touch. *All right, calm down and think.* She couldn't make a plan if she didn't have a clear head. She took three deep breaths. *Assess the situation. Consider your options. Make a plan and execute.* She blew out her breath. *One thousand one, one thousand two…*

Two against one. The odds weren't in her favor, racing down the road at the breakneck speed of thirty-five miles an hour. Opening the door and jumping out would be risky at the ripe old age of seventy-one. She'd probably break her neck or at the very least, her leg. Then they'd stop and drag her back, broken leg and all. *Forget that. Bad idea.*

She reached for her umbrella. She could smack Smitty over the head and… No. He'd likely run the car off the road and the result could be the same as jumping out the door. Again, not a good plan. Maybe she could charm them. Hadn't she always prided herself in being able to handle any man with sweet talk and cookies?

"Smitty. What do you do in your spare time? Do you like to fish?" *That's the ticket. Get him to talk about himself. Create a rapport. People don't usually murder people they like.*

Smitty glanced back over his shoulder. "I like to shoot things. Squirrels, deer, dogs that dump over my garbage cans. That sort of thing. Why do you ask?"

Agnes's heart tumbled. "No reason. Never mind." So much for

sweet talk. Guess she'd have to bide her time. Maybe she could figure out an escape plan when they got where they were going. She shrank down in the corner and recited the Lord's Prayer under her breath.

Scar-Hand squirmed in the front seat, then reached over and punched Smitty's shoulder.

"Hey! Isn't that the kid right there?" He pointed out the window. "That one! There, in the blue striped tee-shirt. I'm sure that's him."

"You're right. Let's get him. He won't get away this time." Smitty steered the car toward the boy twirling a yo-yo.

Agnes gazed at the boy. *He has blond hair like my son, John, God rest his soul.* The memory of John's laughing eyes flashed through her mind. Her heart did a flip-flop. Were these men demented? Now, they were after a child? Why would they want an old woman and a kid? Perverts!

Agnes held her breath as the car crept closer to the unsuspecting boy.

Scar-Hand cracked the front passenger door and as the car pulled up to the curb, he jumped out and grabbed the kid.

The boy twisted from his grasp and took off running down the street.

Run, kid, run! Agnes closed her eyes and clasped her hands in prayer. *Lord, let him get away. Never mind about me. Save the kid.*

Scar-Hand's feet thudded on the sidewalk as he raced behind the boy.

Agnes's heart was in her throat as the car followed about a half-block behind.

Scar-Hand caught up with the boy, grabbed him around his middle, pinned his arms in a vice grip and dragged him, kicking and screaming, back toward the car.

Agnes put her hand on the door handle. Should she take advantage of the scuffle and jump out? In the confusion, she might escape, but how could she abandon this innocent boy? Better she should stay with him until they reached their destination and figure a way for them both to escape.

Agnes patted the boy's arm, put her finger to her lips and whispered. "Don't worry. I'll get us out of this. I've been in worse situations. Trust me." She thought back to the day in Paris during WWI when she and her friend, Mildred, were trapped in a bombed out building for three days during an air raid. They never lost hope then and she wasn't about to start now.

The kid glanced at her with eyes wide. He slithered down in the corner with his hands between his knees. Poor kid didn't say a word. He'd obviously given up and seemed resigned to his fate. But, no way was she going to let these hooligans snatch an innocent kid off the street and...

She couldn't even allow herself to imagine what might happen as the car sped through the countryside, headed for the ocean where they likely planned to murder them and pitch their bodies off the cliffs onto the rocks below.

Somewhere along the ocean road, Agnes cast about for an escape plan until the plot of an old Ellery Queen movie came to mind. Hadn't the heroine managed to fool the kidnapper into thinking she was going to vomit in his car? He'd stopped the car and she escaped. If it worked in the movie, it could work now. At least the boy might get away.

Agnes winked at the boy and whispered. "Get ready. I'm going to try something." She writhed on the back seat, coughed and gagged, and flung her body from side to side.

Scar-Hand turned. "What's the matter, lady? You car sick?"

"You better stop this car," Agnes gurgled, "before I puke all over." She held her breath until she felt as if her face had turned bright red.

"Stop the car, Smitty! We'll catch heck if she barfs in the chief's back seat."

Smitty rolled to a stop on the side of the road.

Scar-Hand opened his door and stepped out.

No sooner had the car slowed almost to a stop than Agnes reached across the boy, shoved open his door and pushed him out. "Go! Go!" She leaned toward the open door as the kid jumped a fence and was off across the sand like a gazelle, even before Scar-Hand could get around the open door. "Now look what you've done, you old bat! We're in for it now. What's the chief going to say when he hears the kid got away again?"

Following a few choice curse words, Scar-Hand pushed her away from the door. "I could strangle you for that."

Agnes leaned back in the seat. This time, her number was up for sure. As Smitty's car lunged along the ocean road toward Boyles Springs, she proposed a contract with God. If He would spare her life, she would never again use the Lord's name in vain, stop telling lies, and would stop using a henna rinse and let her hair go back to its natural color. She shuddered as she murmured the last promise, a huge sacrifice on her part. That should make Him happy.

Just to be on the safe side, in case He was too busy to get the message before she was murdered, she added a codicil to her heavenly contract and ran through a litany of sins, begged forgiveness and resigned herself to her imminent mortal demise. *They'll probably throw my body into the ocean and poor Katherine will never know that I died a hero and saved a boy's life; the scourge of the underworld brought down by heinous criminals.*

Chapter Two

I'm so seldom wrong about anything.

Agnes hunkered in the back seat as the kidnapper's car continued along the ocean road. Over the next thirty heart-wrenching minutes, her thoughts raced from one past indiscretion to another. What would God say at the Judgement Seat later today, when He recounted the number of times she made change out of the church offering basket? She wouldn't even allow herself to think about her disreputable behavior in Paris in 1918, when her husband was in England and she was indiscreet with a fellow undercover government agent…

The terrain changed as the car curved away from the beach and headed inland toward the Boyles Springs Military Base. Sure enough, Smitty turned into the front gate. *What's going on? Why did they bring me here?* They'd have a hard time getting away with murder on a military base.

The gate guard leaned toward Smitty's window. "Papers?"

Smitty stuck out his head. "Colonel Farthingworth is expecting us."

Colonel Farthingworth? What did he have to do with these killers? Uh-oh! Was there a minuscule chance that Smitty and Scar-Hand weren't killers? *It's hard to believe I could have been wrong. I'm so seldom wrong about anything.* Waves of relief swept through her stomach.

Wait! Hadn't they kidnapped the boy, too? Apparently, he was of the same impression as she about these men. He'd never have escaped without her valiant efforts.

The guard waved them through the gate.

Smitty nodded, drove across the base, and stopped the car in front of Headquarters. He turned and grinned. "Okay, end of the road. Get out, Mrs. Odboddy."

Agnes glanced from Smitty to the Headquarters office and back again. "Here? Why didn't you tell me you were taking me to see Colonel Farthingworth? What was all that about the kid? We thought you were kidnapping us."

Smitty chuckled. "Where did you get that crazy idea?"

"Why shouldn't I? You shoved both of us in the car against our will. You never identified yourselves." Agnes's face flushed as her temper flared. "I thought you were planning to kill us and throw us into the ocean. That's why I helped the boy escape, you dimwit!"

Agnes grabbed her umbrella from the floor and smacked it across Smitty's shoulder. They had scared her to death with their stupid spy games, made her believe she was going to die, forced her to make promises to…to…*uh-oh!*

Gulp!

Perspiration prickled her forehead. She shuddered as her mind raced back over her recent bargain with the Almighty. She touched the sterling silver chopsticks in the back of her hair once again, drawing strength from the remembrance of her husband's gift so many years ago.

Hadn't she said something about not swearing? Okay. That was an easy one.

How about promising she wouldn't tell any more whoppers… another one she could live with… What else had she…?

The henna rinse! Her heart sank. Surely *He* wouldn't expect her to stop *freshening* the color of her naturally golden-red hair! Even God wouldn't demand such a price in exchange for her life. Wait! He would have known that Smitty wasn't really a killer and, therefore, He wouldn't hold her to a silly promise about…*umm*…freshening her hair color? Right? *I think I'm okay.*

She shrugged. "Okay, lead on. Whatever Colonel Farthingworth has in mind, I'm game for it."

Maybe he had another assignment for her. Wasn't she successful with one important secret assignment last year? *Humph!* But, the trip across town with Smitty! Colonel Farthingworth didn't have to go through all that cloak and dagger bologna to get her attention. She would have come willingly if Smitty had been truthful with her.

She gathered her purse and umbrella, stepped out of the car and slammed the door. With shoulders back and head held high, she marched up the steps and into Headquarters. *Humph!*

Smitty danced out of reach when she raised her umbrella toward him again.

The bright lights in the front office made her squint. Faded books and baskets full of file folders lined the dusty shelves behind the reception desk. Coffee rings marred the surface beside the old black typewriter where a young man in uniform sat typing, his attention riveted to the document beside the machine.

"Excuse me!"

The young man jerked and turned a pimpled face toward Agnes. The kid wasn't old enough to shave, but he was old enough to defend his country. At least they had the good sense to keep him stateside. He could be sitting somewhere in a European mud hole with a pack on his back and a gun in his hand.

Agnes leaned against the desk, her umbrella resting in the crook of her arm.

"Can I help you?" The kid's voice cracked. How young was he anyway?

"I'm Mrs. Agnes Odboddy. Apparently, I'm supposed to see Colonel Farthingworth. If you'll announce me, please, we can both get on with our day." Up went her nose as she gazed around the office. Dust feathers clung to the blades of a black fan atop the file cabinet. Obviously, there were no women at the Boyles Springs Headquarters.

The kid bounced from his chair. He tapped on a closed door with the name *Colonel Bartholomew Farthingworth* etched on the window.

"Enter."

The pimply soldier opened the door and poked his head in. "There's a Mrs. Agnes Ombididdy here to see you, sir. Shall I have her wait?"

"Mrs. Odboddy? I've been expecting her. Send her in."

Agnes marched through the door. "Colonel?"

Wrinkles in his brow had deepened since last they met and his hair had turned grey over his ears. *It's war that's aging him.* Apparently, things weren't going as well as the newspapers implied. Everyone suspected that the New York Times glossed over the bad news and emphasized the good news. You couldn't believe half of what you read in the papers these days.

"Agnes, my dear. You're looking well. Won't you have a seat?" The colonel gestured toward the chair in front of his desk. He was either a better actor than Humphrey Bogart or he was unaware of the manner in which she had been conveyed to the base.

Agnes huffed and plopped into the chair. "Sir! As I explained when we last met, I would do anything to help the war effort, but I most sincerely protest the rude and insensitive manner in which I have been transported to your office. Do you realize—"

"My dear Mrs. Odboddy. I have no idea what you're babbling about. Surely you must appreciate the fact that I sent a car to fetch you, so you wouldn't have to use your gas ration coupons to drive over. I thought you'd be pleased."

"Pleased? Horse feathers! I was forcefully snatched from the parking lot and shoved in the back seat of a car. Your minions refused to tell me where they were taking me. I thought I was being kidnapped and they intended to murder me! And tell me, sir, who is going to pay for the two bags of groceries that were dumped in the parking lot in the process?"

Colonel Farthingworth's face flushed. His hand went to his mouth. His shoulders shook.

"Why are you laughing? There is nothing funny about this, sir." Agnes's nose was up so far, she had to lower her chin to see the scoundrel's face.

The Colonel sat upright, struggled to straighten his mouth and licked his lips. "Of course, you're right. I apologize for my men. I'm sure they thought it was a huge joke. I'll speak to them, I assure you." He sucked in his breath, obviously hoping to defuse the tension in the room. "So, you met my son, too. I hope he wasn't rude. We've had a dickens of a time getting him to the dentist. I thought, since the guys were picking you up in town anyway, they could—"

"Your son? The dentist?" *Oh, dear God in Heaven.* What had she done this time? All that time she'd thought they were going to be murdered and made that ridiculous bargain with God... With luck, God would forgive her. Colonel Farthingworth? Maybe, that was a different story.

She shook her head. "Well, sir, you see... It's this way. Since I thought we were being kidnapped, I sort of...well..." Agnes's cheeks were on fire. Perspiration puddled between her breasts. Her stomach lurched.

With her eccentric notions and unfettered mouth, the townsfolk of Newbury thought she was a nutcase, but it had been a while since she'd made such a serious fool of herself. She squirmed in her chair, twisted her hands and lowered her head. "I'm so terribly sorry. I truly believed the boy was in danger. I thought I was saving his life and..." Her voice faded to a whisper. "I helped him escape."

"Excuse me, what's that about Billy escaping?"

She lifted her head and raised her voice. "I said I helped him escape because I thought I was saving his life!" She thrust out her chin, her eyes narrowed. "What else do you suppose I would think, the way your men grabbed the kid and shoved him into the car? Your boy neglected to mention anything about a dentist."

"Of course, he wouldn't. That's my Billy, stubborn like his mother, Edith. I'm sorry, Agnes. This has been a terrible misunderstanding. I do hope you will..." His lips twitched and his eyes crinkled. His shoulders jiggled and he started to laugh. "I'm sure it was terrible for you, but...

you thought you were being kidnapped?...and saving my boy's life?" He held his stomach and stifled a chuckle. "Now that it's over, I hope you can see how funny..." Colonel Farthingworth's chuckles burst into guffaws.

"Well, when you put it that way..." Agnes smiled. "I guess I did let my imagination run away with me, didn't I?" She chuckled. The sound of the Colonel's chortles tickled her funny bone. "Your son sure put up a good fight. He must really hate the dentist!" She burst into laughter. "I thought I was saving his life!"

Colonel Farthingworth picked up the receiver with a final chuckle and pushed a button on the telephone unit. "Buzz. Could you please bring us some coffee?" He turned to Agnes. "Do you use cream or sugar?"

"Black is fine."

"Two black coffees, Buzz." He hung up the phone. "Now, Mrs. Odboddy, the reason I brought you here..." He wiped his hand over his mouth, erasing the last vestige of a grin. "I heard through the grapevine something about a trip to Washington, D.C. with Mrs. Roosevelt."

Agnes nodded. "Oh, you heard about that? Yes. It was quite a surprise. You see, Katherine and I volunteer with the Red Cross, you know, well, maybe you didn't know, but we do. Apparently, Mrs. Roosevelt is planning a goodwill tour to visit the troops in the Pacific Islands. She wanted a couple of Red Cross volunteers to accompany her. She remembered me and Katherine from our unusual encounter last summer. You recall the details. Unfortunately, when your wife got involved with—" Agnes turned at the sound of a knock on the door.

Pimply Buzz came in with a tray and set it on the desk. "Will there be anything else, sir?" He saluted and backed toward the door.

"Thanks, Buzz. That's all."

Buzz pulled the door behind him, leaving it slightly ajar.

"Go on, Agnes... You were saying?"

"Well, Mrs. Roosevelt wrote to ask if Katherine and I wanted to join her goodwill tour. Of course, we said yes. Who wouldn't want to go to Washington and meet the President and travel with Mrs. Roosevelt? It will be just like the movie stars on those USO tours. We're both very excited."

"I can imagine. I understand it's all quite *hush-hush*—" Colonel Farthingworth handed a coffee mug to Agnes. "Shouldn't let the press know about Mrs. Roosevelt's plans. It's safer that way. So, to get to the point. Considering your previous experience as an undercover agent during WWI, I wonder if you would consider coming out of retirement to handle a job for the government. Your trip is exactly the reason I wanted to see you."

Agnes opened her mouth to speak. No words came out. *The chance to really do something for the war effort! What a thrill! Knitting socks is fine, but to actually—*

Colonel Farthingworth sipped his coffee and grimaced. "I can never get used to Buzz's coffee." He shook his head. "Anyway, I have a package I need to send to President Roosevelt." The Colonel opened a desk drawer and pulled out a parcel wrapped in brown paper and tied end over end with string. "I don't trust the mail between here and Washington these days. Since you and Katherine are going to Washington and meeting with Mrs. Roosevelt anyway, you could deliver this directly to the President for me. What do you say?" He held up the package.

Agnes stood, threw back her shoulders and saluted. "You can count on me, sir. No one will touch this package until I personally put it into Mr. Roosevelt's hands. *Probably some top-secret papers he doesn't trust to the security pouches going to Washington. What safer way to deliver a package to the President than to have an innocent old lady hand-carry it?* She placed it into her purse. "If that's all, sir, I'll let you get about your business. I have some shopping to do, since my bags were spilled all over the parking lot."

"About that, Agnes. Again, my sincerest apologies." He reached for a message pad, wrote a brief note and signed it with a flourish. "Smitty will drive you to the commissary. This pass will allow you to buy anything you want there, and then he'll drive you home."

Agnes snatched the note. "That sounds wonderful. Do you suppose they have meat?"

"I wouldn't be at all surprised. Thank you for taking my package. It's important that it get there before August 20th. It means a lot." He stood and thrust out his hand.

Agnes grinned and shook his hand. "How is your dear wife, Edith? We haven't seen her at knitting circle for quite a while."

"I'm afraid she's been away, visiting her sister in Portland. That business last summer left her very shaken. She hasn't been herself since. She's too embarrassed to face the church ladies."

"Nonsense. We all make mistakes. I should know. I make more than most, don't I? If you'll give me her address, I'll write to her and let her know she's missed."

"That would be very kind." Colonel Farthingworth scribbled out an address and handed the paper to Agnes. "I'm sure she'd love to hear from you." He moved toward the door. "Thank you so much for your assistance, Agnes." He stepped into the outer office and escorted Agnes to the door.

"Oh Buzz," Agnes turned to Buzz at his desk. "Try some Hydrogen Peroxide on your face! It works wonders."

Buzz's blush turned his pimples bright red. "Thank you, ma'am. I'll do that."

Smitty stood by the car, his head down, his hat in his hands. He saluted as Colonel Farthingworth and Agnes approached the car.

"Private Smithers, I gave you the whole day off because you offered to do me a favor while you were in town. The next time you pull a shenanigan like you did with Mrs. Odboddy, you'll see the inside of the brig. Do I make myself clear? What do you have to say for yourself?"

"Yes sir. I'm sorry about your son, sir." He ducked his head. "Sorry about the prank, Mrs. Odboddy. Me and my buddy were just goofing around. Didn't think you'd take it so serious." His cheeks flamed. He glanced up and then lowered his gaze.

"Don't worry about it, Smitty. I forgive you. Colonel Farthingworth says you can drive me to the commissary. Let's go! I hear there's a steak with my name on it."

Chapter Three

Except for a stewpot, what can you do with four Bantam roosters?

gnes sat at the kitchen table with a piece of ink-stained stationery, a bottle of red Parker *Quink* ink and an ebony fountain pen. *I hate writing letters.* "Katherine, how do you spell *arained*?" Is there one 'r' or two?" She laid down the pen and wiped her fingertips on an old tea towel. Her fingers looked like they were dipped in blood, bringing to mind last night's dream of an airplane crashing into the sea somewhere over the Pacific Islands. *Forget it. It was just a dream.* She hid her hands under the table.

Katherine laid her movie magazine featuring Veronica Lake, the Hollywood starlet of the month, on the table. "Who are you writing to, Grandmother?" She stood and placed a tea ball filled with loose tea leaves into a teapot and filled it with boiling water. She set the gold Fiesta teapot on the table, then took a turquoise mug from the cupboard and slid back into her chair.

"I'm writing to Colonel Farthingworth's wife, Edith. Apparently, she's still distraught over last summer's events. One 'r' or two?" Agnes touched one of the silver chopsticks crisscrossed through her red-hennaed bun.

Katherine's smile crinkled the freckles on her nose. "Let me see." She reached for Agnes's letter, glanced over it quickly and sighed. "You didn't spell *arraigned* right. Here let me show you." She wrote *arraigned* across the top of Veronica's head on the magazine. "There's two 'r's and a 'g.' Why are you using red ink?"

"Edith shouldn't take on so for an honest mistake. No one should." Agnes wadded up the letter and tossed it on the floor.

Agnes's Siamese cat, Ling-Ling, jumped at the ball of paper and gave it a swipe across the kitchen.

"Do you think using red ink will make much difference, Grandma? She'll know how you feel when she reads the letter."

Agnes pulled another piece of stationery from the box. "I want it to look nice without ink blotches and misspellings, but, look at this. The fountain pen is leaking all over my fingers." She held up her hand.

Katherine shook the red curls she had inherited from her grandmother and reached for the teapot. "Do you want tea? It's that nice lemon-orange tea Myrtle gave me for my birthday." She waved the pot in front of Agnes.

"It sounds wonderful." Agnes stood and retrieved a flaming orange Fiesta cup from the cupboard. *My darling girl. How blessed I am that she shares my home and my life.*

"Edith will appreciate knowing that she's missed. You're a saint."

"No, I'm not. Do you want to hear what I wrote?" She retrieved the wadded paper from Ling-Ling and smoothed out the wrinkles.

Ling-Ling hopped into Agnes's lap. She smooshed the long hair on the cat's back as she read.

Dear Edith:

I talked to your husband, Colonel Farthingworth, today. He said you were visiting your sister and that you are depressed about the mix-up last summer. You are not responsible for the actions of someone pretending to be your friend, but isn't. Don't worry. She has been arraigned and will be going away for a long time. We were all glad to see her go, but not you. Please come home soon because I never could get the hang of that argyle sock pattern. You were the only one who could do it right, so we need you here.

Sincerely, your friend, Agnes Agatha Odboddy

"Well, what do you think, Katherine? Does that sound okay?"

Katherine's eyes opened a bit wider as Agnes finished reading.

She cleared her throat and sipped her tea. "*Umm*...well, Grandma. It's certainly a nice letter and with the red ink, she should know it comes from your heart. That's the best kind of cheer up letter."

Agnes wrote the date on the top of another sheet of stationary. August 10, 1943. The 'three' trailed across the page as the pen ran dry. "Oh, *pshaw*! When will they invent a pen that doesn't run out of ink or leak all over your fingers?" She reached for the bottle of ink.

Katherine laughed. "Let me do it. Last time you tried, you spilled it all over the table." She opened the jar and inserted the nib. Then, she pulled the silver clip on the side of the fountain pen, squirting out any fluid remaining inside. Releasing the clip created a suction effect, sucking ink up through the nib into the reservoir. Katherine wiped off the pen with the old tea towel. "There you go. All full again. And, see?" She turned her hands from front to back. "Not a drop on my fingers. I really must go or I'll be late for work." Katherine stood and hurried toward her bedroom.

"Bet you can't do it again without getting ink on your hands." Agnes muttered as she lifted the Siamese cat off her lap and dropped her to the floor.

Outside the kitchen window, one of the four roosters crowed. Mrs. Whistlemeyer, Mildred, Myrtle and Sophia were named last summer before she realized they were all roosters. The boys darted around their small enclosure, bickering and fighting. "Whatever am I going to do about those squabbling roosters, Ling-Ling! They're making a fuss again."

Agnes tromped across the lawn and rapped on her next-door neighbor's door. "*Yoo-hoo*, Mavis. Are you home?" She turned and waved across the street to where Mrs. Williams was replacing the flag covered with blue stars beside her door, with another covered with gold stars. Agnes's smile faded. The flag with blue stars signified a family member in the military, and now…

Four months ago, against the wishes of his widowed mother, Jimmy Williams had enlisted in the Army on his eighteenth birthday.

Last week, shrieks had brought Agnes flying out her front door. As soon as she saw the two uniformed men at Mrs. Williams's door, she knew why they were there. Hadn't two uniformed men stood on her own front porch years ago when her husband, Douglas, died during WWI? A few months later, a phone call from Katherine's mother had relayed the same message about her son, John, Katherine's father.

Her heart had wrenched as she raced across the street to Mrs. Williams's porch, once again feeling the pangs of a mother's broken heart. Her words of comfort hadn't made much difference. The news was grim. Somewhere on an island whose name no one could pronounce, enemy machine gun fire had ended young Jimmy's life. They'd buried him there with the three other young men killed that day. How pathetic, the little flag with gold stars, flying on Mrs. Williams's porch, calling Jimmy's name to all who would hear, representing his supreme sacrifice.

Agnes closed her eyes, whispered a quick prayer for Mrs. Williams's comfort and rapped on Mavis's door again. "It's me. Agnes. Are you home?"

The door squeaked open. "Come on in. I'm up to my elbows in dishwater." Mavis jerked her head toward the street. "Have you been over to see Mrs. Williams?"

"Katherine and I took her a casserole a couple days ago. I haven't been back. Poor thing. Her sister came from San Francisco day before yesterday. She'll stay for a while." Agnes shook her head. "It's hard to lose a son. I should know." She followed Mavis into the kitchen, pulled out a chair and shoved her handbag under the table. The brown paper-wrapped parcel peeked from the top. She'd promised the Colonel not to let it out of her sight and that's exactly what she intended to do.

Mavis plunged her hands back into the dishpan. "Go ahead and make yourself a cup of tea. I want to finish up these dishes before the water goes cold. It is a tragedy about Jimmy, isn't it? He was so young. *Tch Tch!*"

"I watched that boy grow up. He used to deliver my newspaper. Half the time, it landed on the roof. The world has lost a good boy."

"The world is losing a lot of good boys, Agnes." Mavis sighed and dashed her wrist across her eyes.

"Yes…" Agnes glanced around the kitchen, Jimmy's memory so tangible, she almost expected to see him in the corner eating one of Mavis's raisin cookies. Agnes shook her head, took two cups from the cupboard, filled a tea ball and poured boiling water into her cup. The clinking of her spoon in the quiet kitchen erased the sense of Jimmy's presence. "Well, then…"

Mavis swished the dishrag through the soapy water and set the dishes into a wooden drainer. "So, what's on your mind, Agnes? Everything okay at your house?" Mavis emptied the dishpan and reached for a towel.

Agnes sipped her tea. "We're fine. In fact, better than fine. I have something to tell you, but I need you to keep it under your hat."

Mavis put the tea ball in her cup and added hot water. Her eyebrows raised, she glanced at Agnes. "You doing another secret mission for the government, like last summer?"

Agnes waved her hand dismissively. "Not really. Well, sort of." How much did she dare confide to Mavis, considering her reputation as the town gossip? Perhaps about the trip with Mrs. Roosevelt, but certainly not about the package she was to deliver to the President.

"It's like this. Katherine and I are traveling to…" It was no secret what the town thought of her conspiracy theories and previous tomfooleries that usually ended in humiliation. It seemed likely that her mention of the goodwill tour with Mrs. Roosevelt might be met with the same disbelief. Perhaps it would be best to keep quiet about all the details. "You see… Katherine and I are taking a…a…vacation and we'll be gone for a while, and—"

"A vacation? In the middle of war? Where on earth are you going?"

Where, indeed? Just traveling with the wife of the most influential man in the world to visit military bases in the Pacific Islands under constant Japanese attack. That's all.

A chill raced up Agnes's spine as she thought of the risks they might encounter on their *vacation*. It was one thing as the self-appointed scourge of the underworld to take such risks, but what about Katherine? Perhaps she should discourage her from making the trip. On the other hand, if the government kept a press blackout on Mrs. Roosevelt's plans, the enemy would have no idea that a particular island held such an attractive target. No! She had no intention of passing on the adventure of a lifetime and she had no right to deny Katherine such an opportunity.

Not that she would have had much success discouraging such a strong-willed young woman as Katherine. Where she got such a bull-headed, devil-may-care attitude was anybody's guess…

"Agnes? You didn't say where you and Katherine are going. Is it another secret mission? *Heh! Heh!*"

"*Umm…* No, don't be silly. We're going to…to…Washington, D.C. to visit the Smithsonian Institute and see the cherry blossoms. Yes. That's it. Washington. That's why I came over. I wondered if you would take care of Ling-Ling and feed my chickens while we're gone. They need to be—"

"Yes and no." Mavis put up her nose and stared out the kitchen window.

"What does that mean?" Agnes's eyebrow twitched. Was there about to be an unexpected glitch in her plans? If Mavis wouldn't take care of the animals, who could she ask? Mildred was leaving to visit her daughter next week, too. Without a caretaker for the animals, how could she leave town? Her entire trip was in jeopardy.

"Yes, I'll take care of Ling-Ling but, no, I'm not taking care of those gol-darned roosters. Every blasted morning at sunrise, they start crowing. In fact, Agnes, I've been meaning to speak to you about them. You shouldn't keep roosters in this neighborhood. All the neighbors are complaining—"

"Really? Apparently, behind my back." Agnes's head jerked up. "This is the first I've heard about it. Why didn't someone tell me they had become a nuisance?" Her face warmed as she pondered the problem. The roosters were the result of another hair-brained scheme. By the time she learned they were all roosters, they had become pets.

In truth, since the four roosters had reached maturity, their method of *bringing in morning* was getting on her nerves, too. Every morning, at 5:30 A.M., she pulled her pillow over her ears to drown out a chorus of crowing. The boys needed a better living arrangement, but she had put it off. It was hard to give up one's pets, even when it's necessary.

"So, the way I see it, Agnes, I'll be happy to take care of Ling-Ling, but you need to do something about those pesky *dawn-busters.* Maybe you could throw a block party and serve them as the main course." Mavis put her hand to her mouth and gasped. "Oh, I'm sorry, Agnes. I didn't mean to say that out loud. You're not mad, are you? Tell me you're not mad." Mavis laid her hand on Agnes's arm.

Mavis's wavering smile was hard to resist. Even though her solution was unthinkable, it wasn't hard to understand the complaint. *Except for a stewpot, just exactly what can you do with four grown Bantam roosters?*

"You're right. I should have done something before they got to be such a problem. I'm not mad. I'll figure out something before we leave." She squeezed Mavis's hand. "I'll bring over the key later. Maybe Ling-Ling can come and keep you company once in a while." She stood and shoved her chair under the table. "Thanks for the tea. I should get home. I need to wash a load of clothes and hung them out on the line before Katherine gets home."

Mavis walked her to the front door. "Okay. I'll see you. Think I'll bake some cookies and take some over to Mrs. Williams later."

"Sounds like a good idea. Give her my best." Agnes waved, crossed the lawn and stepped through the row of rose bushes between her and Mavis's front yard. *I should cut a bouquet of roses for Mrs.*

Williams… Maybe I should make a few calls about the chickens first.
She paused, her hand on the front doorknob. She cocked her head and listened. What was that? Something crashed inside the house. A chair scraped across the floor! *Someone is in there!*

Chapter Four

Now, if I only had a gun!

Agnes bolted through the front door, stomach churning, feeling as though a chunk of ice was crushing her chest. "Who's in here? Show yourself or I'll shoot!" *Now, if I only had a gun!*

Cushions from the sofa were spread across the rug. The console television-phonograph was pulled away from the wall. Framed photographs from the mantle lay on the floor.

A chill raced up her spine. She clutched her purse to her chest. Did she dare check in the bedrooms or could the burglar still be back there? Where was Ling-Ling?

Slam!

The back door! She dashed through the kitchen and shoved open the door. Just a glimpse of a checkered shirt disappeared over her back fence into the neighbor's yard. *He's gone! What was he looking for?*

A little moan escaped her lips as she stared around her kitchen. The intruder had strewn cans, boxes and bags of food over her counter. Pots and dishes were scattered across the floor. He'd made a hasty, but methodical search of the living room and kitchen. Apparently, the crook hadn't been concerned for the noise he made as he ripped things asunder. A wonder they didn't hear the racket clear over at Mavis's.

Agnes set her handbag on the table, reached for the phone and dialed the beauty shop where Katherine worked.

"*Curls to Dye For.* Myrtle speaking. How can I help you?"

"Myrtle. It's Agnes. I need to speak to Katherine. I have a situation."

"Of course. Hold the line. Katherine, your grandmother's on the phone." She mumbled something Agnes couldn't hear.

"Grandma? What's wrong? Are you all right?"

"I'm just peachy, *punkin*. But we've had a break-in. He's gone now, but the house is a wreck. I wonder if you could—"

"Don't say another word. I'll cancel the rest of my appointments and be right home. Why don't you go over to Mavis's house and wait until I get there?"

"I've just been to Mavis's. That's where I was when the crook broke in. I was only gone for maybe fifteen minutes. How did he know…?" Agnes's hand flew to her mouth. "Katherine! He must have been watching the house and saw me leave. He must have been after…" She paused, her brain clicking along faster than her tongue. "Let's not talk about it on the phone. I'll call Chief Waddlemucker. Hurry home and we'll talk when you get here. Good-bye."

She snapped the receiver back on the wall phone. "My chickens!" Had he hurt her pets? She raced to the kitchen window and peeked out. Mrs. Whistlemeyer, Sophia, Chicken Mildred and Myrtle huddled in the corner against the wire, apparently stressed by the slamming of the back door and the rapscallion rushing past their coop.

Agnes took a bag of chicken feed from the back porch and scattered a small handful in the chicken yard, cooing and gurgling to the Bantams. Her familiar face, or more likely the unexpected treat, assuaged their fears and brought them scrambling from the corner. "That takes care of the chickens. Now, where's my kitty?" Locating Ling-Ling took priority over reporting the break-in to Chief Waddlemucker.

She marched back through the kitchen, toward the bedrooms. "Ling-Ling! Come out, sweetheart. The wicked man is gone. Come to Mommy!" A quick glance into the bathroom and the two bedrooms confirmed that the thief had not gotten to the back of the house. She lifted the corner of her bed skirt. Nothing but several dust bunnies drifting aimlessly about.

"Ling-Ling. Please come out." Maybe Ling-Ling ran through

the door when the scoundrel ran out? She went to the back porch and called, but to no avail.

Tires screeched to a stop in the front yard. Was Katherine home already? She must have left her client dripping in the sink and left the salon the minute she hung up the phone. Agnes hurried back into the kitchen.

Katherine smashed through the door and raced inside. She stopped short when she saw the mess in the living room. "Oh, Grandma. This is terrible." She threw her arms around Agnes's neck. "Are you sure you're all right? Have you called the police?"

Agnes patted her back. "Not yet. I'm looking for Ling-Ling." Her breath caught in her throat. "I can't find her anywhere." Tears prickled her eyes. "You don't suppose he—"

"Everything's going to be all right, Grandma. Give Chief Waddlemucker a call. I'll look for Ling-Ling." She gave Agnes a little shove toward the telephone.

"Okay." Agnes dialed the police department. "Chief Waddlemucker, please?" He wouldn't be happy hearing from her again, considering their history, but this was a legitimate complaint. While she waited for the chief, she called back over her shoulder. "Better not touch anything until I talk to him. He might want to check things out first."

"Right! I'll look in the back yard. Maybe Mavis has seen her." Katherine went to the back door. "Here, chick, chick. Have you seen the pussycat?"

Mrs. Whistlemeyer's responding *er..er..er..er..er* made Agnes smile. The worthless little rascals. She had intended on locating a new home for them this afternoon. If she had lingered at Mavis's a little bit longer, who knows what the hooligan might have done? Chickens were in short supply at the butcher shops these days. She shivered at the thought.

"Hello? Chief Waddlemucker here. What is it this time, Agnes? Another Nazi spy moved in across the street? *Heh...heh!*"

"You don't need to get cheeky, chief. As it happens, a burglar broke into my house and made a prize mess of things while I was next door. I thought I ought to bring the matter to the attention of the authorities. But, if you're too busy, I suppose I'll just give Colonel Farthingworth a call at the military base, next."

"What? What has the military got to do with it? A burglar, you say? Any idea what a thief was looking for?"

Agnes glanced at her purse on the table. "Maybe you should come and see for yourself."

"I'll be right over. Agnes, this springtime, don't fudge a sting."

"What say?" Agnes shook her head. "What does that mean? Don't fudge a sting? How could I—"

"What? I didn't say anything about... I said, in the meantime, don't touch a thing! Agnes, every time we have a conversation... Did you ever get that hearing aid like I told you?"

"Well, if you'd just speak up and stop mumbling! I need to go. I'm beginning to think the hoodlum stole my cat!" The telephone line crackled.

"Stole your hat? What's this about a hat?"

"I said, cat! Cat! Stole my cat! Oh, good grief. And you think I need a hearing aid? Good-bye!" Agnes slammed down the receiver.

Wasn't that just typical? A law-abiding citizen, a warrior on the home front, calls for just the teensiest bit of assistance from the local police and she's accused of having a hearing disorder. Of all things! "Katherine. Did you find Ling-Ling?"

Katherine pulled open the back door, Ling-Ling cradled in her arms. "Here's your baby, Grandma. I guess she got scared and ran up the apple tree. I had a devil of a time coaxing her down." She handed Agnes the furry bundle.

Agnes buried her face in Ling-Ling's beige fur and peered into her crossed blue eyes. "Thank goodness, you're safe."

"Now, tell me, what on earth was this character looking for in our house? We don't have anything anyone wants, do we?" Katherine gestured toward the mess in the kitchen. "He must have been after something specific."

Agnes ducked her head. Her gaze darted around the room, and then settled on her handbag. Her cheeks glowed. *We should have talked about this last night. Something tells me this isn't going to be easy.*

"Grandma! What on earth is going on?"

"It's rather a long story. You see, yesterday morning, I..." The siren screaming up the street indicated the arrival of the police. Any story, short or long would have to be postponed. "We'll talk after the police are gone."

"This better be good. I can't wait to hear what kind of monkeyshines you're mixed up in this time."

Chapter Five

The truth, and nothing but the truth...mostly.

orty five minutes later, after a thorough search of the house and innumerous questions, Agnes closed the door behind Chief Waddlemucker. *I can't believe he came himself and didn't send a flatfoot.*

"Okay, Grandma. What gives? What do you know that I don't know? Tell me what you didn't tell Chief Waddlemucker. You were dancing around all his questions."

Agnes turned to face Katherine, standing with arms akimbo, eyebrows pulled down, tapping her foot on the flowered living room rug. "Oh! You startled me. I didn't see you walk up behind me."

"I wasn't sneaking. What was the thief after?" Katherine picked up a cushion from the floor and replaced it on the sofa. She sat and patted the cushion beside her. "Sit! Speak!"

Agnes stared at her, her eyebrows raised. "You don't need to speak to me that way. I'm not a dog."

Katherine's cheeks flushed. "I'm sorry. I didn't mean to infer…" Her mouth turned down. "Now, don't think you can change the subject. You're not getting away from me that easily. Tell me what you know about all this. What was the thief looking for?"

Agnes's frown melted. She sat beside Katherine and patted her knee. "Had no intention of it, *punkin*. If you'd just run into the kitchen and make us a nice pot of tea, we can sit and discuss everything from beginning to end." *And give me time to figure out exactly how to put this.*

With a nod and a reluctant sigh, Katherine left the living room. "Don't you move a muscle. I'll be right back."

Agnes sucked in her breath and blew it out. Best to cogitate the situation for the next few minutes. Just exactly how much should she share with Katherine and how much should she keep secret?

Colonel Farthingworth hadn't sworn her to secrecy about President Roosevelt's package. All he had asked was that she should deliver it personally. Since Katherine would also be traveling to Washington, telling her about the package itself wasn't exactly the problem. The problem was sharing the manner in which she was conveyed to the military base and her absurd reaction.

Katherine would never understand how she thought Smitty had kidnapped her and the boy. But, if she didn't explain all of it, how could she account for the trip to the military base PX and the extra groceries? Five pounds of sugar, two pounds of coffee, half a dozen bananas, a frying chicken and two packages of stew meat certainly wouldn't escape Katherine's notice for very long, even though Agnes did most of the cooking. It was probably best to stick as close to the truth as possible, lest she slip up somewhere along the line. Katherine would be furious if she caught her in another fib.

"Here we are, Grandma. It's lunchtime and I thought you might be hungry." She set a tray on the coffee table, poured two cups of tea and settled back on the sofa. She handed Agnes a cup and held up a plate with two sandwiches cut in triangles.

"Thank you, dear." Apparently, Katherine had not noticed the fresh fruit in the icebox, nearly impossible to buy these days. How had she missed the coffee and sugar so insidiously scattered across the counter? "I *was* hungry." Agnes stood. "Maybe we should clean up just a bit before we eat."

"Oh, no you don't. Sit down. It won't take long to eat a sandwich and tell me what you need to say. We'll clean up later." Katherine grabbed Agnes's arm and pulled her back onto the sofa. "What's going on here?" She gestured around the living room, where magazines still lay strewn across the floor and pictures hung askew on the walls. "The kitchen looks like a tornado went through it."

Agnes sighed. "Yesterday, Colonel Farthingworth summoned me to the military base. He asked me to personally deliver a top secret document to President Roosevelt when we go to Washington. After we talked, he let me shop for groceries at the PX. Someone must have heard us talking and broke in to steal the package. Fortunately, I had it in my purse when I went to Mavis's house this morning. That's the whole story." Agnes smiled at Katherine. *That should do it. The truth, the whole truth, and nothing but the truth…mostly.*

Katherine's face looked like the beach on a cloudy day. She shook her head, sighed and stood. She walked toward the kitchen without a word.

"Where are you going? I thought you wanted to talk about this." Agnes stood with her hands outspread.

Katherine turned at the kitchen door. "I have no intention of sitting here and listening to another one of your *cockamamie* stories, Grandmother. I told you before, I was through with that. If all you can do is make up baloney, I'm going to clean up the mess."

Agnes followed her to the kitchen. She grabbed several cans and shoved them back into the cupboard. "You don't believe me? Katherine, I swear, it's the God's truth, every word." She slammed the cupboard door, reached for her purse, revealing the brown paper package tied with string. She pulled it out and laid it on the table. "See? Here it is. Just like I said."

Katherine looked at the package, her mouth still pinched into a pout. "So? It's a package." She picked it up. "I don't see President Roosevelt's name on it. It could be anything. It certainly doesn't look like top secret documents." She tossed it back on the table and began to wipe up the spilled flour and sugar on the counter. "Why don't you find someplace to go, Grandma? I'd just as soon clean this up by myself. I don't really feel like talking to you right now."

"But, Katherine! You don't understand. It's true! Colonel

Farthingworth asked me to take it to Washington. It must be what the prowler was looking for."

Katherine snapped her head around. *Humph!*

Of all things! For the first time, she told almost the whole truth and Katherine didn't believe her…*well, maybe not exactly the first time, but close enough…* She wasn't going to stand around and be insulted.

Agnes grabbed her purse and stomped out the front door, climbed into her Model A and started the engine. She backed down the driveway and chugged off down the street. *Where should I go? What should I do?* Her heart pounded like an oil rig as she drove aimlessly down her block and turned left at the corner. *If she doesn't want my help, she can just clean up the mess herself.*

Miffed and seeking vindication, she drove toward town. *I wonder if Mildred is home.* Several blocks from her house, she glanced in her rear view mirror. A black sedan followed about half a block behind. Was it following her?

Perspiration pricked her underarms. Maybe it was the burglar! *Don't be ridiculous!* She sucked in her breath and pressed her foot harder on the gas pedal, turned left at the next corner and right two blocks later. The black sedan, staying a half-block behind, continued to follow at each turn.

The First Church of the Evening Star and Everlasting Light was several blocks away. Agnes attended there somewhat irregularly—in spite of good intentions of a Saturday night—often discarded of a Sunday morning. She made a right turn and sped up the street toward the church, pulled into the parking lot and stopped the car.

The black car crept past The First Church of the Evening Star and Everlasting Light, and then continued down the street.

Pshew! I'm probably imagining things again. This darn package is making me suspicious of a local citizen! She reached for her purse and groped around inside. Where was the package? Her thoughts jerked back to the recent argument with Katherine. There! Her package lay on the table, where Katherine tossed it beside her purse. If the thief went back to the house, he'd find Katherine alone and the package on the table. *I have to get home!*

"Mrs. Odboddy?"

Agnes jumped several inches off the seat cushion. Her heart fluttered. Right outside the driver's side window, a man had leaned down and peered through the window glass. Her heart pounded. Had the black car circled around and come back when she wasn't looking?

Agnes blinked and then her vision cleared as she recognized the figure beside the car. "Oh! Pastor Lickleiter! It's you." Her hand flew to her heart. "You startled me." She rolled down the window.

"Why, Mrs. Odboddy. You look upset. Is there something I can do to help? Do you want to talk?" He gripped the edge of the window frame.

"No. No. I'm fine. I was driving across town and I thought someone… Well, never mind what I thought. You know me! Always imagining things. I was on my way to see my friend, Mildred, so if you'll excuse me, I'd best be on my way." Agnes pushed in the clutch and shifted into first gear.

"Will we see you Sunday? We've missed you at services recently."

"*Umm.* Well, no. Actually, Katherine and I are off on a trip to Washington, D.C. We'll be gone for a month or so. I'll tell you all about it when we get back. Bye!" She waved, touched the gas pedal and pulled away.

Pastor Lickleiter called, "Have a nice trip!"

Hope so. If I live to tell about it.

Katherine peered out the kitchen window overlooking the chicken yard. Wasn't it a beautiful day in their perfect little California town? Now she had let all this trouble and her quarrel with Grandma spoil it. The sun lit up the red roses on the bushes across the back fence. Robins hopped across the clipped lawn, pulling worms from the damp grass and flitted up into the trees to enjoy their brunch. Yes, it was a beautiful summer day. She scowled. It was *not* the kind of day that should be spoiled, dealing with burglars and cranky old women given to falsehoods and fabrications. Maybe she should go back to work and let Grandma clean up the rest of the mess.

She tossed the soiled dishrag onto the back porch with the heap of clothes waiting to be washed. What should she do about Grandmother? Her tall tales were getting worse by the day. Imagine! Saying she was delivering a package to the President of the United States! What a preposterous story. Maybe it was time to suggest a rest home. *I can't be responsible for what Grandmother might do while I'm at work.*

She shoved the sugar canister back into its place in the corner. Why was it so heavy? They were almost out of sugar a couple days ago. She opened the canister. Almost full to the brim. *Where did that come from?*

Grandmother said something about sugar, fruit and meat. Katherine opened the icebox and pulled out the meat tray. Two white butcher-wrapped hunks of meat lay in the tray. She pulled out the vegetable tray. Bananas and oranges! *Where on earth...?*

They hadn't tasted an orange for months and buying sugar required a ration coupon which they didn't have until their next ration book arrived on the first of the month.

Grandmother *said* she'd shopped at the military base. Maybe it was true. The military PX was the only place that might have fresh fruit these days. Certainly not at Wilkey's Market, even *with* a ration coupon.

So, if that part of Grandmother's story was true... Katherine turned. The brown package tied up with string lay on the table where she had tossed it. She reached for the package. *Do I dare?* Maybe just a tiny peek inside? If it was military papers, she wouldn't really read them. If it was something else...well, there was always that rest home.

She shivered. Was the thief still out there, spying on her from the back yard? She could almost feel eyes staring at her. She glanced out the kitchen window. Sure enough, Chicken Sophia and Chicken Myrtle sat on top of their coop, peering at her through the window.

Katherine grinned and tapped the glass. The Bantam roosters hopped off their little house and picked at bugs in the dirt.

She glanced around the kitchen again and slid the string off the package, holding her breath as the paper fell away, revealing a typed letter on top of a box. *One quick glimpse won't hurt.*

Not daring to touch the paper and leave a smudge or a fingerprint, she leaned over the table, and read.

Dear Franklin,

Knowing the importance of the event almost upon us, I'm asking a reliable woman to deliver this package directly into your hand. Its contents should help hasten the day until the hostilities are over and we'll once again be able to schedule a golf date.

Your Partner in Arms, Colonel Bartholomew Farthingworth

"This isn't right. I shouldn't read this." The box *must* hold top secret military documents! "Dear God in Heaven!" Katherine wrapped the brown paper around the box and threaded the strings over the corners. "Everything Grandma said is true! And I sent her away."

Katherine examined the rewrapped package. It looked okay. She scooted the package about three inches to the exact spot where Agnes left it when she went out the door.

Warmth crept up her cheeks. She not only insulted and quarreled with Grandmother, now she had breached National Security and read secret documents…almost. Hopefully, no one would know except Chicken Sofia and Chicken Myrtle, and she doubted they would tell anyone.

Chapter Six

Someone will only get this package over my dead body!

Agnes sped back across town at the dizzying speed of forty-five miles per hour, squealing her tires around corners and giving every stop sign a cursory rolling, California stop. Katherine was home alone with the package! It didn't take a Ph.D. professor to determine what the burglar was looking for. He couldn't have guessed that she had followed Colonel Farthingworth's instructions, 'Don't let it out of your sight,' when she visited her next-door neighbor.

Hadn't she even taken it with her into the bathroom last night when she took a bath? And, now, only a day later, she'd failed her assigned duty and rushed out of the house, mad as a wet hen, leaving it unprotected on the kitchen table! *Agnes, you are not to be trusted with a simple task. Hardly a warrior on the home front, and a poor scourge of the underworld.*

Another stop sign disappeared in her rear view mirror without so much as an attempt to slow down since there were no cars in the intersection. Good thing Chief Waddlemucker's henchmen were nowhere in sight.

Agnes skidded into her driveway and yanked on the handbrake, leaped from the car and slammed the car door. *Dear God. Please let Katherine be all in one piece and the package still safe on the kitchen table.* If anything happened while she was gone, how could she ever forgive herself?

She dashed up the sidewalk and threw open the front door. If

Katherine was still mad, she'd just have to get over it. "Katherine!" The package had to be secured in a safe hiding place. It was too vulnerable to carry around for the next few days, not to mention dangerous to whoever carried it. She knew how important the papers were, even if the Colonel hadn't specifically said so. The big black car that followed her around town was all the proof she needed. What if they'd caught up with her? What if they had cornered her, hoping to make her give up the package? Today, it wouldn't have mattered because she'd left it on the kitchen table, but just the same, if she continued to carry it around…

"I'm back, Katherine. We need to talk."

Katherine hurried from the kitchen, a smudge of flour on her cheek.

Thank God, she's all right. Agnes reached up and brushed her cheek. "You have—"

"Oh, Grandma. I'm sorry we quarreled. I don't know what's wrong with me lately." Katherine grabbed Agnes's hand from her cheek and pulled it to her lips. "Come and sit down. I'm sorry I was so rude. Forgive me?" She pulled Agnes into the kitchen. The cans and boxes of food were back in the cupboard. Chairs were shoved neatly under the table and all the flour was wiped from the kitchen counter. Only a shadow of flour still lay scattered across the linoleum.

Agnes raised an eyebrow. "Of course, dear." She sat. "Glad you agree with me. Get mad, get over it. That's what I always say. What made you change your mind?" She reached for the package and stuffed it back into her handbag, then brushed crumbs from the tablecloth onto the floor, her gaze wandering around the kitchen floor and out the window.

"Oh, nothing specific. I just thought about what you said. I figured you wouldn't lie about something so important. If Colonel Farthingworth wants you to take the package to the President, then, that's what we'll do." Katherine sucked in her breath. The color faded from her cheeks. "Oh! Do you think that's what the burglar was after?"

Agnes nodded. "The question is, how did he know *I* had it? Maybe Colonel Farthingworth has a spy in his office. Lucky I had the package with me this morning when the burglar came. But, I don't think I should carry it around for the next few days. I could be wrong, but I thought someone followed me downtown today. We need to hide the package somewhere safe until we leave for Washington." She gazed around the kitchen. "Where's a good place no one would think to look? The thief might come back." Agnes tapped her lips. "I know. I'll put it in Chicken Mildred's little house. No one would ever think to look there."

She pulled the package from her purse and carried it down the back steps into the back yard.

Katherine followed her out the back door and whispered. "Grandma. Really? Are you sure? In the chicken coop?" She scanned the yard and then nodded to Agnes. "The coast is clear."

Agnes unlatched the gate and stepped inside the twelve-foot square wire fence that held her four roosters. Chicken Sophia sat on top of the little wooden coop house, under the kitchen window.

Agnes shooed Chicken Mildred, Sophia, Myrtle and Mrs. Whistlemeyer off to the side. "Hey, little darlings. How are Mama's babies this morning? Mama wants you to keep something safe for her, okay?"

With a final glance around the yard, she leaned down and shoved the package as far as she could reach into the little chicken house. "That should do it. No one will think to look for it there," she whispered.

Mrs. Whistlemeyer flapped to the top of the little house and picked at Agnes's sleeve. She stroked the red feathers on his head. "Now, don't think you're going to get fed again. You had your breakfast this morning."

Agnes retraced the few steps across the chicken yard, latched the gate and tromped up the back stairs into the kitchen. She scrunched her face into a frown. "We have to find the boys a new home before we leave for Washington. Mavis said the neighbors are complaining about their crowing." She turned on the kitchen sink faucet, washed and dried her hands.

"I hate to say it, but they're right." Katherine ambled back into the house. "But, where can we take them?" Katherine grabbed the broom and swept the remnants of the flour into a pile on the floor. She gathered it into the dustpan, then dumped it into the garbage can and returned the broom to the closet.

"Don't worry. We'll find a good place. They'll not end up in anyone's stew pot, that's for sure." As hard as it was parting with the colorful Bantams, she knew it was for their own good. They would be much happier in a bigger yard. Just where that might be was the question.

Katherine glanced at Agnes and then looked away, her cheeks pinking up. "Do you have any idea what's in the package you put in the coop?"

Agnes cleared her throat and sat down at the table. She and Katherine were in this thing together. As long as they were both traveling with the package, she should know the whole story and the risk involved. "I don't know for sure, of course, but I've checked the package over pretty good. It feels like a box. The way I figure, it must be secret war documents for the President's eyes only. I'm thinking that Colonel Farthingworth didn't trust the teletype or regular mail delivery." She ducked her head and lowered her voice. "General Farthingworth is probably in contact with General McArthur. Maybe they're planning some big military plan and these are the maps and—"

"Oh, Grandma. You can't be serious." Up flew Katherine's eyebrows. "Like an invasion?" Her face paled. "Why on earth would he trust such important information to someone like...*uh*...?"

Agnes's mouth turned up in a little grin. "Someone like me? What better way to deliver the documents to President Roosevelt? Who would suspect a crotchety old lady traveling across country on a train?"

"Then again, apparently somebody did. Why else would he break into the house the very next day after the Colonel gave you the package? Maybe you should call Colonel Farthingworth and tell him what happened. He might want to send the documents another way—"

"Not on your tintype! He entrusted them to me." Agnes crossed her arms over her ample bosom and tossed her head. "The only way someone is going to get these papers is over my dead body!"

"But, Grandma. If they're as important as you think, someone might not hesitate to consider that possibility."

"We'll just see about that. I'll be right back." Agnes hurried down the hall and into her bedroom where she opened a cedar chest in her closet. The scent of cedar tickled her nose. Under the bag of baby clothes, her wedding gown, a box of old photographs and John's baby book, she found a small box. "*Ah!* Here it is." She pulled it out and closed the hope chest lid. How many years had it been since the inside of this box had seen the light of day?

Agnes balanced the box in both hands, carried it like a precious treasure and laid it in the middle of the kitchen table.

"What is it?" Katherine whispered, her eyes wide. She reached for the box and lifted the lid.

"When your grandpa died during WWI, they sent me his personal effects. His watch, the St. Christopher's medal he wore next to his dog tags and his Colt .45 pistol." Agnes nodded toward the box.

Katherine pulled back the cotton covering the item in the box. She drew in her breath. "A gun? What are you going to do, Grandma? Carry Grandpa Douglas's gun in your pocket?"

"Why not? I learned to shoot back in 1918, just like every other able-bodied agent who served. I was a pretty good shot, too, if I do say so myself."

"But, Grandmother, it isn't 1918 anymore and you aren't … You're… you're—"

"You were going to say that I'm not a size eight any more, right? Right?"

"*Umm…*well, yes, I suppose so." Her cheeks took on a rosy hue. "At the very least, make sure you know how to use it."

Agnes lifted the gun from the box. Her hand dropped to the side from the weight of it. "Oh, dear! I had forgotten how heavy it is. I'm afraid this won't do after all!"

"Didn't I say? Grandmother. You need to put that thing back where you found it. The idea of you carrying a gun! Ridiculous!" Katherine took the pistol from Agnes, laid it back in the box and closed the lid.

"It's not ridiculous. It's just the wrong gun. I'll get mine, instead. The one I carried during my courier days." Memories of her courier days in 1918, changing tires in an ankle length skirt, hand-cranking the automobile to start the engine, and her days in Paris during the blitz flashed through her mind. She shivered at the memories. Some pleasant and others best forgotten.

"You carried… You never cease to amaze me."

Agnes scooted back into her bedroom and returned with the smaller, lighter .32 caliber Colt revolver and a box of shells. She hefted the gun left and right. "Now, this is more like it. Bring it on, Nazi spy, and see where it gets you." She squinted one eye, aimed the pistol toward the rooster clock on the wall and pulled the trigger.

Blam!

The plastic rooster clock over the stove shattered and about twenty pieces clattered down onto the top of the burners. The electric cord coiled in a heap around the burners with the plug still attached and hanging from the wall socket over the stove.

"Grandmother! What have you done now? You've shot a hole in the wall and killed your rooster clock!"

"*Whoops!* I told you I knew how to shoot the dang thing. Just didn't remember that it was loaded. If anyone on the train tries to take these documents from me, they're going to feel the business end of old Betsy and end up like that rooster clock."

"As much as I hate to admit it, somehow, I believe you're serious. We still need to tie up a couple loose ends before we leave for Washington."

"Such as…?"

"Picking up our passports, packing our clothes, and finding a home for the roosters!"

Chapter Seven

Fourteen hens was too many for one rooster.

Bantam hens scattered every which way as Agnes pulled her Model A to a stop in front of Marvin Higgenbottom's large red barn. A group of hens were perched on a barrel and others picked bugs from a haystack beside the sliding barn door. Above the door, barn swallows had built mud nests in the eaves, some attached to each other like condominiums, and some single nests along the edge of the roofline. Male swallows flitted in and out, streaked across the barnyard in search of bugs, and then zipped back into their nest where Mrs. Swallow waited, up to her beak in demanding, hungry baby chicks.

Agnes glanced through the rear window at the jiggling burlap sack that thrashed on the rumble seat. "My poor darlings. Bet they can't wait to get out of that bag."

Thank goodness, last night Mildred had come up with a solution to their rooster problem, and contacted her brother-in-law, Marvin, who lived on a farm outside of town. He graciously agreed to adopt the four Odboddy boys. *So here we are, delivering my babies.*

Agnes tapped her horn. The sliding barn door opened and Marvin stepped into the morning sunshine. He pushed back his hat, pulled a piece of straw from his mouth, and smiled, revealing a gap between his teeth. "Good morning, *Misshus* Odboddy." He whistled his S's like a canary. "Been expecting you." Another trill pierced her eardrums. Listening to this guy was as bad as fingernails dragged across the blackboard.

Marvin thrust his hands into his bib overall pockets. He grinned, stepped toward the Model A and opened Agnes's door. "I'm Marvin. Welcome to the Rocking-H Ranch." He offered his hand to help Agnes from the car.

The door of the little clapboard house slammed and a chubby Mrs. Higgenbottom bustled out, wiping her hands on her apron. "Welcome. Welcome. Mildred said you'd be by this morning. I'm Hilda." She thrust out her hand. "I hear you brought us a present."

"I did. Are you sure you want all my boys?" Agnes stepped out of the Model A.

"Absolutely. Since our last rooster died, Marvin's hens are on strike and stopped laying. I think that's where the expression, *frustrated old hen*, comes from," Hilda giggled.

Agnes turned toward the rumble seat. "They're in here. Probably pretty anxious to get out. Where do you want them?"

Marvin hefted the bag over the end of the rumble seat. "Well, let's *shee* these fellows," he whistled. "There are four, right?" He set the bag on the ground and untied the string on top. "I think I'll just turn them *loosh*. With the hens meandering about, I don't suppose they'll run away. They'll likely follow the *girlsh* into the hen house when it gets dark. *Heh, heh.*" He dumped the bag upside down.

The four roosters tumbled out, squawking and fluffing their feathers, obviously annoyed at being hauled across town so unceremoniously in a sack.

Mrs. Higgenbottom stepped back as the four stumbled around her feet.

Agnes beamed at her boys. All four were the picture of health. They looked nothing like the scrawny pullets Nurse Rachet had pawned off on her last summer.

"This is Mrs. Whistlemeyer. That's Myrtle and Sophia over there." Agnes pointed to the various roosters. "This one is Mildred, and...." *Oh, goodness. What are they going to think?* Warmth crept up her cheeks. She glanced up at Hilda.

"Mildred?" Mrs. Higgenbottom raised her eyebrows. "Why on earth would you name a rooster after my sister-in-law, Mildred?"

Agnes gulped. "Their previous owner assured me they were hens, so I named them after my friends and neighbors. The boys know their names now and come when I call."

"*Huh!* They'd come to anybody with food in their hand," Marvin warbled. "Doesn't mean they know their *namesh.*"

Agnes laughed. "You're probably right." She gazed around the yard. Her boys had already mingled with the hens, clucked happily and looked as if they'd spent their whole lives on the farm. "How many hens do you have? I wouldn't want the boys to squabble over the ladies."

She chuckled at the thought of the tussles her four hunky roosters might have, all trying to woo the same hen. *My babies should be happy here.*

"We have fourteen hens. It was too many for one rooster to handle," Hilda said.

"What do you think killed him?" Marvin muttered, slapping the dust from his hat.

A swallow dive-bombed Agnes's head. "*Whoa!* Look out!" She ducked and then her gaze followed the bird back up to the eaves.

"Oh, you get used to it when you live here. They're annual visitors." Marvin pointed up to Barn Swallow City where dozens of the feathered citizens flitted in and out of mud condominiums, bickering and wrangling over prime real estate. "They come back every year, refurbish their old nests or build a new one."

"The nests almost look like wasps nests. How do they get the mud to stick to the eaves like that?" Agnes craned her neck and peered at the architectural marvels.

"They gather mud pellets in their *beaksh* to build the exterior and then line them with grasses, feathers, algae or other *shoft* material. If you want to know how they know what to do, you'll have to ask them, 'cause I never figured it out." Marvin laughed.

"It's one of God's miracles, to be sure." Hilda nodded.

"Well, I should let you get about your work." Agnes gazed around the barnyard where the Odboddy boys mingled with the hens. "They look happy enough, already." Agnes sighed and opened her car door. "But, let's make sure we understand each other, Mr. Higgenbottom." Her eyebrows squinched together as she raised her finger. "You promise the Bantams will have the run of the place and never be put into a stewpot?"

"Of course, Missus Odboddy. Look how happy they're making my *girlsh*. Maybe they'll start laying again. A couple might even sit a clutch of eggs. Rest assured, they're most welcome."

Hilda nodded. "Don't worry. I promise we'll take good care of them."

"Then, I guess there's no reason to hang around." Agnes slid into her car.

Marvin closed her car door and gave it a slap. "I'll let you know if we have baby *chicksh*. You can come back and visit your grand-*chicksh* anytime. Give Mildred my love."

Agnes nodded. Her gaze followed the Odboddy boys around the barnyard. She doubted they would miss her one tenth as much she'd miss them. Each of them already had a glint in his eye she had never seen before in her little chicken yard. And, each had picked out a fat hen to follow around the yard. Not one looked back or seemed to care whether they ever saw Agnes Odboddy again.

She started the car, waved to Marvin and Hilda and drove down the dirt driveway toward home. "Just like a man. Give him a slick chick to chase around and he forgets everything the old broad has ever done for him. Typical!"

Chapter Eight

He looks like a Nazi spy to me.

K atherine, honey. Aren't you ready yet? Mildred will be here any minute. Now, where did I put those tickets?" Agnes rifled through her purse, spilling its contents onto the kitchen table: her Maybelline Crimson Bow lipstick, mirrored compact with the ormolu cover and the turtle shell comb Mildred gave her last Christmas. Her lace-edged hankie dropped on top of the .32 special, alongside Colonel Farthingworth's package.

Agnes's heart raced. *Where are those blasted tickets?* What if the bus pulled out of the station with them standing in the parking lot, digging through her purse for the missing tickets? She'd have to tell Katherine that she had misplaced them. They might have to pay for another ticket on a later bus. What if they missed connections with the train in San Francisco and on down the line until they missed the plane leaving for the Pacific Islands with Mrs. Roosevelt? They'd be left in Washington D.C. in an unexpected snow storm in the middle of August, and their luggage might be stolen as they stomped the dark streets, shivering and cold through—

"Are you daydreaming, again? Mildred just drove up. What are you looking for?" Katherine stood in the kitchen doorway, her overnight case in one hand and her purse in the other. "I thought you were ready."

Agnes pawed through the items on the table, shoved them back and forth as panic constricted her chest. "I can't find the bus tickets! I was sure I put them in my purse." Perspiration beaded on her upper lip.

Katherine would be so mad. *I'm just a silly, careless old woman.* Of course she had let her imagination run amok, but the risk of having to purchase more tickets and missing their connections was all too real if the tickets weren't found.

Katherine lifted her purse. "Don't you remember? You gave them to me and told me to keep track of them because you were too care…um…because you might lose them."

"Oh! Yes, now that you mention it, I do seem to recall—"

"I see you didn't lose Colonel Farthingworth's package, though it looks a bit worse for wear."

Agnes picked up the bedraggled parcel that lay amidst her personal items. She pulled a chicken feather from under the ragged strings, thanks to Mrs. Whistlemeyer and Chicken Myrtle and their attention to an unfamiliar object left unattended in their coop.

She ran her fingers over the dark and light spots that wouldn't wash off the brown paper wrapping; tell-tale proof that on several occasions, the package had been used as a perch.

"*Uh-huh.*" Agnes brushed at the tattered package. "I tried to get it clean. You don't think he'll notice, do you?"

"Not at all. Well, come on. Mildred is waiting."

Bags and suitcases were loaded into Mildred's sedan and within fifteen minutes, the ladies pulled up to the bus station. "Now, do you have everything, dear?" Mildred turned off the engine and set the brake. The ladies exited the car. "Did you bring galoshes and a raincoat? You never know how the weather will be in Washington D.C." Mildred lifted Agnes's suitcase from the trunk and waved to a porter. "And sandwiches? Did you bring a lunch? I hear that food is very expensive on the train these days."

The porter rolled a trolley over and loaded the luggage onto it. "Tickets? Ma'am? I can check them for ya' and you can jes' climb on board."

Katherine handed him the tickets.

He glanced at them. "Hope you ladies have a nice day in San

Francisco." The porter handed them back.

"We're catching a train there, headed for Washington. D.C." Agnes said.

"You on vacation?"

"Not exactly. We have business in Washington."

He jerked his head toward a war propaganda sign on the wall that read: *Millions of troops are on the move…is your trip necessary?*

"Now, that second bus over yonder," the porter pointed toward a large grey bus across the covered garage area. "That's the one you ladies will be takin.' It's got lovely tall windows, so you sit real high, the better to see the sights. Now you have a pleasant trip, hear? Ma'am?" He touched his hat and shoved the trolley toward the bus where a porter loaded luggage into large open doors beneath the bus.

Agnes hugged Mildred. "Thanks for the ride, dear. We'll give you a call when we get back. If you aren't home—"

Ahooga!

Agnes jumped and turned toward the sound. A big black sedan plunged toward the front door and stopped just short of driving onto the sidewalk. "Why, that looks like…" She stopped short. *Could that be the same car that followed me around town several days ago?* The one she hadn't mentioned to Katherine. Should she bring it up now? She clutched her overnight bag to her chest, aimed an air kiss toward Mildred and grabbed Katherine's arm. "We better get on board, *punkin.* Others are boarding. We'll want to get window seats, now won't we?"

Katherine craned her neck to gaze over the crowd.

Agnes shoved Katherine toward the bus with the large greyhound dog painted on the side, careful to keep her back toward the black car.

Looking back over her shoulder, Agnes noted a man and woman climbing out of the sedan. He was dressed in a black business suit and vest with matching tie and handkerchief. He carried a black Homburg hat in one hand and a briefcase in the other. *He looks like a Nazi spy to me.* Didn't they all try to look like ordinary folks so no one was the wiser?

The woman looked younger. She wore a smart form-fitting light green suit. The fox fur wrapped around her shoulders must have come straight from a New York fashion show. A cute little box hat sat on her peroxided hair. *I would never dye my hair like that!* The blonde pulled a compact from her purse, powered her pert little nose and smacked her blood-red lips. *Disgusting!* Then she leaned down to straighten the seam on the back of her silk stockings.

Agnes hated her on sight. It wasn't jealousy, mind you. It was disgust. With so many refugees, widows and orphans, struggling families and homeless puppies, how could one woman waste so much money on one outfit? The price of that outfit would keep orphans in milk for months.

Agnes followed Katherine up the steps of the bus and chose seats near the front.

Katherine settled next to the window where she continued to twist and stare through the window at the passengers in the bus station. "Donald said he'd try to come to the bus station to say good bye. We're going to leave before he comes, I just know it." She pouted.

"I suspect he got tied up at the hospital and couldn't get away, dear. I'm sure he would have come if he could."

Katherine's lip turned down. Her head drooped. "I know. I talked to him last night on the phone. He said he was on duty this morning, but he'd try to get away."

"Cheer up, dear. You're going to love sleeping on the train tonight. Of course, I've traveled by train on several occasions over the years, but I hear ours is a diesel-powered streamlined train."

"Won't we be changing trains several times before we reach Washington?"

Agnes nodded. "And several places, we'll have a layover for some hours before the next train."

Katherine grimaced. "In this modern day and age, why isn't there just one train that goes all the way across the country?"

"Maybe someday, *punkin*, but not this time. It makes for an interesting journey and lots of time to see the sights." Agnes peered at the couple from the sedan who appeared to be arguing beside the ticket window.

Agnes scooted down in the seat, lest they see her through the window. *Which one was traveling? The woman? The man? Or both of them?*

The young woman shook her head and gestured toward the sedan.

Her companion grabbed her arm and shoved her toward the bus.

Agnes half rose in her seat and then sat back down. *They're both coming on this bus!* How far would they have to travel with that couple? Hopefully, just to San Francisco. Was it a coincidence they should show up on the very day she and Katherine were traveling? *Or are they following me?* It looked as if the frowsy woman wasn't too keen on making the trip.

Agnes clutched her purse to her chest. Scenes from *Alice in Wonderland* jumbled in her thoughts. In her mind's eye, the package in her purse warmed and grew larger, like the cake in *Alice in Wonderland* that screamed, 'Eat me!' But, her package seemed to scream, 'Here I am! Steal me!'

The imaginary scene switched to *The Wizard of Oz*, and she heard, 'Don't mind the woman holding the purse. She can't protect me. Can't you see? I'm full of secret documents?' She shook her head to clear her ruminations and chuckled. *Don't be ridiculous, Agnes. They're not following you. Stop imagining things.*

"What's so funny, Grandma?"

Agnes shrugged. "Nothing, really. Just thinking."

Chattering voices approached. She looked up. The Fancy-Dan man and his moll took seats directly across the aisle! Another coincidence? Agnes pulled her purse tighter to her chest. Her cheeks tingled as she looked away.

The moll flopped around, a scowl marring her pretty made-up face. She removed her mink stole and squirmed until she found a comfortable spot in the window-seat, leaving the gentleman sitting not two feet from

Agnes's hip. He shoved his briefcase under his seat, leaned forward, grinned at Agnes and nodded a greeting. "Good morning."

Agnes nodded back, made a futile attempt at a smile and turned her head. *He's the one, all right.* The very same Nazi spy that followed her across town several days before!

Perhaps along the way to Washington, D.C., he thought he could waylay her and steal President Roosevelt's secret documents. Well, he hadn't counted on Agnes Agatha Odboddy, the scourge of the underworld. *Only over my dead body!* She reached into her purse, ran her hand over the package tied with twine, then downward and was comforted by the touch of cold steel.

Chapter Nine

Is living with a conspiracy theorist contagious? I'm as paranoid as she is.

atherine perused her fellow bus passengers. Would there be any interesting people to meet? If only they didn't have to take the train all the way to Washington, D.C.! Mrs. Roosevelt would have provided airline tickets if Grandmother had asked. But, no, she wouldn't hear of it. Grandma had said, "Traveling by air is far too expensive, dear. The country is at war, and we must economize every possible way. We'll travel by train. Just think! We can see the country. Won't that be fun?"

Fun, indeed! The thought of spending three days with Grandmother as her sole companion was daunting. What could they talk about? *As much as I love her, she is not a very stimulating conversationalist.*

"I hope the chickens are happy at the Higgenbottom farm. I'm going to miss them terribly."

Katherine rolled her eyes and glared out the window. *There! See? She wants to talk about chickens.*

Agnes shifted her purse on her lap. "I'm so excited! I just can't believe that we're actually on our way to Washington, D.C. with the 'you-know-what.'"

Why didn't I sit on the aisle? At least I might have had a chance to talk about something other than those…oh dear…oh dear. Katherine twisted her hankie. *Why did I ever peek inside that package?*

"Are you okay, *punkin*? You mustn't worry. You know, riding in a bus is very safe these days."

Katherine nodded. "I'm fine." Were they fine? What were they involved in? Someone had already broken into the house. Would they make another attempt on the long train ride? She gazed at the man across the aisle. He looked normal enough. But, the wannabe *Mata Hari* beside him suggested otherwise. *I can believe her as a secret agent, with her spike heels, pancake makeup and fur stole.*

Three rows back, a young woman traveled with a little girl. The child leaned over a coloring book. The woman had pulled a magazine from her purse and was already deep into its contents. Not much chance of engaging her in a conversation. *Wonder if they'll transfer to the train in San Francisco?*

Katherine turned in her seat and watched as passengers boarded the bus and found their places. She scanned the parking lot, still hoping Donald would at least make an appearance to wave at the bus. She had so hoped to be his priority this morning, as busy as he was at the hospital. But wasn't that about par for the course with Don these days? Always too busy...

Toward the rear of the bus, two Negro soldiers sat with their heads together, reading. One of them reminded her of Jackson, Grandmother's friend, who ran the elevator at the police station and had built their chicken yard last summer.

A smile tickled her cheeks. She was going to miss those silly chickens, now that they were settled on the Higgenbottom farm. Probably not as much as Grandmother, but they were cute... Until 5:30 A.M. when they started crowing. She wouldn't miss that.

"All aboard!" The driver slid the door closed and started the engine. The bus jerked forward.

A female attendant rose from the front seat and came down the aisle. "Present your tickets, please." She stopped by the couple across the aisle. "Tickets, please. Thank you." She punched the tickets and handed them back. The attendant stopped beside Grandmother. "Tickets?"

Katherine leaned over and handed her the tickets. "We had ours checked outside." The attendant nodded and moved down the aisle toward the woman and child.

"We're actually on our way to the Pacific Islands. Aren't you thrilled, Katherine?"

"*Shh!* Grandma," Katherine whispered. "We aren't supposed to talk about that. It's supposed to be a secret." Katherine patted Grandmother's arm. "Just sit back and enjoy the scenery. We'll be in San Francisco in a couple hours. That should be exciting. I haven't been to San Francisco in years." She pulled an Agatha Christie novel from her bag and opened it in her lap.

"*Psst!* Katherine." Grandmother put her hand to her mouth. "Did you notice that couple across the aisle? I've seen him before."

Katherine glanced at the couple. *The Fancy-Dan and his moll?* "That's not surprising. You've probably seen him around town—"

Shrill words from the strumpet across the aisle interrupted her comment. "Stop touching me. I don't like it!" The young woman half-rose from her seat.

"Be still. You agreed to be my wife. Now, sit down, do you hear me?" Her companion replied in a stage-whisper and grabbed her arm.

What on earth? Katherine stared at the couple. Heads turned. Was the young woman in danger? Wasn't that all they needed? A domestic free-for-all right here on the bus.

The woman rose and tried to push her way past her husband.

He shoved her back down in the seat. "I said, sit down and behave. People are staring," he snarled between gritted teeth, and then looked around at all the faces turned his way. "Nothing to worry about, folks. Just a nervous bride." He forced a toothy grin.

Who was he kidding, pretending that she was suffering from honeymoon jitters?

The young woman scooted down in her seat, her cheeks aflame, her face lowered, trying to avoid the stares of her companions.

"That man is making me nervous," Agnes whispered. "Let's move so we can talk." She picked up her purse, shuffled three rows down the swaying aisle and slid into one of the empty seats across from the woman and child.

Katherine shrugged, gave the man a shy smile and followed Grandmother. *What choice do I have? I have to go with her.* Reaching the new chosen seats, she crawled over Grandmother's legs and settled next to the window. "Why did you do that? You've embarrassed me to death. He's going to think you moved because they were arguing."

"Let him think what he wants. Listen to me. Remember, the other day when we quarreled and I went for a drive and left the package on the table? That man…" She tossed her head toward the couple, "… followed me around town in his black sedan. He's trying to steal the *you-know-what.*"

Katherine shrugged. "Really, Grandma? All black sedans look alike. Are you sure? We just saw the car for a minute when they drove up."

"It was the same car. I'm sure. It had a dent in the left front fender."

"Maybe he was just going the same way you were going."

Agnes shook her head. "No. I changed directions several times and then stopped at the church. I'm telling you, he followed me."

Katherine nodded. She was half-inclined to believe Grandmother's conspiracy story. She knew what the package contained, something her grandmother only suspected. *Maybe living with a conspiracy theorist is contagious. I'm getting as paranoid as she is.* "So, does he think he can steal it here on the bus? What if they're going to Washington, D.C. too? That gives him a full three days. Oh, dear! What are we going to do?" Katherine twisted her hands. Why was it that every day with Grandmother was like an afternoon at the Saturday Matinee with the Three Stooges?

The journey that started out as a boring three-day trip to Washington might change to a three-day test of will between two helpless women and a Nazi spy, bent on stealing national secrets that could affect the outcome of the war. Katherine continued whispering. "Suppose we lay over in San Francisco and take another train to Washington tomorrow?

Or call Colonel Farthingworth and tell him what's going on."

"Let's not be hasty. We don't even know for sure that he's going on to D.C. Maybe he's just on his honeymoon in San Francisco. Beside, at this late date, I doubt we could lay over a day and still get to Washington in time to meet Mrs. Roosevelt's plane."

Agnes squared her shoulders. "Listen. Between us, we'll make sure the package is never out of our sight. We can handle it." She threw back her head and squared her jaw. She covered her mouth and whispered, "The only way that traitor will get his hands on this package is over my dead body."

Katherine lowered her head. "You've said that before and that's what I'm afraid of. You might have agreed to sign onto this job, but I didn't. I'll support the war-effort as much as the next guy, Grandma, but this is ridiculous. Maybe I'll take the next bus back to Newbury."

"Katherine. You can't mean that. Aren't you going to help me see this thing through?" Agnes's face paled. She grabbed Katherine's hand. "I really need you. I can't do it alone."

Grandmother needed her all right, but how could they match wits with a trained Nazi spy? She could see the headlines now. *Two Women Mysteriously Fall from Moving Train.* If she agreed to help Grandmother, they were committing to a life or death struggle of wits and courage. A chill raced through her body and her fingers tingled. A smile twitched at the corner of her lips.

The thought of matching wits with a criminal and living to tell the tale *was* exhilarating. In that moment, the interior of the bus brightened with an unexpected glow, like when candlelight reflects through a crystal chandelier. The buildings rushing by all looked freshly painted and the neon signs seemed to have new light bulbs. The sun streaming through the window glinted off Grandma's sterling silver chopsticks and cast a flickering streak on the ceiling. Katherine could almost smell the flowers on the gun-moll's perky little hat, so like the yellow roses in their own garden.

Yes, the prospect of engaging in a life and death adventure *was* exhilarating. Adrenaline rushed into her chest. Was this why people pursued dangerous sports? Why men jumped from airplanes or drove fast cars, or volunteered to join the FBI and track down Nazi spies?

Yes, I'll help Grandmother. An invigorating idea, but, at the same time, terrifying. She'd never felt quite so full of life since the night Stephen proposed marriage. And yet, look how that turned out. The Japs bombed Pearl Harbor and Stephen died and... *I won't think about that now!*

Katherine threw back her head. "I'm going to help you, Grandma. Between us, we'll get this damn...*er*...darn package to Washington, if it's the last thing we ever do."

"Why, Katherine, for shame. There's never any call for a lady to use vulgar language. I'm surprised at you. I raised you better than that."

Katherine ducked her head, the blood rushing in her ears and warming her cheeks. *What just happened? Did she really say...?* "Yes, Grandma."

Chapter Ten

What a mean-spirited woman!

gnes and Katherine rode in silence, watching the surrounding scenery. Highway 1 meandered along the crooked Sonoma County coastline. As beautiful as the ocean was, the hairpin curves high above the ocean made Agnes's stomach lurch. What if the bus should pitch off the narrow road and crash into the sea? There wouldn't be much left of the passengers and who would know to get the package to President Roosevelt? *What a crazy thought!*

Eventually, the road turned inland toward Santa Rosa where it wound past farm land, apple orchards and fields filled with black and white cows. "Thank Heavens, we're beyond that part of the highway. It's beautiful, but wouldn't you think there'd be a better road inland from Newbury to Santa Rosa? I didn't think my stomach was going to survive those curves."

Katherine laughed. "I wish I hadn't packed my camera in my suitcase. Did you see the seals on the rocks?" She smiled at the young woman across the aisle.

Somewhere around San Rafael, Agnes caught the young woman's eye. "Hello. I'm Agnes Odboddy. Are you going far with your daughter?"

The woman jerked her head up, looked quickly around the bus and then gazed at Agnes. Her face paled. She blinked several times. *Why is she so nervous?*

"Oh, she's not my daughter. I'm her nanny." Her shoulders relaxed somewhat. "This is Madeline and my name is...*uh*..." She lowered her voice and glanced around the bus again. "*Uh*...Miss Grafton." A big truck whooshed past as she spoke.

"'Scuse me?" Agnes leaned across the aisle. "I didn't quite catch that. Did you say Miss Griffin?"

"Close enough." The nanny pursed her lips and turned back to her magazine.

How rude. I guess she doesn't want to socialize. "Well, excuse me for interrupting. I thought it might be nice to get acquainted, but I see you're not interested. I won't bother you." She straightened her shoulders and stared straight ahead.

"Oh, I'm sorry," the nanny stammered. "I didn't actually mean to be rude. I...I'm just a very private person. I don't usually speak to strangers." The woman turned toward the child. "I'm taking Madeline to her father in Washington, D.C. She spends the school year with him and the summers in California with her mother. I take care of her while they work."

"Oh, I see. That's nice. She gets to see both sides of the country and you get to move around. That sounds quite exciting for both of you."

"It can be. Though it's hard for Madeline to make friends, and then has to leave for months at a time. Since her father is a Senator, this is the best way to handle visitation since the divorce."

"*Tch... Tch...* A shame, but at least she has you, one stable adult she can count on."

Miss Gifford, or Grifson or whatever her name was, blushed. Her hand trembled.

Agnes peered at her pink cheeks. *What did I say? I wonder if there's more to this story than she's telling me.*

"Grandma! Look. There's the Golden Gate Bridge. Look at the skyscrapers up ahead. And, there's Coit Tower. Oh, this is so exciting."

The bus rattled across the Golden Gate Bridge. Agnes gazed at the sailboats scattered across the bay. "Look! They look like toy boats in a pond."

"There's Alcatraz!" Katherine leaned toward the window as they passed the San Francisco landmark island. Across the bridge, the road curved and followed the shoreline through town.

Agnes pointed out the window. "See that round building? That's the Palace of Fine Arts. It was built especially for the 1915 Panama Exposition."

"Isn't this where they held the San Francisco World's Fair in 1939? I hated missing it, but I was in college in Boston then." Katherine craned her neck to peer out the windows on the opposite side of the bus.

"That was across town." Agnes leaned toward the child. "Did you know they built an actual island in the Bay to hold all the exposition buildings? It was named Treasure Island. The plan was to turn it into an airport after the Fair closed, but then the war started. Now, it's a naval base."

"Is it still there? I'd like to see a treasure island." Madeline jumped up and down in front of her seat.

"No, sweetheart. The Fair was only open for four months, then again for four months the next year. The exhibitions and shows debuted the technology of tomorrow."

"Like rocket ships and things?" Madeline asked.

Agnes shook her head. "No. But I did see a *television*. They broadcasted President Roosevelt's speech on the opening day of the Fair. It played every day, so every day all the visitors could see it." She turned to Katherine. "I wish you could have been there. You'd have loved it."

"Television? I've read about them. There's one at the department store downtown. How does it work?"

"It's a mystery to me, but somehow, it picks pictures out of the air, like radio waves or something. They claim that someday every home will have one, but that sounds like hogwash to me. How many times would folks want to listen to Roosevelt give the same speech?"

"Oh, Grandma. He'd give other speeches and they'd get other people to give speeches. Maybe even have orchestras or something."

Agnes put up her nose. "Just the same. I'll keep my radio, thank you very much. But I will say, movie stars and musicians put on some great performances at the Fair. Esther Williams had an Aquacade show. She was great."

"It must have been wonderful. I'm sorry I missed it." Katherine leaned close and whispered. "Look how excited Madeline is, seeing all this for the first time."

The chatter increased as the bus passed through downtown San Francisco.

Agnes leaned toward the nanny. "If Madeline wants to come over here on our side, we can squeeze together and make room for her. She could see the sites better."

The child bounced up and stood in front of her seat, looking hopefully between the nanny and Agnes.

"I don't think so." The nanny placed a possessive hand on the little girl's arm and pushed her back down. "She can see just as much from over here."

Madeline's shoulders slumped. She sniffed, sat back and turned toward the window, wiping her eyes.

What a mean-spirited woman. Did she think I was going kidnap the kid?

"She's sure got that poor child on a short leash," Agnes whispered to Katherine. "I wonder what she's so afraid of."

Katherine shrugged. "Look! Look! There's a cable car." The car wound its way down a street with passengers clinging to the sides. "Wouldn't it be fun to ride a cable car, Madeline?"

Madeline leaned in front of her nanny, smiled and nodded.

Several blocks later, the bus pulled into the train station. The driver stood and shoved a lever, and opened the door. "Here we are, folks. San Francisco Union Station. If you'll exit the bus and wait alongside, we'll have your luggage out in a jiffy. Once you've collected your bags, head on into the station. The ticket booth is on your left just through the double doors. Restrooms on your right. Information booth is straight ahead. Hope you enjoyed the ride." He tromped down the steps, opened the double baggage doors, and pulled out suitcases from under the bus.

"This is it, Katherine. Are you ready? We're really on our way now." Agnes patted her purse, gripped the handrail and stepped off the bus.

The man and his bride lingered in their seats—the last ones off the bus.

Chapter Eleven

That sleazy lady is putting more lip rouge on her Clara-Bow lips!

A hubbub of noise in the train station nearly drowned out the voice on the loud speaker. "Arriving, Track C, Los Angeles to San Francisco. Departing, Track A, San Francisco to Bakersfield."

"What did he say?" Agnes gripped Katherine's arm. "It's like a zoo in here. It's giving me a headache. I could barely understand what he said for all the babbling."

"He was announcing some trains' arrival. Not ours, I don't think."

The huge room trembled with mixed human emotions that ran the gambit from joy to sorrow—travelers, vacationers, business men, squalling children and frazzled mothers, uniformed men and women, exuberant hello hugs and tearful, clinging good-bye kisses.

Agnes checked her tickets. "We have a while before our train leaves. Let's find a seat and eat our lunch." She pushed the cart loaded with their luggage, led Katherine to a somewhat quieter section of the station, and plopped onto a wooden bench. "My feet hurt!"

She rummaged in her purse and pulled out two liverwurst sandwiches, carrot sticks and a crumpled oatmeal cookie from the bottom of her handbag. "We should eat our sandwiches before we get on board. I hear the price for food is dear on the train. We'll have enough of that over the next three days. We mustn't waste money on food when we're at war. Carrot stick?"

Katherine mumbled something unintelligible around the bobby pin in her mouth that had tumbled from the victory roll in her hair.

Agnes munched on her sandwich as she watched the hubbub rushing hither and yon, buying tickets, mothers weeping as young men went off to war, girls throwing themselves into soldiers' arms, babies shrieking. She shook her head and mumbled, "It's sad, isn't it? So many young men going off to war."

"Which track is our train on, Grandma?" Katherine clutched her overnight case with one hand while she nibbled on the crust of the day-old bread. "Wish you'd thought to bring a thermos of coffee."

Agnes opened Katherine's purse and pulled out the tickets. "*Umm…*We take the train headed for Phoenix, leaving from Track B at 12:45 P.M." She glanced at her watch. *12:10 P.M.* She leaned toward Katherine and raised her voice to be heard over the din. "We have time to visit the restroom and wash our hands. Then we best find Track B." *If I don't get to the restroom in about one minute, I'm going to explode.*

She hailed a porter rushing by with a pushcart filled with luggage. "Sir! Sir! Excuse me. Can you direct us to the ladies' washroom?"

He pointed across the congested station. "Just under that big American flag there, ma'am."

"Can you see that our luggage gets on board the train to Phoenix?" She gestured to the cases on the pushcart near the bench.

"Sure can, ma'am. I'm heading to Track B with this here load now." The porter grabbed their suitcases and stacked them on top of his load.

"That's very kind of you." Agnes pulled a dime from her purse and handed it to the porter.

"Thank you, ma'am. Much obliged." He rushed off with the trolley, headed across the room.

At the long line of ladies outside the restroom, Agnes pushed her way toward the head of the line. "Excuse me. Pardon me. Can you let us through here, please?"

A rather large blonde woman with a ruddy complexion glared at her. "Hey! Pardon your own self, lady. We've all been waiting for nearly ten minutes!"

"If you don't mind, we have a train to catch. Can we step in front of you?" Agnes flashed her most charming smile and nodded, hoping to gain approval, while mentally measuring the distance between the line and the nearest bathroom stall.

"As a matter of fact, I do mind. We all have a train to catch. Wait your turn. Who are you? Some kind of celebrity or something?" The woman thrust out her chin and moved forward a few feet as another woman exited through the swinging door and the line shifted a step.

Agnes turned and caught Katherine's eye. "Someone left her manners home today. Guess she doesn't know about our important mission." She pulled her face into a smirk, crossed her feet at the ankles and…

"Grandma! *Hush!*" Katherine swatted Agnes's arm. Her cheeks pinked up. She shook her head, stepped away and turned her back, distancing herself from her grandmother.

The woman in line stared at Agnes.

Agnes glared back. "That's right. I'm on official business for the President. What's your name? If I don't make that train, he'll want to know which inconsiderate, unpatriotic upstart kept me from making my connections."

The woman in the line stepped back. Her cheeks paled. She sputtered. "*Er…uhh…*I'm sorry. I had no idea. Please. Go on ahead of me. I can wait." She lowered her head, not able to meet Agnes's glare.

"Come, Katherine. We don't want to miss the connecting train to Washington." She grasped Katherine's arm and bypassing the ladies in line, stepped into the restroom.

Agnes entered the next vacant stall and closed the door. She chuckled as she hung her purse on the peg, draped her jacket over top of the door and hiked up her skirt. *Oh, thank goodness! And not a minute too soon.*

"Thank you. That was most kind of you." Katherine called to the women at the front of the line. Her voice sounded almost apologetic.

Agnes stared at the graffiti written on the back of the door. *Mary loves Gregory... Agnes loves Gerald... What! Who's Gerald?* Katherine didn't need to apologize. The woman was being rude, wasn't she? And, they *were* on their way to Washington, weren't they? And, it was official business, wasn't it? Why were people so rude these days? Not at all like folks during WWI when everyone was so thoughtful and kind. Back then, if you asked for a favor, anyone would fall all over themselves to oblige.

Agnes adjusted her clothing, retrieved her jacket and purse, and stepped out toward the sinks. *Oh, my gosh! Isn't that the sleazy woman from the bus, painting more gaudy red lipstick on her Clara-Bow lips? Should I speak to her?* Where was Katherine? Probably still in one of the stalls. Before Agnes could come to a decision, the young woman looked up from the sink.

"Hello. I guess we're traveling on the same train. Going to Washington, D.C., right?"

Agnes started. *"Umm...*yes, it seems so." She reached out her hand. *So, they were going on to Washington. No big surprise!* "Agnes Odboddy..." She turned as Katherine stepped up beside her. "This is my granddaughter, Katherine. And, you are...?"

"Geraldine Ledbetter...*er...*Scruggs." She smiled and put out her hand. "We just got married. We're on our...*umm...*honeymoon." She shook Agnes's hand. "I hope I didn't give you the wrong impression. I mean, about our tiff on the bus?" A crimson flush crept over her cheeks making her face look more like a marionette than ever.

She's lying. I can't believe she's married to that creep.

"*Uh...huh.* I see. Of course. Newlyweds. Well, we'd best be on our way. So nice to meet you. See you on the train." She took Katherine's arm. "Come dear, we must hurry." Agnes turned and pulled Katherine out the door.

"Grandma. How could you? I've never seen you so rude. What's gotten into you?" Katherine said, glancing at Agnes.

"You didn't buy that story about them being on their honeymoon, did you?" Agnes looked back over her shoulder as she hustled Katherine away from the washroom. "Now, where exactly is Track B?"

"Don't change the subject, Grandma. You know what I'm talking about—all that malarkey before about being on government business? You can't toss that information around just to get to the head of the washroom line." Katherine shook Agnes's arm. "I've never been so embarrassed."

Agnes stopped walking and spun in a circle, checking out the signs high on the walls indicating various points of interest. "There. Track B. Due north." She pointed, and then checked her watch. "It's 12:30 P.M. Step lively." With the determination of Lewis and Clark searching for a route across the western half of the continent, Agnes plunged through the crowds toward the sign indicating Track B.

"Well? You have nothing to say?" Katherine trudged beside her.

"I say that it worked, didn't it? Stretching the truth is the best way to get what you need in this world. We would never have gotten through that line and made the train at the rate we were going. Besides, I had to... Never mind. Did I say anything that wasn't true?"

"Grandmother. What am I going to do with you?"

Before Agnes could respond, a harried woman with a baby on her shoulder pushed between Agnes and Katherine. It appeared that life was dealing unkindly with her at present, if the stress lines in her face were any clue. Perhaps she was meeting a relative or sending a loved one off to war. Most likely, the latter. Agnes's heart went out to her.

"*Yoo-hoo.* Mrs. Odboddy! Wait up! *Yoo-hoo!*"

Agnes stopped in her tracks and turned. *Uh-oh!* That all too familiar voice.

Geraldine licked her lips and shoved her way through the crowd. She tottered over on her spike heels until she stood beside Agnes and Katherine. Her hand rested gracefully at her breast as she heaved a delicate sigh. "Thank goodness, I caught up with you. Can you help me? My husband has our tickets. Somehow, we got separated. I'm not exactly sure which train to take. Do you mind if I tag along with you?" A muscle twitched beside her mascaraed eye, quite evident of her bogus excuse to join them. *What a phony act! She would put Lillian Gish to shame with that performance.*

Agnes exchanged glances with Katherine. Would it be considered consorting with the enemy or doing someone a wartime favor if they allowed Geraldine to accompany them to Track B? Hadn't she just admonished the lady in the washroom for not granting a favor to a stranger? And, for that matter, what choice did she have? Could she have said, "Oh, I don't think so, you painted floozy. I know what you're trying to do. Find your own way across the crowded room..."

Agnes painted a grin on her cheeks and nodded. "Of course, dear." She took Geraldine's arm. "We're headed for Track B, in case we're separated." She glanced at her watch. "And, we'd best hurry! The train leaves in ten minutes. I'm sure you'll find your...*umm*...husband waiting for you there."

"Oh, that's right. Silly me. I remember now. He did say to meet him at Track B."

"I thought you said you didn't know which train to take." *Just as I thought. She's just trying to get close to us so she can steal our package.*

"Oh, I did say that, didn't I? Well, I guess I'm a bit befuddled. I have a nervous condition, you see. Being in a crowd makes me very anxious."

Her face was pale and her hands trembled slightly. Perhaps she was telling the truth. More likely she was embarrassed for being caught in a lie.

Of course you do. "Well, never mind. Come along with us. We'll see you safely to the train." Agnes used her purse to shove through the crowds as she strode ahead with Katherine and Geraldine trailing behind. Two young ladies with completely different agendas.

Katherine—to join Mrs. Roosevelt's goodwill Pacific Island tour and deliver a package of secret documents to the President.

Geraldine—to intercept *said package* through any possible means. *We'll deliver the package in spite of Geraldine and her husband's efforts.* If she was right about the contents, depending on the outcome, General McArthur's successful invasion might well hang in the balance. And Agnes was never wrong. Hardly ever…

Chapter Twelve

Chicken and Pickled Beets—ninety cents!

Gnes gripped Katherine's arm as they approached the train on Track B. Steam *swooshed* from beneath the engine and the bell clanged loud enough to raise a mummy from its grave.

Geraldine's stiletto heels clicked on the tiled floor as she pranced beside Agnes.

A porter assisted the women up the steps and directed them to the observation car where about half the seats were occupied. "Watch your step, ma'am. Just there, the car to the left." Soft recorded music from the overhead speakers cast a spell of quiet calm after the hectic station.

Agnes nodded to Madeline, seeing Miss What's Er' Name settled in the front row, next to the door. *I must clarify the nanny's name. I can't go on calling her that.*

Agnes moved to the third row from the front and directed Katherine into the window seat. Even from the aisle, she could easily view the mountains and trees through the windows that curved halfway over the roof. She leaned toward the window to gaze at travelers still bustling on the platform. A mother picked up her fussy child. A soldier kissed a young woman and dabbed tears from her cheeks.

"Oh, there's Irving now!" Geraldine waved and started down the aisle to meet him. She called back over her shoulder, "Thanks for walking with me, ladies."

Agnes watched until Geraldine scooted past Irving's legs and sat next to the window, four rows behind her.

Seated in the rear behind Irving, the black soldiers whispered together, their heads down, as though trying not to attract attention. *Where are they going and where have they served? Bet they have some stories to tell.* The military had only recently integrated the troops. She hoped to get a chance to speak to the soldiers later.

Agnes ran her hand over the velvet rose-colored cushions. Such luxury! She leaned back against the headrest as passengers trickled past and filled the empty rows. Men and women in groups of two and three came down the aisle, sometimes brushing her shoulder as they passed. She glared at the newcomers and scooted closer to Katherine as more people filled the car. Voices grew louder with the growing numbers. *So much for a quiet peaceful trip across the country!* Maybe some of them would disembark at their next stop, Phoenix, Arizona. Others were likely heading to points east and perhaps some, all the way across the country.

She must make an effort to meet some of the ladies, perhaps make a new friend. At least there was safety in numbers and not likely that Irving would try to take Agnes's package by force while they were on the train. By guile was something else again.

The afternoon passed uneventfully. Agnes napped and Katherine read the popular Agatha Christie mystery novel, *And Then There Were None.*

Along about 2:00 P.M., the porter strolled up the aisle passing out menus. "Here's your dinner and your breakfast menu, ma'am. We'll be servin' supper in the dining car about five o'clock. May I check your tickets, please?"

Katherine retrieved the tickets from her handbag and exchanged them for the menus.

"I sees you ladies will be 'commondatin' with us all the way to Salt Lake City. I'll pass back this way in a few minutes to take your evening and morning meal orders." The porter marked their names in his little book, handed the tickets back to Katherine and moved on to the next row of seats. A badge on his jacket indicated twenty-five years of service on this railway. How many miles had he traveled during that time? How many meals had he served? How many people had he met? The numbers were mind-boggling.

Katherine patted Agnes's arm. "Wake up, Grandma. We need to select our dinner order." She tapped the menu.

"Let me see." Agnes lifted the menu and straightened her glasses. "Oh my, look at the prices! Do they think we're all millionaires?" She perused the menu and read aloud. "Breast of Chicken and Pickled Beets—ninety cents! My stars! I could practically buy a whole chicken for ninety cents, if Mrs. Wilkey had one to sell. Grilled Lake Superior Whitefish—a dollar!" Agnes's mouth dropped open. "At these prices, we'll be broke before we get to Washington. Now, aren't you glad I made up a lunch for us today?"

Katherine's face paled. "I only brought $50 cash for the whole trip. At this rate… What are we going to do? We can't go without food for three days," she whispered.

"I knew the food on the train was pricey. I guess we'll just have to *make do* tonight. Tomorrow, there's an hour layover in Albuquerque when we change trains. Maybe we can find a grocery store where we can buy some cheese and crackers, or sliced bologna." Agnes patted Katherine's hand. "Don't worry. We'll get by. So, what if we're a little hungry? It won't be the first time.

"Why, I remember one time in WWI, Myrtle and I were in Paris. We were stuck in a bombed-out building with nothing to eat but two candy bars and a thermos of coffee between us. It was two days before they dug through the rubble and—"

"You ladies make up your mind what you want for dinner?" The porter stood by Agnes's seat, smiling down at her.

"Oh! You startled me." She glanced up at him and opened the menu. "Could we please just have a bowl of vegetable soup and perhaps a piece of bread or a dinner roll?" Agnes's gaze dropped from the porter's face to the floor. A warm flush crept up her cheeks. She squared her jaw and lifted her head. *Just because we can't afford their exorbitant prices is nothing to be ashamed of. I dare you to make a comment.*

The porter smiled and leaned down to whisper. "In case you don't recollect, you ladies have a $75.00 food voucher attached to your tickets. You can order most anything you want off the menu. It's already paid for."

"Are you serious? Did you hear that Katherine? God bless Mrs. Roose...*umm... Humm*...let me see here..."

Katherine's elbow dug into her ribs.

Agnes opened the menu again. "I'll have the breast of chicken dinner, please, and coffee. Katherine?"

"I'll have the same. And, if you have some fresh fruit, that would be lovely." She handed the menu back to the porter and squeezed Agnes's hand. "Isn't this wonderful? I'm so excited!"

"And, for breakfast?" The porter touched his pencil to his tongue. "We're serving bacon and eggs, all kinds, and hot cereal with maple syrup."

"That sounds fine. Bring us two of that. And a couple of soft-boiled eggs please."

The porter nodded, touched his cap and marked their order in his booklet. He moved on up the aisle to the next row and then to Madeline and her nanny.

Nanny handed the menu back to the porter and shook her head, a blush tinting her cheeks. "Nothing, thank you." She dropped her chin and turned away.

"Did you see that?" Agnes whispered, "Miss *Whoo-Zits* isn't ordering any dinner for her and Madeline." Agnes nodded toward the pair.

"Maybe she packed food in her carry-on bag."

"Possibly, but everyone else is ordering something, even if it's only soup. I wonder… Maybe I should go and ask—"

"Grandma. Don't do it. You can't take on the problems of the whole world. You'll just embarrass her if she can't afford anything."

"Why would a Senator send off his child without enough money to buy food on the train? I can't sit here and eat a chicken dinner and watch a child go hungry. I'm going forward to the restroom. I'll see if she's given Madeline something to eat."

"Grandma, now don't…"

Agnes marched up the aisle and stopped beside the nanny. "Hello, again, Miss… *umm*. Hello, Madeline. Are you having fun? Won't it be fun to eat dinner on the train?" Agnes flashed a disarming smile toward the pair. That should get some reaction from Nanny to clarify the situation.

"Nanny says we can't order dinner because—"

"Madeline! Sit still and don't interrupt." The nanny gave the child's shoulder a swap.

Madeline cringed against the window. She hung her head, her shoulders slumped.

The nanny glared at Agnes. "It's really none of your business, Mrs. Odboddy, but if you must know, we aren't eating dinner because we had a big lunch. People eat far too much. The child is on a strict regimen of exercise and a specialized diet. I have food for her in my bag. She is my responsibility and I'll thank you to keep your opinions to yourself."

Agnes reared back. "What opinions? All I said was, it would be fun to eat dinner on the train. There's no reason for you to get all uppity about it. I meant no harm." Agnes jerked open the door on the restroom, turned and glared at the nanny. *What's her story? I was only being pleasant. And maybe just a little bit nosy.*

Madeline had her head in her lap. Her shoulders shook with tears.

What a witch. Agnes stepped into the tiny room and slammed the door. The space was so small, that an obese person would have difficulty turning around. She couldn't get the situation out of her mind. Was there some way she could let the father know how his child was being treated? Perhaps she should speak to the porter about it.

Agnes washed her hands in the tiny sink, unlatched the door and stepped back into the aisle.

The couple in the row across from Madeline nodded a greeting. Agnes smiled back.

Madeline's nanny had her head bowed, reading her book. No doubt she was avoiding Agnes's gaze as she passed their aisle. *She should be ashamed of herself, talking to me that way.*

"*Humph!*" Agnes held her head high. She glanced back at Madeline.

Madeline turned her head and smiled.

That poor child. What on earth could she do to help her?

Agnes slid into her seat beside Katherine. "Did you hear what that old biddy said to me? The nerve!"

"Didn't I tell you not to interfere? Now you've just made things worse. The nanny probably won't feed Madeline anything, just to prove her point."

"What about breakfast? She didn't order anything for the morning, either. Well, I won't have it, I tell you. I'm going to speak to the conductor and tell him that the child is hungry. I'm going to wire her father at the next stop, and—"

Katherine put her hand on Agnes's arm and shook her head. "You'll do nothing of the sort. If you do, the nanny might take it out on Madeline. You don't even know the Senator's name. We'll ask the conductor Madeline's last name. If her father is a Senator, it shouldn't be hard to locate his office. We'll tell him what we witnessed here on the train. Madeline's safety could be compromised if you interfere now. In the meantime, you need to keep quiet."

"Why, Katherine. I'm surprised you would question my intentions. You know very well that I never stick my nose where it's not wanted."

Chapter Thirteen

Oh, the rotten eavesdropper heard every word.

By the time the train reached Arizona, Agnes had bored Katherine with an opinion of most of the passengers on the train, speculating on their life stories. "And, about the soldiers in the back? Where do you suppose they're going?"

"I wouldn't know, Grandma." Katherine sighed and laid her magazine in her lap.

"Do you think Geraldine and Irving made up? They stopped quarreling."

"You didn't need to be rude when he spoke to you. We're all in this together for the next few days. You might as well be polite." Katherine thumbed through her magazine and nodded toward Geraldine, now napping with her mouth wide open. "She's asleep."

The train stopped in Phoenix. Some of the passengers departed and others took their places, headed for points east.

Near sunset, Agnes looked up at the sound of a bell.

The porter stood at the front of the car. "Dinner is served in the dining car, just next door. If you aren't dining with us, you can stay here or visit the club car, two cars back." He gestured to the rear of the train. "Some of you may wish to visit the smoking car where we have alcoholic beverages. That is three cars forward."

"Passengers with sleeping accommodations will be notified of your sleeping car assignments. The sleeping cars are toward the front of the train, that-a-way." He pointed toward the front of the car. "If you have questions, please ask any porter and we will help you." He smiled and opened the door connected to the dining car. "Please watch your step."

The room hummed with conversations as Agnes stood, gathered her purse and stepped into the aisle directly in front of Irving and Geraldine.

The train swayed as it wound around a wide curve. Agnes stepped back to catch her balance and bumped into Irving.

He touched her shoulder and steadied her.

"Oh, I'm so sorry. Please excuse me." Agnes's cheeks warmed. The idea! *Practically throwing myself into his arms like that.* What would he think?

"No problem. My pleasure." His arm still rested on her shoulder. "Moving about on a train can be a challenge."

She pulled away. "Thank you." She turned to see that Katherine had moved alongside her. "Here, dear, move in ahead of me." *There, now the package is safe between us.*

Katherine stepped in front of Agnes.

The crowd proceeded down the aisle toward the dining car. With the door open, clatter from the wheels drowned out conversations. The breeze cooled the interior of the car. Agnes drew her jacket closer around her neck.

Thankfully, not all the passengers were going to the dining car. Madeline and her nanny were still seated. As Agnes passed their row, the nanny abruptly stood and lurched into Agnes, as though the train had thrown her off balance. *What on earth? Is she drunk?*

Agnes put up her hands to steady the woman. They rocked together for a moment, the nanny's hands and arms flailing around like she was having a seizure. Her hand streaked toward Agnes's handbag, and then fell to her side.

Agnes jerked back, still grasping Nanny by the shoulders. "Are you all right? What's the matter?" She glanced at Madeline. The child's mouth had opened with surprise…or, was there a hint of fear in her eyes?

The nanny's face paled. Her eyes fluttered and her wild gestures ceased. She crumpled to the floor.

Irving moved past Agnes, put his arm around the nanny's waist and eased her back into the seat. "Step back, folks. There, now. Just relax. You're okay." He looked up at Agnes and Katherine. "Can one of you ask the porter to bring a glass of water? She's fainted."

"*Huh!*" Agnes mumbled, "No doubt from hunger." She glanced at the woman's pale face and then over to Madeline. "She'll be okay, honey. Don't worry."

The porter halted the crowd, creating space around the seats. "Give her a bit of room, folks."

Everyone hung back, whispering and gesturing.

The porter fanned a menu toward Nanny's face. Another porter appeared with a glass of water and handed it to Irving.

He held the glass to Nanny's lips. "Here, drink this. You'll feel better."

The porters directed the crowd, one at a time, past her seat where she lay slumped. Within a minute, only a few passengers remained in the car.

Katherine loosened Nanny's collar and patted her hands while Agnes stood by the door. *Just what was that all about? Was it real, or a performance to get attention?*

One of black soldiers stepped forward and tapped Katherine's arm. "Anything I can do to help, ma'am? I worked at the Travis Air Force Base Infirmary. I know a little about medical issues." He pulled off his cap and tossed it into an empty seat across the aisle.

Katherine stepped back. "She's looking better. I think she's coming around now."

The soldier felt the woman's wrist. "Her pulse is normal and her color is improving. I think she'll be all right." He stood, picked up his cap and sat in the empty seat.

Agnes took Katherine's arm. "There's nothing more we can do here. Let's go on into the dining room." She glanced at Madeline and then lowered her eyes. She felt like a heel, going in to eat a chicken dinner. But, Katherine was right. She had no right to interfere while the nanny was in charge. It didn't make her feel any better knowing there was nothing she could do. *Aha!* A thought! She smiled and then moved on into the dining car.

She and Katherine chose one of the little tables. "This is nice." China plates monogramed with the name of the railroad, cups with saucers and water goblets were placed on a white tablecloth. Monogramed silverware lay on cloth napkins.

The porters scurried back and forth, checking tickets, carrying trays of food ordered earlier that afternoon. The chatter of voices, clanking glasses and silverware soon filled the dining car. The delicious aroma of food and beverages made Agnes's mouth water. When the porter arrived with their dinner, she slid two dollar bills toward him.

"A lady just fainted back in the observation car. I'm sure she'd feel better if she had a cup of tea and something to eat. The child with her should have a sandwich and a glass of milk, as well. Tell her that the conductor insists that it's the train policy when anyone is ill. Please don't mention that I made the request. Can you do that?" She shoved another dollar toward him. "This is for your trouble."

He grinned, nodded, and picked up the money. "Yes, ma'am! I'll see to it right away."

As Agnes's gaze followed the porter down the aisle, Irving caught her eye, several tables away where he and Geraldine were sitting. He lifted his cup, nodded and grinned.

Oh, the rotten eavesdropper. He heard every word. No matter. Hopefully, he'd keep quiet. One has to respect a gracious opponent, German spy or otherwise. Their little game of cat and mouse was *on* and the prospect of outwitting him in his attempt to get her secret documents exhilarated her to no end.

A little smile twitched her lips as she turned away. Steam rose from the plate as she lifted the lid from her dinner tray. "Oh, my, Katherine! Doesn't that chicken smell good? Potato salad, pickled beets and a dinner roll." She smacked her lips, then took her knife and fork and cut into the chicken breast. For the next few minutes, the only sound was silverware clanking against china, sounds of smacked lips and a few appreciative murmurs about the flavor of the food as it disappeared from her plate.

Katherine buttered her roll and took a bite. She picked up the teapot. "This should be steeped enough now. That was a lovely thing you did, Grandma, especially after she was rude to you," she added in a whisper. "I should have thought of it myself. She'll have to let Madeline have the sandwich, if the conductor sent it." She giggled and filled their cups.

"Did you find her behavior odd? I've seen a number of ladies faint in my day and I've never seen anyone react quite that way. It almost looked contrived, but, of course, I'm sure—"

The porter leaned down. "The lady was a bit embarrassed when I brought the tray, but when I explained that the conductor insisted, she accepted it right away. The child seemed most appreciative, ma'am. I thought you'd want to know."

"Thank you...*umm*... What's your name?"

"Jackson, ma'am."

Agnes chuckled. "That's easy to remember. We have a dear friend back home in Newbury named Jackson."

"Thank you, ma'am. Can I bring you anything else?"

"Miss Katherine ordered fresh fruit."

"Indeed. I'll be back in a jiffy." Jackson touched his cap.

"After dinner, shall we go back to the club car and see if we can set up a card game? I brought a deck of cards." Agnes leaned down, brought her handbag into her lap and reached inside. "Well, I declare, will you look at this?" She opened the top of her bag and tilted it toward Katherine. Colonel Farthingworth's package poked out of her purse with a rip in the side, as though something had torn the paper away. "When do you suppose that happened? I don't remember the paper being torn when I took it into the kitchen sink to clean up the streaks from the chickens."

"Well, no harm done. Perhaps your comb gouged it there in your purse. You can always rewrap it when we get to Washington. For that matter, why didn't you rewrap it at home when you saw the mess Mrs. Whistlemeyer left on it?"

Agnes's cheeks warmed. "I…I don't know. Of course, I should have done. I guess old age and senility is creeping up on me quicker than I thought. Good thing I have you around to keep me from running naked through the streets."

"Oh, Grandmother. You're such a caution. Here's Jackson now with my fruit." Katherine's eyes glowed like a child on Christmas morning when he set down the bowl of strawberries floating in a golden puddle of cream.

Agnes shuffled the cards and dealt them to Katherine, herself and the two elderly women they had convinced to join them.

The ladies across the table appeared ready to do battle in a rousing game of Whist.

Agnes pulled off her jacket and laid it across the back of her chair.

Katherine gathered her cards and fanned them, holding them close to her face. She laid down the first card. "We should introduce ourselves. I'm Katherine and this is my grandmother, Agnes Odboddy. Where are you ladies from?" She drew a card from the stack and rearranged the remaining cards in her hand.

Agnes glanced across the aisle as Geraldine and Irving settled at a small table. He waved to the porter and ordered drinks.

Agnes jerked her head and snapped her attention back as the older of the two ladies put out her hand.

"I'm Evelyn and this is my sister, Winnie. We're from Oakland. We're on our way to Alabama to visit my daughter." She straightened the collar on her navy blue suit, and then moved two of her cards from left to right in her hand.

Winnie's gaze passed from Katherine to Agnes. "I'm curious, dear. Pardon me, but why are you wearing those silly chopsticks in your hair?" Winnie stared at Agnes. "It appears a most odd way to dress your hair, being as you're not Oriental. Of course, we see such odd ways of doing things in the movies, but I declare, I've never seen anyone of your social standing wearing such a hair ornament. And, your hair is such an unnatural color. How is it possible—"

"Winnie, dear, *shhh!* You mustn't be impertinent." Evelyn patted her sister's arm. "It isn't polite." She glanced up at Agnes. "Forgive her. Sometimes she speaks a bit out of turn. Winnie isn't…well. I've always looked after her, you see. She suffers from…*umm*…" Evelyn's face pinked up as she glanced at her sister, who was still staring at Agnes's hair. "Well, Winnie is…you know." She lowered her eyes and cleared her throat.

"It's okay, I don't mind. Winnie dear…" Agnes glanced from Katherine to Winnie.

Winnie stared at her cards, as though lost in some private reverie, apparently unaware that her inappropriate questions had created an uncomfortable moment for her companions.

Agnes fluffed her hair and touched the chopsticks crisscrossed through her bun. "My husband gave me the silver chopsticks the day he left for Europe in 1918. He never came home. I've worn them ever since to remember him. They come in handy opening the mail and on other occasions!"

Katherine and Evelyn giggled. The embarrassing moment had passed.

"Now that we've got that settled, it's nice to meet you ladies. Winnie. Evelyn," Katherine nodded, "shall we begin?" She pulled two cards from her hand and laid them on the table.

Agnes turned at the sound of a chuckle from Irving. *Eavesdropping again!* She caught his eye and frowned. He seemed to be hovering close by, no matter where they went, watching and listening to every word. *Probably looking for an opportunity to grab my purse!*

Agnes moved her handbag a bit closer to her feet. And, suppose he was successful. How did he think he'd get off the train with the secret documents, while traveling down the track at the astonishing speed of sixty miles an hour? What about tonight? How could she keep the package safe all night? She couldn't stay awake for three days. The minute she closed her eyes, he might take the opportunity to snatch her handbag.

The game proceeded for a few minutes until Irving and Geraldine's angry voices interrupted Agnes's concentration! Arguing *again?* Conversation ceased. Heads turned toward the couple.

Geraldine's face flushed as she snarled. "I've had enough, I tell you! I'm going straight to the—" She tried to stand.

Irving's face darkened. Had he reached his limit with his bride? What kind of marriage goes awry on the honeymoon? Why had they gotten married in the first place?

Irving grabbed Geraldine's arm and shoved her back into her seat. "No, you won't. You'll see it through if I have to—"

Geraldine gave Irving a shove and pushed past his legs. "You can go to the devil for all I care." She rushed down the aisle, her fox cape trailing off her shoulder and onto the floor. She flung open the door and stepped onto the platform.

Clunk-clunk, clunk-clunk.

The door slammed behind her.

The lady nearest the exit grabbed her hat as the rush of air from outside threatened to send it flying. She reached down and picked up Geraldine's cape and carried it down the aisle. "Your wife will want this when she calms down." She blushed and handed it to Irving.

He scowled and tossed it into Geraldine's empty chair, mumbling. "I don't give a damn if she does. *Uh*...thanks."

Agnes smiled and ducked her head. Maybe Irving would be so busy chasing after his celibate bride, he wouldn't have time to snatch Agnes's package, after all.

Chapter Fourteen

That woman exasperates the very heck out of me!

ow, wasn't that interesting? Agnes put up her hand to hide a smile. Not that she would *ever* intentionally eavesdrop on a private conversation, mind you, but how could she help it? Spatting honeymooners were hard to ignore. Not much hope for that marriage, to be sure. On the other hand, she almost took delight in Irving's discomfort since he was a spy after all, and deserved none of her sympathy.

Agnes lifted her gaze from her cards. Again, Jackson, the porter, stood near the door ringing his bell. The mumbles that rose after Geraldine made her grand exit had ceased.

"I'll be passing amongst you passengers with sleeping 'commendations, handin' out cards. The numbers and diagram on the card is your assigned sleeping car and your berth is outlined in blue. Even numbers is for upper berths and odd numbers is for lower berth. When you retires, please find your berth quietly so as not to disturb the other passengers. There are two bathrooms labeled *Ladies* and *Gents* at front and rear of each sleeping car. Bathrooms has commodes and wash basins. You'll have to share these 'commendations, so please be courteous with your time in the washrooms.

"We has placed your luggage in your berths. A porter will be stationed in each sleeping car all night, so don't worry about your possessions as you sleep. Are there any questions?"

For a minute, no one spoke and then Winnie raised her hand.

"Suppose I need to get up in the night? Will you leave the lights on so I can find my way to the bathroom?"

Chuckles erupted among the passengers. A few women nodded, as though they had wondered the same thing but hadn't the courage to speak it out loud.

"There will be a nightlight burnin' all night, but not so bright as to keep you awake with your curtains pulled. If you need anything, just wave and your porter will come to your berth to assist you."

Winnie questioned, "How will I get into the upper berth if I'm assigned that one? I'm not as spry as I used to be." She glanced around the car, her face beaming, relishing all the attention as all eyes had turned to her again. Several elderly ladies again nodded in agreement.

"Don't worry, ma'am. We has a ladder for the upper berths and the porter will help you get up and down when you wants to. Now, the folks what don't have overnight 'commendations can stay here or go back to the observation cars and we'll get you all a piller and a blanket, but we only has so many pillers, so best be askin' for one as soon as possible. Any more questions?"

Several passengers shook their heads. Murmurs traveled through the car.

The porter strolled down the aisle calling names and handing cards to specific passengers. He approached Agnes's table. "Misses Winnie and Evelyn Stubblefield?"

"Here!" Winnie waved.

The porter handed her the card. "You ladies are in car seven, berths nine and ten. You have the upper and lower berths."

Evelyn glanced at Winnie. "I'll take the upper one, dear, since you need to get up in the night more often than I do."

The porter moved on, then turned back. "Agnes and Katherine Odboddy?"

"Here!" Katherine showed their ticket stubs and took the card. She glanced at the diagram. "We're in car six, numbers three and four. Oh, dear. That puts us pretty close to the washroom. Folks will be coming and going all night. Well, so much for getting much sleep."

"Don't worry. You can sleep late tomorrow morning." Agnes called out to the porter. "Excuse me, sir. What time do we have to get up in the morning?"

"9:30 A.M. at the latest, because we stop serving breakfast at 10:00 A.M. Some of you will be changin' trains in Albuquerque long about 11:00 A.M., so we has to get you up and out of bed in time.

"One final thing, folks. The train will make a ten minute stop about 2:00 A.M. at Gallup, New Mexico, to take on mail and again, later, to take on water. If you have any letters or telegrams to send, let us know before then and we'll see they get sent."

"Thank you, Jackson." Agnes unpinned the watch from her lapel and glanced at it. "It's 8:45 already. I think I'll go to bed early." She laid the watch on the table and glanced at the porter's card. "Katherine, are you coming, or do you want to stay and play another hand with Evelyn and Winnie?" Agnes stood, gathered her handbag and suit jacket. "Perhaps if I go now, I'll get into the washroom before the others come to bed. I'll see you ladies tomorrow."

"It's a bit early for me, Grandma. I'm not sleepy yet."

"Shall I leave the card with you, or can you remember car six, berth three and four?"

"I can remember. I'll take the upper berth. I'll be along shortly. I'll finish out this game and then I'm going to find a comfortable sofa and read for a while."

Agnes waved to Evelyn and Winnie as she started down the aisle toward Jackson. He opened the door and stepped across the platform to hold the door into the adjoining car.

Agnes stepped across the landing and opened the door into sleeping car six. A rustling sound further down the aisle and the prominent backside of a woman leaning into a lower berth suggested that someone else had decided to come to bed early. Madeline and the nanny! *Wouldn't you know it?*

A child's voice from behind the curtain verified her suspicion. "I'm not tired, Nanny. Why do I have to go to sleep now?"

"Because it's almost nine o'clock and little girls should be asleep by nine. When you get your pajamas on, I'll pop you up into the top berth like a bird in a nest. Won't that be fun?"

"*Uh-huh.* Can I read my book for a little while?"

"For a little while. I think the rocking of the train will soon put you to sleep. I'll be right down here. If you need to get up, just call me." Nanny pulled her head out from the curtain and stood, turned and looked down the aisle. Her smile faded when she saw Agnes. She looked quickly away.

How rude. She acts as if we've never met. What is wrong with that woman?

Agnes slid back the curtain on berth three. As Katherine had guessed, it was only two berths down from the ladies' washroom. There would be noises of flushing and water running half the night. *Just our luck!*

The porters had folded down the seats inside the berth. By placing sheets, blankets and a pillow across the seats, they created a sizable and comfortable bed. At least it was better than sitting up all night with a pillow behind your head, as some of the passengers would do. Bless Mrs. Roosevelt for upgrading their tickets with a meal credit and sleeping accommodations. The woman was a saint.

Agnes's two suitcases were stacked at the foot of her bed. She pulled the top one toward her, opened it and retrieved her nightgown, robe, slippers and her travel bag containing toothbrush, comb, talcum, tooth powder and cold cream.

As she pulled the curtain of her berth closed and turned toward the bathroom, Nanny pushed past Agnes and rushed down the aisle, as if her life depended on reaching the washroom ahead of Agnes.

"Excuse me! We aren't running the Indianapolis 500 here,

you know."

Nanny jerked open the washroom door, leaped inside and slammed the door.

"Well, I never!" Agnes returned to her berth. A little lamp over the window cast a warm and inviting glow across the bed. Through the windows, telephone poles flashed past, almost in a blur. She pulled her Bible from her suitcase and laid it by her pillow, then stacked one suitcase on top of the other at her feet.

She slid under the blanket and fluffed the pillow behind her head. Since she had to wait for *Miss Britches on Fire* to get out of the bathroom anyway, she thought she might as well catch up on her reading.

It was her almost regular nightly practice to hold the Bible in her lap and let it fall open to see if the message on the page spoke to her in some meaningful way. This time, it opened to Genesis 28:20. She read, *"Then Jacob made a vow, saying, 'If God will be with me and watch over me on this journey, and will give me food to eat and clothes to wear so that I return safely to my father's household, then the Lord will be my God.'"*

Now, wasn't that propitious? Just like she and Katherine, Jacob was going on a journey, and expected God to provide food and clothing.

Talk about prophetic! Mrs. Roosevelt had provided them a meal credit and by wearing Red Cross uniforms, not many clothes were needed, a boon due to the forty-pound-luggage-per-passenger limitation on the military airplane. Not that she compared Mrs. Roosevelt to God. But, to be on the safe side, Agnes had every intention of honoring the Lord on their overseas journey.

A little wave of guilt washed over her, as she remembered her mean thoughts toward Nanny. *Oops! Heart adjustment! Best to put away such mean thoughts if I mean to honor God. Even though that woman exasperates the very heck out of me.*

Footsteps in the aisle drew her back to the present. She peeked out the curtain as Nanny hurried past Agnes's berth.

Agnes flung her legs over the side of her bed and stood. She hurried down the aisle before anyone else could beat her to the washroom. After brushing her teeth, washing her face, and smearing cold cream across her face, Agnes glanced into the mirror. She chuckled, noting that her white face now resembled a clown. Mid-chuckle, her smile faded. My purse! *I left it in my berth, with the package inside, unattended!*

Agnes flung open the door and plunged down the aisle, heart pounding, cold cream smeared over her face, staining the collar of her bathrobe. What had she done? She was so committed to not letting the package out of her sight and here she'd left it sitting in the middle of her bed! *Oh, Lord above. Protect this idiot from my foolish ways.*

The empty cubicle shrieked its condemnation at her carelessness and neglect. *Oh, dear God!* Her purse was nowhere in sight.

Oh, nooooo! Was anyone still lurking in the corridor? Empty! Where was the porter who was supposed to be on guard, watching their belongings?

Agnes raced toward the far end of the car and found the porter tipped back, his chair balanced against the wall, sound asleep, his head lolled to the side.

"Porter! Wake up!"

The young man jerked, the legs of his chair slamming to the floor. He jumped to his feet, his eyes blinking. "Yes, ma'am?" He straightened his back and touched his cap, his eyes scanning wildly from left to right. As he came to full wakefulness, he peered at Agnes, her cold-creamed face contorted in rage. His eyes looked like black marbles floating in pools of milk. He stepped back, with his trembling hands outstretched. "I's sorry. I won't do it again!"

Agnes put her hand on his shoulder. *What's wrong with him?* "Porter! Did you see someone getting into my berth? I'm the second one from the end." She turned and pointed down the aisle, toward the ladies' washroom.

The porter's face turned several shades lighter. "No, ma'am. Sorry ma'am. I...I... I'm afraid I fell asleep." He hung his head. "Are you going to tell my boss?" He lifted his head. "Is you a ghost?"

Agnes reached up and touched her cheek. "Oh, my goodness!" *I didn't even wash my face. No wonder I scared the living daylights out of him.* Or was he just rattled because she caught him sleeping? She pulled a tissue from her pocket and wiped at her cheeks. "I left the bathroom in such a hurry… But, then I discovered my purse missing from my berth!" Her heart raced as she uttered the dreadful words. *And vanity clouded my good judgment! I'm such a fool.*

His mouth trembled again. Was he more worried about her missing purse or getting caught sleeping on the job? "Missing? You're sure you didn't misplace it? Show me." He hurried down the aisle toward her berth.

Agnes followed on his heels. She paused when she passed Nanny and Madeline's berths. Could they have heard something? She'd check with Nanny later.

The porter yanked back Agnes's curtain and glanced around her bed. Only the Bible lay on her pillow where she had left it. The purse was gone. What had she hoped for? Its magical reappearance like a magician's rabbit?

The porter slid the suitcases from side to side and tossed the pillow to the other end of the bed. "Have you checked in your suitcase? Maybe you put it away and forgot."

"Don't you think I'd remember if I put it in my suitcase?" Agnes huffed. *What kind of an idiot does he think I am?* On the other hand, what kind of an idiot was she to leave her purse sitting on the bed with secret documents inside and run around the train with cold cream smeared on her face? Chill bumps raced up her arms as the realization of the loss hit home. What kind of a scourge of the underworld loses track of her parcel practically the first day out? She had failed Colonel Farthingworth and she had failed the President of the United States of America. She blinked to hold back tears as the porter rifled through both of her suitcases. To no avail, of course.

"Can you describe it, ma'am? What was inside?"

Agnes shrugged. "It was black and contained valuable…*um…*

well, never mind what it contained. It had my wallet and my money and…and…my train ticket and passport." Tears trickled down her cheeks.

The porter looked almost as sad as she felt. "I'll question the passengers before I make a report to the conductor." His face contorted again. Probably worrying about losing his job. *Aren't we two of a kind? Both of us brought low by our own carelessness.*

"I'll finish up in the washroom while you look."

The porter nodded and hurried off, leaving Agnes to return to her interrupted ablutions.

Now, wasn't this a fine kettle of fish? The secret documents aside, how could she get to Washington with no money and no train ticket? Perhaps the railroad would allow her to finish the journey with a promissory note when she could access her funds at home. Or would they recall that she had a ticket when she came onboard? If she had to buy another ticket, what would it cost? Did she have enough money to pay for one?

Living on a limited Social Security income and a bit of interest from Douglas's life insurance was tenuous. If it wasn't for Katherine sharing household living expenses, she would be hard-pressed to make ends meet.

Agnes washed the cold cream from her face and stared into the washroom mirror. The wrinkles in her forehead had deepened over the past few minutes and the sparkle that folks said she carried in her eyes seemed to have abandoned ship.

She reached up and patted her hennaed hair, catching her finger in one of the silver chopsticks protruding from her bun. She turned her head from side to side as the light caught the trinkets and shimmered in the mirror. Once again, as so often over the years, she remembered Douglas's admonition. *Don't lose heart, old girl. We've gotten through tougher times than this. We'll muddle through again. I'm here, watching over you. Things will be all right, my darling.*

Agnes straightened her shoulders and forced a smile. She gave her hair a final pat and stepped out the washroom door, climbed into her bunk and pulled the curtain. She laid her head back on the pillow, clutched the Bible to her chest and began to pray.

Chapter Fifteen

I could have talked all day without saying that.

Katherine ordered a glass of wine, put her feet up on the hassock, and laid her sweater across the arm of her chair. The clack of the train wheels drowned out the hum of conversation around the club car as she began to read. She was soon immersed in the storyline of her novel.

Some twenty minutes later, she yawned and crossed her legs. Just sitting on a train all day could wear you out. Maybe she should go to bed early, too. She needed to speak to Grandmother about a serious matter, anyway. She squirmed to find a more comfortable position.

"Ma'am? Your sweater?"

Katherine looked up. "What?"

One of the Negro soldiers held out her sweater. "You dropped this on the floor."

"Thank you. I didn't even notice. How careless of me." Katherine laid the sweater across her lap.

"Not at all, ma'am. What are you reading? You were so engrossed in your book, I almost hated to disturb you."

Katherine held up the novel. "*Grapes of Wrath*. Steinbeck. He's one of my favorites."

"Mine too. Probably the best he's written. Reading the story now from the migrant worker's point of view is an eye-opener for California folks. They didn't understand how dreadful things were for the mid-westerners. The locals viewed the migrants as invaders taking away jobs. Steinbeck made the situation so clear. Too bad the book wasn't published during the Dust Bowl. Things might have been easier for the migrants."

"My! You know a lot about the situation."

"It was part of a course I took at the University. I had to write a paper on the Dust Bowl. By the way, I'm Samuel Dillard and this is my friend, David Copperhead." He gestured to his friend at the next table. He stood and reached his hand toward Katherine.

She shook hands with them. *College? How interesting. Grandmother should meet these two young men.* "I don't mean to sound prejudiced," Katherine said, "but I've never met a…a…Negro who attended college. The colored folks in Newbury rarely go beyond high school."

David grinned at Samuel. "We both went to Howard University in Washington D.C. That's a Negro college. The Army recruited us into an experimental program. We're on our way to Tuskegee, Alabama, to train as pilots."

My Stephen was a pilot. A surge of tightness swept through Katherine's chest. "Really? That's interesting." She cocked her head. "But, I thought the military was still…*um*…sort of…segregated. How will that work?" Her cheeks warmed. "I…I…mean, not that I agree with that notion, mind you, but I thought that's how things were."

Samuel leaned forward. "Don't be embarrassed. You're right. But, two and a half million colored men and women signed up in the military after Japan bombed Pearl Harbor. With that much manpower, the government realized they needed to integrate us into fighting positions. We have a right to fight for our country too, not just drive trucks and peel potatoes."

Katherine nodded. "That's a valid point." *That's just how my Stephen felt. He wanted to fight for his country. See how that turned out.*

Several other passengers appeared to be listening, but none had joined the conversation. Samuel continued. "The government started a training program for Negros. They're finally going to let us fight! We'll be trained as pilots, gunners and navigators and all the other supporting fighting positions, although we'll serve in special units. We'll still be segregated from the white troops. The Negro units are already doing a darn good job too, from what I see on the newsreels at the movies. Maybe someday things will change and we'll all be together."

"I can't wait to get up there and take on some of those Jap planes." David smacked his fist into his palm.

"So, how do you happen to be on a train coming from California?" Katherine asked.

"We had a two-week furlough before we start the program. David is from Newbury, California. He wanted to go home and visit his family. I just came along for the ride."

Katherine raised her eyebrows. "That's where my grandmother and I live. We have a…a…*umm*…good friend named Jackson Jackson. You wouldn't happen to know him, would you? He helped us build a chicken coop last summer. He works at the Newbury Court House."

"Wait! I think I know Jackson," David said. "He's sort of a shirt-tail relative. We met at a barbecue my mother held last week. He's a great guy."

Katherine smiled. "Yes, he is. Well, it's a small world, isn't it? Wait until I tell my grandmother. I'm so glad we got a chance to talk. Can I buy you a cup of coffee and piece of pie?"

David glanced at Samuel and then ducked his head.

"What? What is it? You don't like pie? I thought all Ne… I mean, I thought all men liked pie." She blinked as warmth coursed up her cheeks. *I could have talked all day without saying that. Good heavens!*

"Oh, we love pie, ma'am. Truth is, if you're so inclined to buy us something, we'd rather have a sandwich. Prices are so high on the train, we sort of skipped—"

"David!" Samuel laid his hand on his friend's arm. He shook his head.

David lowered his gaze. "I guess I talk too much."

"That's terrible. Didn't they give you any traveling money?"

Katherine shook her head. "Don't be embarrassed. If our friend hadn't paid for our train ticket and a meal credit, we might have skipped dinner too." She waved. "Porter? Bring a couple of ham and cheese sandwiches and cookies to my friends, would you? And two cups of coffee. Put it on my account. Katherine Odboddy."

A woman, listening nearby, leaned over toward the porter. "In the morning, porter, let's have some bacon and eggs for the gentlemen, on Melvin Hickenlooper's account, please. Our soldiers deserve the best." She grinned.

"Thank you, ma'am. Much obliged. You're too kind." David nodded.

"It's the least we can do for our fighting men," Katherine said.

One of the porters passed down the center aisle, glancing from side to side as he moved by each seat. He paused by Katherine's sofa, then turned and hurried through the door into the next car.

Katherine's gaze followed him out the door. Wasn't that an odd thing to do? *I wonder who he was looking for.*

She stood and gathered her belongings. "Gentlemen, it's a pleasure to meet you, but I have an errand I must attend to. I'm sure we'll get a chance to talk again."

The two men stood as she moved toward the sleeping cars. Before she reached the door, the porter and a uniformed officer stepped through. The insignia on his badge indicated some sort of security. The porter grabbed Katherine's arm and directed her backward toward the nearest chair. "If you'll just stay for a minute, ma'am. We have a couple of questions for you."

What's this all about? Is it a crime to buy a soldier a sandwich? Katherine's heart raced.

Sam and David stood and moved closer. David clenched his fists.

Do they think I need bodyguards? Katherine plopped into the chair. Her pulse quickened and her hands trembled. She glanced from face to face. *What have I done?* "What on earth is going on?"

Chapter Sixteen

Did I say something about not coloring my hair?

Agnes closed her eyes, and tightened her grip on her Bible. "Lord, I really need You to find my purse or I'm a cooked goose with Colonel Farthingworth. This time it's really important. I promise, if You will help me get my purse back with the package safe and sound, I'll stop arguing with Joe the butcher about the price of chicken wings. I won't gripe at Mrs. Williams about her dog barking in the middle of the night and…and…*um*… I'll even stop coloring my hair. Amen."

This was serious. Not that she truly believed making such promises would make much difference. Wasn't this the second time in so many weeks she had engaged in such bargaining with God? For that matter, it hadn't even been necessary last time, as the reason for her prayers turned out to be a mistake. But, it seemed that at every crossroad and rough patch in the road, she had this bargaining session with God. And, things usually turned out okay. Apparently, God was still trying to get her attention. Perhaps He took these opportunities to set her on the straight and narrow.

In any event, it was worth a shot. She would be remiss in her duty to Colonel Farthingworth not to explore every avenue in an effort to retrieve the package. "Oh, P.S. And, Lord, I promise to stop criticizing Chief Waddlemucker and saying that he's as stupid as a rock. Please God, if you could see fit, just this once more, to make a miracle and find my package, I'd be ever so good from now and forevermore. Amen."

"Grandma! If you're asleep, you better wake up, now!"

Katherine? Agnes's eyes flew open. She sat straight up on the bed. Oh, dear God. In all her prayers to save the package, she had neglected to ask God to save her from Katherine. *What will she say when she learns I left my purse on the bed and it was stolen?* Agnes's heart thumped against her chest. Not only would Katherine be furious, but Agnes would have to admit she hadn't behaved like a good warrior on the home front. She was toast!

Agnes reached out a shaking hand and pulled back the curtain. "Katherine, I…"

Two porters stood beside Katherine, holding her arms like some sort of prisoner. *Was that a badge on that guy's chest?* "What's going on?"

"Would you by chance be looking for this?" Katherine glared at Agnes and held out… her purse! "Would you please tell these gentlemen that I did *not* steal it?"

Agnes hopped out of the berth into the aisle. "My purse! Where did you find it? Who took it?" Her cheeks warmed at the expression on the porter's face. She grabbed her robe, thrust her arms into the sleeves and yanked the belt tight around her middle.

"No one *stole* it, Grandma. I came back to the berth to get my sweater and found it sitting right in the middle of your bed. You were nowhere in sight so I took it with me for safe-keeping. Where were you?"

"I guess I was in the bathroom washing my face. I'm sorry." Agnes's cheeks flamed.

"So, you're saying your purse wasn't stole, after all?" The porter's face squinched into a scowl. "We been runnin' around like bald chickens, lookin' for a purse that wasn't stole?" He released Katherine's arm, glanced at Agnes and then at the security guard. He shook his head, and sighed. Was he relieved that the purse was found, or more relieved that he wasn't responsible for it going missing on his watch?

The security guard spoke. "So, Parker, how is it that you didn't see this young woman getting into Mrs. Odboddy's bunk when she took the purse?"

Uh-oh! Looked like Parker was busted, after all.

"I...I...guess I was—"

Katherine turned to the porter. "I believe I saw him helping Madeline with the ladder when I came back. I doubt he saw me."

Parker's shoulders slumped and he breathed a heavy sigh. "Thank you, Jesus," he whispered.

Agnes smiled and nodded. With her purse and the package safely returned, and her heart full of gratitude, she felt relieved and penitent enough to keep quiet about Parker sleeping on the job. Hopefully, he had learned his lesson.

Double uh-oh! What about her bargain with God? Yet again, she had jumped to conclusions, petitioned God's favor, and made promises that must now be evaluated.

Humm. What *had* she said? *Stop arguing with Joe, the butcher.* She could probably do that, though it was hard with chicken wings a whopping fourteen cents a pound.

Stop griping about Mrs. Williams's dog. Sleepless nights were hard to deal with. Most likely the dog missed Mrs. Williams' son. Maybe the dog realized the boy wouldn't ever come home again. *I'll have to ponder how to deal with that one.*

Stop criticizing Chief Waddlemucker. How could she stop doing that? He *was* stupid as a rock. Telling the truth wasn't exactly criticizing, was it? There! That should get her off the hook.

Didn't I say something about not coloring my hair? Now, hold it. Enough was enough. Surely God would understand that she had uttered such a vow in the haste of a desperate moment. Besides, she didn't actually *dye* her hair. She *freshened* it with a colored shampoo formula. Even God should understand the difference between dyeing and freshening, and wouldn't hold her to such a ridiculous promise... Well, time would tell because there was no way she intended to stop *freshening* her naturally auburn hair and allow it return to...to...some other color.

"Grandma, are you going to stand here in the corridor staring into space, or are you going back to bed?"

"Oh! I was just thinking how glad I am to get my purse back. I'm so embarrassed to make such a fuss about it. I've inconvenienced everyone." She leaned forward and whispered. "I was almost ready to accuse Nanny of stealing it. Thank goodness you came back when you did. I would have really made a prize fool of myself if I'd done that."

"Well, those porters certainly gave me a few interesting moments. They even threatened to lock me in the Mail Car and turn me over to the sheriff in Albuquerque!" Katherine chuckled. "It's pretty funny now, but it wasn't a few minutes ago."

"I'm sorry, Katherine. I was careless, but I've learned my lesson. The package won't leave my sight from now on, even when I go to the bathroom!"

Agnes sighed and turned in her sleep. The *clack-clack* of the train wheels had become the sound of a beating drum on a battlefield. Agnes ran back and forth between soldiers marching forward, with guns drawn. Sweat poured from their pale faces. The sun blazed down on red jackets as they marched toward an outline of men in buckskin hiding behind rocks and trees. Redcoats? Buckskin? A battlefield?

Agnes jerked and twisted, thrashing her pillow. How did she get in the middle of a Revolutionary War battlefield? *I don't belong here! Wait. I can't be here. The field will soon be littered with dead and dying men.* She turned and tried to run. *I must be dreaming! Wake up! Wake up!*

Someone grabbed her arm, dragged her from the line of fire and pulled her down behind a rock. Her heart pounded. Perspiration pricked her forehead. Crouched so close beside the men, she smelled the sweat on their clothes. Her legs cramped. The older soldiers' lined faces suggested they knew what was coming. Younger soldiers, their guns trembling in their hands, appeared terrified of the unknown as the enemy advanced, step by step to the beat of their drums. Outnumbered by the advancing troops, the advantage still lay in the ragtag soldiers' favor, as they hid behind the cover of trees and rocks. Ramming power and balls into their long rifles, the men in buckskins squatted in the dirt, waiting, waiting as the formidable enemy advanced closer and closer. The drums beat louder.

I've got to get away. This can't be real! Wake up, Agnes. Wake up!

The drumbeat stopped. Silence! She peeked around the rock.

Guns at the ready, the enemy stood immobile on the field, feet in mid-step. The flag drooped unmoving, despite a brisk breeze. The young drummer's drumstick hovered in mid-air… Overhead, a bird hung motionless, frozen in time.

Agnes lifted her head toward the brilliant sky where patches of clouds were suspended as if from wires. *What happened?*

She opened her eyes, blinked against the darkness in the train berth. The *clack-clack* of its wheels had stopped. The train stood still. *I was dreaming!* Dreams were, after all, just snatches of thoughts and memories, sounds and sights stored willy-nilly in one's mind and pulled into a fractured scenario to haunt a restless night. She shuddered at the thought that on a day, not unlike this, her dream had been another's reality.

She turned toward the window. Rivulets of rain streaked the glass, curving and twisting as it traversed the pane. Outside, buildings shifted and wavered through the etched designs in the glass.

Agnes put her hand to her pounding heart. *Calm down. It was just a dream. Everything is fine.* Her fingers sought her purse, tucked safely beside her pillow. The package was safe and sound inside. *Just a dream.*

What time is it? Her suit jacket lay at the foot of the bed. Bringing the jacket to her chest, she moved her hand up and down the lapel, feeling for the watch pinned to the collar. Where was it? A gift from Douglas on their first anniversary, the tiny round watch hanging from a platinum silver bow edged with diamonds was one of her favorite pieces of jewelry. She saved it for special occasions, such as Easter Sunday and formal events. She had pinned it to her suit jacket just before leaving home to wear on the trip and when she met Mrs. Roosevelt.

She flicked on the lamp beside the window and turned the jacket inside out, feeling in the pockets. No watch! *Oh, no! Now, take a breath. Remember how crazy you got when you thought someone stole your purse.* There must be a logical explanation. Think. When was the last time she saw the watch? Her thoughts returned to earlier this evening.

She had pulled the watch off her jacket when they were playing cards. She must have left it on the table when she came to bed. Katherine probably picked it up and put it in her pocket. Hadn't she done the same with her missing purse? Odd that she hadn't mentioned it when she returned the missing handbag. She must have forgotten in all the excitement. Yes, that's it… Or perhaps the porter picked it up and took it to lost and found.

Agnes tossed and turned, trying to find a comfortable position. The lumpy berth wouldn't win any prizes for comfort. She fluffed her pillow and stared out the window at the rain. Where were they? Most likely, somewhere in New Mexico.

In her mind's eye, her beloved watch still lay on the table for anyone to see. Weren't people sitting up all night in there? Anyone could take it. Should she wake Katherine and ask if she picked it up? Probably. On the other hand, wasn't Katherine already peeved at her about the purse? If she woke her up now to ask about the watch, no telling what she might say.

It wouldn't take but a few minutes to run back into the observation car and check the table. Otherwise, she'd lay awake and worry about it all night.

Agnes pushed back the curtain and stood. Wait! Her purse! She wouldn't make that mistake again. Better take it along with her this time.

A fluttering of curtains down the aisle suggested someone else was awake. Probably woke up when the train stopped, like she had. She donned her robe, grabbed her purse, pulled the curtain closed and headed toward the observation car. Just a quick look on the table would ease her mind.

The dimmed lights in the observation car cast a glow across the lumps of bodies huddled into their pillows. Most folks were trying to sleep or read by the light of their individual lamps. She tip-toed through the observation car toward the club car where she and Katherine played cards with Evelyn and Winnie. The train jerked as each car's couplings clanked together, and then lurched forward. She nodded to the porter, standing beside the exit.

He opened the door onto the platform between the cars. "Watch your step, ma'am. The train is pullin' out. The footing is unsettlin'."

The chill and fresh scent of rain swept into her face as she stepped out onto the landing.

A man in the shadows leaned over the railing, clutching something in his hand. He leaned over farther and released the object. It fluttered and then disappeared into the night.

What was he doing? Throwing something off the train? The clanging bells and *ssshhhh* from the engine drowned out her gasp. Couplings beneath her feet clunked and then engaged. The platform swayed as the train picked up speed. Her gaze moved from the man's dark figure to the handrail connecting the two cars. She grabbed it, catching her balance.

Buildings slid past. She reached up to wipe drops of rain from her face. A chill passed through her body. She yanked open the door and stumbled into the club car. Its lights, too, were dimmed and the warmth from the pot-belly stove warmed her cheek.

She sucked in her breath and glanced toward the table where she and Katherine had played cards with the elderly sisters. Hoping against hope that her watch would still be there, she approached the table. Cigar smoke circled the heads of the two men sitting there. Red and blue poker chips dotted the table. Half-filled liquor glasses sat in puddles where her watch should have been, but wasn't. She wrinkled her nose against the noxious fumes of cigars and liquor.

Agnes's heart tumbled. Did one of these men pick up her watch? They looked so tough and uncooperative. Dare she confront them? Trepidation filled her heart. Her chilled fingers tingled.

She didn't want to repeat the recent embarrassing episode with her purse. Should she go back and talk to Katherine before she approached the men? She turned and then stopped.

Hold it! Wasn't she a self-proclaimed scourge of the underworld? Hadn't the Colonel trusted her with secret military documents to be delivered to the White House? Surely, she was capable of approaching two thuggish-looking men and asking a simple question. Where's the harm? Not to mention that the porter stood twenty feet away and would come to her rescue if the conversation got out of hand. How hard would it be to handle a couple of old coots playing cards?

She threw back her shoulders. Wasn't she a warrior on the home front even in a red checkered flannel bathrobe, no make-up and pink curlers in her hair?

She stepped up to the table, cinched her bathrobe tighter and leaned down. *Be brave, Agnes. Smile.* "Excuse me, gentlemen. Did either of you see a silver pendent watch here on the table? I'm afraid I left it here by mistake about 9:00 P.M. this evening." Best to begin the conversation by putting one's best foot forward. Her heart thumped.

The burly guy with the white beard peered at her face. He snickered. "What you made up for? Halloween?"

His friend slapped down a card on the table and chuckled. "That's a good one."

How dare they? Hadn't she smiled and asked politely? They were acting like a couple of high school brats. She folded her fists on her hips. Her eyebrows squinched, and her mouth turned down. Common sense prevailed. *Now, Agnes. Calm down.* No need to get belligerent. One catches more flies with honey than with vinegar. She switched her purse to her right arm and stood up straighter. "I'm sorry. I think we got off on the wrong foot. I'm Agnes Odboddy and I left my watch here on the table earlier this evening. Did either of you gentlemen happen to see it?" *There!* Now, how much nicer could she be?

"Beat it, lady. You're interrupting our game."

Tears pricked her eyes and tumbled over. "How dare you speak to me like that, you crass bully!" As she raised her hand to swipe the tears off her cheeks, her purse caught on the edge of the table, swept across and sent poker chips and liquor glasses flying.

Whiskey flowed across the table, wicked into the cards until the paper swelled and the dyes bled together. A stream of liquid trickled toward the edge of the table. Several ice cubes skidded and landed in one man's lap. He bounded up from the table and grabbed Agnes's arm.

She struggled to free herself. Her purse fell to the floor with a thump.

The porter rushed toward the commotion. "Here, now. None of that!" He freed Agnes's arm from the man's grasp. "Sit down over here, Mrs. Odboddy," he said, shoving her into a sofa chair. "Now, what's the problem?" He picked up her purse and set it in her lap.

Two pudgy fingers pointed toward Agnes. "That woman slandered our good names and then assaulted us." A slight exaggeration, but basically true from the man's perspective.

"I didn't mean to! It was an accident!" Agnes's mouth opened and closed like a baby bird. *Now, what have I gone and done?*

"She accused us of stealing her watch." The bearded man wiped at his wet pants with a napkin.

The porter glared at Agnes. "You been having a lot of things stole tonight, Mrs. Odboddy. What is it this time?"

"I left my watch right there on the table. These hooligans say they didn't see it, but I know different." She jabbed a finger toward the table, where liquor had created an amber pool around the remaining poker chips. The colors on the face cards had faded from bright red and black to pink and grey. This game was definitely over.

The porter sighed. "Seems to me I heard this same story regardin' your purse not *anower* ago. Perhaps you've just misplaced the watch, Missus Odboddy. You'd best go back to your berth and let me sort this out with these here gentlemen. I'll speak to you in the morning if we find your watch."

Humph! Agnes rose from the sofa, stalked toward the door where she turned. "I left it right there! Right there on the table—"

"Missus Odboddy?" The porter pointed toward the door. "Now, gentlemen. Let's see if we can clean up this mess."

Agnes slammed the door and stepped onto the landing between the two cars. She gasped as the memory of the man she had seen on the platform when she came into the car flashed back into her mind. Recognition finally dawned. It was Irving who had stood on this very platform, leaning over the railing, and it was Geraldine's fox fur cape that he threw from the train!

Chapter Seventeen

Where will he go, rocketing down the track, sixty miles an hour?

Agnes stood on the platform for a moment recapturing the image of the dark figure she had seen. Irving! Why would he throw Geraldine's fur cape overboard? Where was Geraldine? Had they quarreled again? Was he getting even with her? How juvenile. Or sadistic! In either case, it was totally unacceptable.

She'd get to the bottom of it in the morning. Right now she needed some sleep. Upon reflection, her behavior in the observation car was a bit unacceptable, too. She shouldn't have let the conversation with the men get so out of hand. She had no proof they stole the watch. Katherine might have picked it up, like she had the purse. *Shame on me!*

Now she'd have to say her prayers all over again and ask forgiveness for acting like a crazed nut case. *When will I ever learn?*

She opened the door to her sleeping car and stopped dead in her tracks. Someone was leaning into her berth and from the size of the protruding rear end, it wasn't Katherine.

"Hey! What are you doing? That's my berth!" Agnes rushed up and yanked back the curtain, revealing…Nanny!

Nanny shot out of the berth, her face looking flushed, even in the dimmed light. Her hair hung down over her shoulder in a single night-time braid. Her bathrobe was tied loosely around her middle. Her feet were bare. "I…I…*um*… Isn't this my…"

"No. It's not! It's mine." Agnes shook Nanny's arm. The woman looked drugged or half-asleep. "Are you all right?"

Nanny looked around, her eyes staring and fixed. Maybe she was sleep-walking. Or had she gotten up to go to the bathroom and climbed into the wrong berth by mistake?

"Mrs....Odboddy?" Nanny's eyelashes beat against her cheeks. "Where am I?"

Agnes took her arm and walked her down the aisle. "*Shh.* It's okay. Here's your berth, dear. Now, climb right in and go back to sleep." She pulled back the covers.

Nanny sat on the bed and then lay down.

Agnes drew the blanket up to her chin. "Good night, now. Sleep tight." She tugged the curtain closed and hiked back to her berth. Poor woman wasn't well. Likely, she was half-asleep.

At her berth, Agnes tossed her purse toward the window and climbed into bed. All the blankets were pulled loose from the cushions. Her suit jacket lay in a heap on top of her Bible in the corner. The suitcase latches were undone and stacked crookedly. Strange. She didn't remember the berth being in such disarray when she left for the observation car. Hadn't the porter straightened everything after they searched for her purse? It almost looked as if someone had *tossed* the berth searching for something...but, that was impossible, wasn't it?

Agnes slept fitfully the remainder of the night, hearing the frequent shriek of the train whistle as it passed through town after town. With the dawn, the morning light seeped around the edges of the window shade and streaked across her face. She blinked. *What time is it?* The question brought to mind her missing watch and her heart plummeted again. If Katherine was awake, she could get the answer right now.

"Katherine?" Agnes whispered. She dared not raise her voice, lest she wake the passengers in the surrounding berths.

The flush of water from the bathroom nearby indicated at least one of her fellow travelers was awake. She reached for her robe, stood and peeked between the curtains into Katherine's berth. Empty. *Ah-ha!* She was already awake. Maybe it was she in the ladies' bathroom.

Agnes retrieved her overnight bag with comb and toothbrush and her clothes and hurried to stand outside the bathroom door, eager to be next to use the facilities. *Ooh, hurry, whoever is in there!* She squirmed at the door and then knocked. "*Yoo-hoo!* Is that you, Katherine? Can you hurry, please? Nature calls and this old lady can't wait much longer."

The door cracked open. Katherine peeked out. "Good morning, Grandma. Go on in. I'll finish my hair in my berth."

"Thank you, dear." Agnes pushed past Katherine and slammed the door. Now, why hadn't she asked about the watch when she had the chance? No matter. She'd know in a few minutes.

Agnes dried her hands, ran a comb through her hair and hurried to dress in deference to the other passengers. Another lady might be standing outside the door doing the pee-pee dance. *I know how that feels!* Pulling on her girdle and stockings was no easy task in the tiny bathroom, but at last it was completed. She stepped out of the bathroom fully dressed with the seams on the back of her hose only slightly crooked.

Katherine was not in her berth when she returned. *She must have gone ahead into breakfast. Hope she was able to get a table.* She glanced toward her lapel to check the time, to no avail. Habit! Of course, Douglas's watch was not there. Agnes's heart seized again at the loss, but, only for a moment because now that she had slept on it, she was sure Katherine had picked up her watch. *Isn't she always looking out for me?*

Agnes hastened through the sleeping car and observation cars toward the dining car. She plunged through the door and breathed in the aroma of coffee, waffles and bacon. Lovely! How long since they'd had bacon for breakfast? How had the railroad convinced the government to let them buy all the wonderful food for the passengers?

Her gaze passed over the passengers and paused momentarily on the two soldiers enjoying their breakfast. And, there was Irving, sitting alone at a table, stuffing ham and eggs into his mouth. Where was Geraldine? He looked up, caught Agnes's eye and nodded.

She nodded back and then frowned. As curious as she was to question him about last night's odd behavior on the train platform, her stomach twisted at the thought of such a conversation. Oh well, there was plenty of time after breakfast.

She waved to the soldiers seated at the far end of the dining car. Where was Katherine?

Agnes moved down the aisle past all the tables full of passengers. Perhaps Katherine was in the observation car. They could dine together later when a table was available. As she passed Irving's table, he wiped a napkin across his mouth and stood. "Won't you join me, Mrs. Odboddy?" He nodded toward the empty seats around his table.

Now, really! Should she accept an invitation from the man, knowing it was his intention to steal Colonel Farthingworth's secret documents? Her hand went into her purse. She touched the string wrapped around her package. Safe and secure. Was it tempting fate to place the parcel within three feet of her adversary? On the other hand, how risky could it be in a room full of people? Was he likely to knock her on the head, grab her purse and run…where? Stuck on a train rocketing down the tracks, sixty miles an hour? Where would he go? And, hadn't she wanted to speak to him, anyway? Now was as good a time as any.

She glanced around the room again. Had she somehow overlooked Katherine? No.

Irving pulled out her chair.

Agnes sat. "Thank you. That's very gracious. I'm looking for my granddaughter. You haven't seen her anywhere, have you?" She set her purse on the floor between her feet. *Let the mental game of wits begin. A secret agent he may be, but I can play this game as well as he can.*

"No. Sorry. Haven't seen her. Shall I call your waiter?" Irving raised his hand and waved at the porter.

"Thanks. Katherine and I pre-ordered breakfast yesterday. I can't imagine where she is." Her gaze roamed the dining car again.

The porter appeared, acknowledged Agnes and hurried to fill her order.

"So, I hear you ladies are headed for Washington, too. Business or pleasure?" Irving buttered his toast and spooned a dollop of strawberry jam on top. "I hope you don't mind if I continue eating. I hate to eat cold food."

"Of course. Feel free. My food will be here soon." She took a deep breath. *Onward and upward!* "Where is your lovely bride this morning?" She raised her eyes to meet his gaze, the innocent look of a newborn kitten plastered on her face. She lifted the napkin from under the silverware and laid it in her lap. Now, just exactly how should she approach the delicate question of why he tossed Geraldine's fur cape off the train?

"*Umm.* Geraldine. *Umm*…yes…well, you see…" Irving cleared his throat, the color rising in his face. "I might as well tell you, Mrs. Odboddy. We weren't actually married…*umm*…well, not exactly. I thought it prudent for appearances sake to *say* we were newlyweds. You understand how things are, don't you, being a woman of the world—"

"Excuse me? I? A woman of the world? Really, sir, I must object. I'm almost a regular church-goer and I certainly don't condone such… such…an immoral relationship." Agnes's face warmed. The very idea! Woman of the world, indeed! It was downright scandalous. "So, where is she?" Agnes leaned forward and grinned. *Look at him squirm.* This was more fun than a car full of monkeys at the circus. A real scandal, right in her lap. Her grin spread wider. *Probably has a wife and six kids back home.*

"We quarreled during the night. I thought it best to send her home. She got off the train when we stopped during the night."

The warmth in Agnes's cheeks cooled. Her smile faded. *Got off the train…* That wasn't possible. Hadn't the train stopped in the middle of nowhere, taking on water at a water tower or something? No one would willingly leave the train at such a place. A chill worked its way up her spine. She grabbed her purse. What kind of *hogwash* was Irving peddling? Where was Geraldine?

"You can't be serious. She got off…" Agnes stood, suddenly light-headed. *I think I'm going to faint!* She felt an overwhelming urge to flee. "Excuse me. Please have the waiter send my breakfast to the observation car. I can't…" She plunged down the aisle, bumped into a man stepping away from his table. "Sorry! Sorry." She rushed on and yanked open the dining car door, and stepped onto the platform between the cars. She leaned on the rail and sucked in the fresh air. Fields full of cactus rushed past as the train bumbled through the countryside. She felt so faint. What brought that on?

Without a doubt, it was Irving's trumped up excuse about Geraldine's whereabouts. *He's lying. I'm sure of it.* A dainty creature like Geraldine who wore spikey high heels, floppy hats and a fox fur cape would never willingly leave the train at a water stop in the dead of night… *Dead! Dead!* The word echoed through her head.

Was Geraldine dead? Had Irving thrown more than her cape off the train last night? And, if he had, what should she do about it? *He must have seen me cross the platform between the train cars when he was concluding his murderous deed.* Wouldn't he want to eliminate any witness to the murder of his mistress?

On the other hand, why would he tell her such an unlikely lie? Couldn't he have said she was sleeping late, and claim later that she had left at Albuquerque where they would stop in only a few hours? A much more believable tale and less likely to make him a suspect in her disappearance.

It might be days or weeks before someone found Geraldine's body somewhere along the railroad tracks in the middle of nowhere. Or never!

Agnes filled her lungs with crisp morning air, clearing her head, but the questions kept swirling around. Should she report her suspicions to the conductor? Or wait and go to the local police department in Albuquerque? *Oh, dear, what should I do?* Where was Katherine when she so desperately needed to talk to her?

Her heart skipped a beat as the dining room door opened. *Who!* Agnes put her hand to her heart. Irving! *Oh, my dear God in Heaven. He's come to kill me!*

Irving stepped onto the platform and stood in front of the door, blocking her way back into the dining car. "Mrs. Odboddy! What's wrong? You looked positively ill. Did I say something to upset you?"

Agnes gripped the rail. Wasn't he the cool cucumber? Did he say something…? Guess he was going to keep running his bluff. Well, she could run a bluff as well as the next mistress-killer.

"Oh, my, Irving. I'm just fine now. You know how it is with women of a certain age. We get hot flashes and *tetchy* at the most inconvenient times." She put her hand to her head. "I just needed a breath of air. I feel ever so much better now." She edged toward the door of the observation car, a faint smile pulling at her lips, hoping against hope that her hand wasn't shaking so much that she couldn't turn the doorknob.

Irving grabbed the handle. "Allow me." He opened the door and waved her in.

What? How odd was that? You'd think his conscience was as clear as a newborn babe instead of a man who, just hours before, had murdered his hussy.

Agnes hurried through the door and breathed a sigh of relief at the sight of multiple passengers reading, playing cards and chatting. There was safety in numbers. For now. But, what about later, perhaps when no one was around, or in the middle of the night? Couldn't he just as easily run a knife through her ribs while she slept and her only protection, a canvas curtain and a porter prone to falling asleep on the job?

Chapter Eighteen

I think Irving killed Geraldine last night!

K atherine leaned back in her chair and waved to the porter. The dining car was full of passengers enjoying breakfast.

"Yes, ma'am? Can I help you?"

"May I have more butter, please? And a coffee warm-up would be wonderful."

She gazed around the dining car yet again. Where could Grandmother be? They had agreed to meet for breakfast every morning at 7:00 A.M. *Grandma was still asleep when I got up. After the incident last night, I guess she was all wore out.*

Why didn't any of the passengers in here look familiar? Where were Irving and Geraldine, the two elderly sisters and the soldiers who shared their dining car yesterday? Nanny and Madeline weren't here either. But, then, the old prune probably planned to feed the child a dried up apple from her suitcase.

The porter returned with four pats of butter placed on a small plate with a sprig of parsley and the coffee pot.

Katherine slid her coffee cup closer to the edge of the table. "I don't suppose you've seen Mrs. Odboddy this morning, have you? She was supposed to meet me for breakfast." She glanced at her watch. "I can't imagine what's keeping her."

"I'm sorry. I don't know Mrs. Odboddy. This is my first day in this dining car."

"What do you mean, 'this dining car'? There's more than one?"

"Oh, yes ma'am. We has four dining cars placed *strategimickly* throughout the train, so as to be convenient for the passengers traveling back that-away toward the end of the train."

More than one dining car? Well, no wonder she didn't recognize any of the passengers and Grandmother wasn't here. She was probably waiting in another dining car. Come to think of it, she had walked through several cars before she sat down. Perhaps she had walked the wrong direction from her sleeping car.

Well, no matter. "Thank you, I'll pass on the refill for now." She waved away the waiter, gulped her coffee and pushed away her nearly empty plate. She signed the ticket and grabbed her purse and the piece of unbuttered toast. "I have to run. I think my grandmother must be in another dining car. She's probably fit to be tied that I'm not there."

Katherine hurried toward the door and then stopped. Which way should she go to get back to the one nearest their sleeping car? Which door had she come in? She looked to the front and the back of the car. *I think I came in that way.* What number was their sleeping car? She tried to think back to the conversation yesterday afternoon when the porter handed out the accommodations cards. *We're in car six, berths three and four.*

"Excuse me, porter. Which direction would I go to return to sleeping car six?"

He pointed to the rear of the car. "Through that door and about five or six cars back. Can I help you with anything else, ma'am?"

"No. Thank you. I think I just got a bit turned around. I've got it now." She smiled and stepped out onto the platform where she ran into Agnes, reaching for the handle.

Katherine leaned forward. "Well, there you are. I went to the wrong dining car by mistake. I'm surprised you found me."

Grandmother's face looked as pale as a dandelion in a field full of daisies.

"What's happened? You're as white as a sheet?"

Agnes put her hand to her heart and sighed. "Thank goodness, I found you. I've been looking all over. When you weren't in our dining car, I went from car to car. We need to talk." She cast her gaze back toward the door she'd just come through. Her face suggested, indeed, that something was dreadfully wrong.

"What is it, Grandma? Come on back inside and we'll get some coffee. Have you eaten anything?" She took Agnes's arm and guided her back into the dining car.

Her table had been cleared and the porter was resetting it with fresh linens, silverware and cups.

Katherine pulled out a chair for Agnes and then sat in the seat she had recently vacated. She waved to the porter carrying his silver coffee pot from table to table.

His eyes opened wide when he recognized Katherine. "I thought you left, ma'am. I'm afraid we've taken away your breakfast. I thought you weren't coming back."

"Oh, not a problem. I didn't plan to. Just a change in plans. I found my grandmother. Do you want to order some breakfast, Grandmother?"

"No, thank you. Just coffee. Well, maybe a muffin…with jam. That would be nice."

The waiter nodded and turned away.

"Wait! Maybe a bowl of stewed prunes for my digestion…" Agnes lifted her head and sniffed. "And, a couple strips of bacon. It smells so wonderful." The waiter made notes on his tablet. "Is that all, ma'am? Are you sure you won't be requiring something else?"

"No, thank you. That's fine. I'm not really hungry. How about you, Katherine? Is that all you're having? Just coffee?"

Katherine nodded. "I've already eaten a bit. That's all for now, thank you, Porter. Just coffee with cream, please."

"I'll be right back with your orders." The porter turned and hastened away.

"Okay, Grandma. What's the story? Something has upset you. You haven't lost your purse again, I see. What is it this time?"

"First of all," she reached into her purse. "Take my train ticket. It's best to keep both of them together, don't you think? I don't want to lose it." She handed the ticket across the table.

Katherine raised her eyebrow and reached for the ticket. "Okay. If you say so. I'm sure you're capable of—"

Agnes waved her hand. "Just keep it. I'll feel better knowing you have both of them. Now, here's the thing. It's my pendant watch. I must have left it on the table last night with Evelyn and Winnie and when I woke up in the night, I remembered. So I went back to the car to fetch it. Two men at the table claimed they hadn't seen it." Agnes folded her hands as if in prayer and looked pleadingly at Katherine. "Please, please tell me you picked it up after I went to bed."

"You left it on...? I never saw it. Have you seen Winnie or Evelyn this morning?"

Agnes dropped her chin and shook her head. "No. Actually, the watch is the least of my worries." She leaned across the table and whispered. "It's Irving. I think he killed Geraldine last night, and now he's coming after me!"

"What?" Katherine's voice rang through the dining car.

Heads turned and passengers stared.

"Katherine. People are staring." Agnes lowered her head. "I said, Irving killed Geraldine. Last night when I went to look for the watch, I saw him throw her fur cape off the platform. This morning, he told me they weren't really married, he'd just made that up...oh, it doesn't matter now. He says she left the train at the water stop in the middle of the night. How ridiculous is that? Who would get off at a water stop? That's hogwash."

"Really, Grandmother! *Here-We-Go-Again is leading the pack by a nose, running down the track...*

"It's the only explanation that makes sense. He killed her. I had just stepped out onto the platform. That's when I saw him throw off her fur cape. We have to notify the authorities." Agnes glanced out the window. "We'll be in Albuquerque in a couple hours. We can go to the police department and report the murder."

Katherine shook her head. *I-Can't-Believe-This has taken the lead, running neck and neck with Here-We-Go-Again...* "You're not serious. Not really married... And, you think... Grandma, you know how you are. You're always imagining... I mean... Sometimes you get carried away and... There must be a logical explanation. You can't accuse someone of murder just because you saw him throw something off the train. Maybe it wasn't Geraldine's fur cape. Maybe it was something else, like his newspaper."

"And, maybe Hitler will get religion and stop invading European countries, but I'm not going to hold my breath. Don't you think I know the difference between a newspaper and a fur cape? I may be forgetful at times, and I'm old and have arthritis in my left hip, but I'm not blind. I know what I saw and Geraldine is not on this train. What other explanation is there? Now that he knows I saw him, he'll probably come after me."

Katherine threw back her head and crossed her arms. *...and Good-Grief-What-Now is three lengths ahead of You-Have-Got-to-Be-Kidding...* "Stop being melodramatic. If you go to the police department in Albuquerque, you'll go alone. I'll not have any part of this." Katherine's brow knit and she pulled her mouth down. How many times had they been through this nonsense? Grandma saw boogie-men everywhere she turned and wasn't shy about making accusations, even though she was always wrong. Most of the time.

"Suit yourself. Then, I'll just go—"

"Here's your breakfast, Mrs. Odboddy, just like you ordered." The porter lowered the tray to the table and whipped off the silver lid. The aroma of bacon mixed with strawberry jam rose from the plate.

Agnes sniffed. "*Ahh!* Smells wonderful. Thank you so much." She grinned at the porter.

He filled their coffee cups, set the cream pitcher on the table and backed away.

Katherine looked down at her cold piece of toast. *Why am I still holding...?* She laid the toast on the table, poured cream in her coffee and stirred as Grandmother smeared jam on her muffin. She avoided her grandmother's eyes and didn't speak. The only sound was the murmurs from nearby tables.

"So, are you going into town with me, or not?" Grandmother bit into her muffin.

Now, what should I do? Let Grandmother wander the streets of Albuquerque alone or encourage her poppycock by going with her on a fool's errand? *I'll have to go and try to change her mind.*

Katherine pushed away from the table and glanced at her watch. "It's nearly 7:30 A.M. I'll go back and get our things together for the porter. We'll be transferring to the new train in Albuquerque." She retrieved her purse. "Let's meet on the station platform and we'll go into town together and do a little shopping. We only have an hour and a half layover. Now, don't go off half-cocked on your own. Promise?"

Agnes nodded. "If you say so. There's not much time to shop if I go to the—"

Katherine turned on her heel and stomped away. She glanced back to see Grandmother waving at the porter. *She'll probably order waffles and eggs, because she isn't very hungry.*

Chapter Nineteen

You're welcome, you ungrateful old bat!

Katherine latched the last buckle on her suitcase and laid it on the bed next to Agnes's. The porter would be here soon to move the luggage to their sleeping berth on the connecting train. *I wouldn't mind living like this, waited on hand and foot, eating gourmet meals and seeing the sights on a luxury train.* No stress or worries!

Katherine glanced at her watch. 10:18 A.M. They'd be in Albuquerque in twelve minutes. She'd best hurry, make a quick stop in the washroom and meet Grandmother on the platform before 10:30 A.M. Then, she had to convince Grandmother she was mistaken about Irving. *How can I keep her from looking like an idiot at the police station?* A quick stop at a fruit stand for local fresh fruit and it would be time to board the connecting train for lunch.

Hopefully, the conductor would give clear instructions on their way out the door about where they should go to board the next train. Darn Grandmother's stupid notions and conspiracy theories!

Katherine reached for the handle on the washroom door. Locked! She stood beside the door and checked her watch again. 10:21 A.M. Perhaps there wasn't enough time to wash up after all. She should probably meet Grandmother and use the train station facilities.

She turned to leave. *What was that?* A sob from inside the washroom? She listened. There it was again. It sounded like a child. She knocked. "Hello! Are you all right? Can I help?"

The door sprang open and Madeline flung herself at Katherine, her face pressed into Katherine's skirt. "Katherine. Oh, I'm so glad you're here." Madeline lifted tear-streaked cheeks.

"What's wrong, sweetheart. Where's Nanny?" Katherine looked up and down the empty aisle. Apparently, all the passengers had gathered in the observation car, ready to make a quick shopping trip into town or change trains.

"She left me in the berth." Madeline sniffed. "She said she'd be right back but it's been ever so long and I'm scared. The train whistle keeps blowing and it's so loud." Madeline put her hands over her ears.

How could anyone be so unfeeling? The poor kid. "There, there." Katherine patted Madeline's shoulder. "You're not alone now. I'm here. You come with me and we'll find Nanny together, all right?" She glanced at her watch. 10:25 A.M. Five minutes until the train pulled into the station. If she couldn't find Nanny in the next couple of minutes, she didn't dare take Madeline off the train without permission. Worse yet, she couldn't leave her here alone. *Looks like Grandma might have to go into town alone, after all.*

"Did Nanny say where she was going, sweetheart?" Katherine leaned down and stroked Madeline's hair." *Soft, like a kitten...*

Madeline shrugged. "Maybe she went to get some breakfast?" She lowered her head.

How could Nanny go to the dining car and leave the child in the berth without any breakfast? Katherine clenched her fists. *If I could get my hands on her, I'd wring her scrawny neck.* She forced a smile and reached into her purse. "Here. I have some graham crackers. Would you like one while we look for Nanny?"

"Yes, please." Madeline took the cracker and bit off a large bite. "Good." Her precious smile would make the angels weep for joy.

Katherine's heart seized. Someday, she'd have a little girl like this.

The train slowed. If they found Nanny in the dining car, perhaps there was still time to meet Grandmother. *If not, I'm likely to miss her.* Maybe she would wait for a few minutes on the platform.

The dining room was nearly deserted. Several waiters gathered the white tablecloths and replaced them with clean ones. Another pushed a carpet sweeper back and forth under the tables. Nanny wasn't there.

"Perhaps she's in the observation car. Let's check it out." Katherine gripped Madeline's hand and led her through the dining car, lifting her carefully across the open platform and into the next car. From the platform, they could see the train station slide into view. Brakes squealed and the train screeched to a stop.

As they stepped into the observation car, the outer doors opened. The passengers crowded into the aisles, lining up to leave. Katherine tightened her grip on Madeline's hand and moved into one of the empty rows of seats. There was Grandmother on the platform, looking around, just on the other side of the window. Katherine knocked on the window.

Grandmother was too far away to hear. *Do I have time to jump off the train and alert her to the situation?* It would only take a minute and she and Madeline could get right back on the train.

Madeline began to wail. All the sorrow in her tiny body erupted. Tears spilled down her face.

Katherine leaned down and scooped the child into her arms. "What's wrong now, Madeline. Tell me."

"I'm scared. You're going to leave me, aren't you? What if we can't find Nanny? What am I going to do?"

"Oh, nonsense! Don't cry. We'll find her." *That wretched woman!* "I think it would be best if we go back to your berth and wait for her there. We'll never find her in this crowd. If she returns to your berth and you aren't there, she'll be terribly worried and very angry with me."

She patted Madeline's shoulder, took her hand and threaded her way back through the dining car and into the sleeping car. *Guess Grandma's on her own.*

"Hold it, Miss. What's your name?" A nattily dressed man in a dark pin-striped suit and tie held up a badge, blocking Katherine's way in the narrow hallway. He raised it to eye level. *FBI.*

His companion reached inside his jacket and produced a similar badge.

What on earth? Katherine shoved Madeline protectively behind her. "What do you want?" Her hand felt damp from gripping Madeline. *FBI? What have I done? Surely, Nanny hasn't accused me...*

The man returned his badge into his coat pocket. "FBI, ma'am. If you'll please show us some identification?"

Katherine nodded, reached into her purse and removed her wallet. *Does this have something to do with Madeline's father, the Senator?* "I have a driver's license. Will that do?" She handed the wallet to the tall man. Her heartbeat quickened.

He glanced at the license. "Katherine Odboddy?" He handed the wallet back to her. "You fit the description of someone we're looking for. Sorry to trouble you. Good day, ma'am."

"Good day." Katherine shoved her wallet back into her purse and moved down the aisle toward the sleeping car, breathing a sigh of relief. *Guess I have one of those common, everyday faces.*

Back in sleeping car six, porters gathered suitcases from the berths, piled them onto a luggage cart, and wheeled them down the aisle.

Katherine hailed the porter loading the suitcases from her berth. "Excuse me. Have you seen the woman traveling with this child?"

"Sorry, ma'am. Sure haven't. But, we's pretty busy this mornin' and not payin' much attention to folks comin' and goin'. Is everything all right? Is the child lost?"

"No. Not really. Thank you. I'll watch her until her nanny returns. Do you mind if we sit in her berth?"

"Not a problem. The luggage is already gone from that one. Let me know if you need anything."

"Thank you. We'll be fine." She lifted Madeline into the lower berth, crawled in alongside her, and sat cross-legged on the bed. "Now, let's see what I have in my purse. *Ahh.* Here's something." She spread a deck of cards across the coverlet. "Do you like card tricks?"

Madeline nodded and dashed tears from her cheeks. For the next ten minutes, Katherine pulled cards from Madeline's ear, made the queen magically appear and disappear, and otherwise amused Madeline with various slights of hand.

The curtain yanked back with a snap. Nanny stood glowering in the aisle. "What are you doing here?" Her fists were knotted on her hips.

Katherine stepped off the bed and stamped her feet a few times to restore the circulation. "Oh! Here you are. I found Madeline crying in the bathroom…" She glanced at her watch. "…twenty minutes ago. Why was she left alone?"

"What business is it of yours? Madeline is my responsibility." Nanny yanked Madeline off the bed. "Come with me. I need to make a phone call." She towed the child toward the exit.

Katherine stood in the aisle with her mouth open. *And, you're welcome, you ungrateful old bat!*

Madeline turned and waved. "Bye, Katherine."

Nanny jerked her arm and plunged through the door onto the platform between the cars.

Katherine shook her head. "That poor child." She checked her watch again. 10:45 A.M. *I've surely missed Grandma by now.* She hurried to the exit and stepped out onto the nearly deserted station platform.

Grandmother was nowhere to be seen.

Agnes clutched her purse and peered out the window as the train pulled into the Albuquerque station. Crowds of passengers had cued up in the aisle behind her. Great clouds of steam issued from beneath the engine as it slowed to a stop next to the Albuquerque depot. She glanced around the car. *Now, where is Katherine?*

The porter opened the outer door and the crowd pushed Agnes down the steps. They oozed across the platform and then scattered like roaches in a bright light. Some headed into the station toward the telephone booths and telegraph office. Others, having reached their destination, shouted and waved to waiting friends, while weary porters lugged suitcases to the curb. Still others headed toward the streets of town to sightsee and shop. Several stopped at the corner and retrieved Brownie cameras from their bags to photograph the mariachi players strumming guitars, adding local color to the New Mexico experience.

Agnes scanned the passengers. Where on earth was Katherine? *We only have an hour and a half. That's not much time to get to the police station, report Geraldine's murder and get back to the connecting train.* Besides, Katherine wanted to shop, for what was anybody's guess.

She glanced up at the large clock over the station window. 10:38 A.M. *Katherine, where are you?* She'd wait for two more minutes. *If Katherine isn't here by then, I'm leaving without her.*

Agnes tapped her foot as the crowds rushed past.

10:40 A.M. She couldn't wait any longer. She didn't know where the police station was, or how long it would take to get there, not to mention the time it could take to deliver her testimony regarding Geraldine's murder. Even if the building was right around the corner, she was still cutting it close.

"Porter!" She waved to a young man pushing a wheeled cart loaded with luggage. "Excuse me. Can you direct me to the local police station?"

The porter paused and then pointed over his shoulder. "Go six blocks that way until you get to Marquette. Turn left and it's about four blocks down on the right. Shall I fetch you a cab, ma'am?"

Ten blocks. Not too far to walk if she had more time, but under the circumstances, probably best to take a taxi. *Where the heck is Katherine? Everyone's gone, for goodness sake. This is ridiculous.*

"Yes, please. I'll wait for the cab here."

"Yes ma'am. I'll call for you just as soon as I deliver this cart. Shouldn't be more than twenty minutes."

"Jumping Jehoshaphat! I can't wait that long. We're only here for an hour and a half. Oh, never mind, I'll just hail my own cab." Agnes scowled and started toward the street. Was the whole world out to prevent her from doing her civic duty?

At the end of the wooden platform near the parking lot, Agnes turned. Was Katherine anywhere in sight? Had something delayed her or had they miscommunicated where they should meet? *I'll just have to go to the police station alone.* Agnes scanned the train platform.

Near the ticket window, a man in a dark suit leaned against the wall. When Agnes glanced his way, he ducked behind a stack of luggage about twenty feet from the street.

My stars! Irving?

The man popped out from behind the luggage, bent over at the waist and hurried behind a telephone booth.

What on earth? Agnes's heart pounded. Irving was following her, trying to be undetected and he wasn't doing a very good job of it. He reminded her of years gone by, watching her son, John, play hide-and-seek with the neighborhood children.

Agnes hurried past a parked car and squatted behind the fender. She peeked over the edge in time to see Irving move from the telephone booth to a tree near the edge of the parking lot.

Does the stupid man think I don't see him? He must plan to snatch the package here in town. Or was it more sinister than that? Did he plan to follow her to a deserted location and *rub her out*, like in the James Cagney gangster movie last week? Her heartbeat throbbed in her temples. Drops of perspiration beaded up on her upper lip. *Oh, where are you, Katherine? What should I do?*

Chapter Twenty

Murder must be on the decline in Albuquerque.

inally! Here comes a taxi. Agnes lurched from behind the parked car where she had crouched and rubbed her leg. She sprang in front of the cab and waved, bringing it to a screeching halt about three feet from her knees. She climbed into the cab and slammed the door. "Go! Go! This is an emergency!"

The driver shoved the car into gear. It leaped forward, tires squealing and careened around the corner. "Where to, lady? What's the emergency?"

"There's a man following me. He's trying to kill me. Take me to the police station!"

The cab driver's head jerked around, his face pale. "Yes, ma'am!"

Agnes clutched the armrest as he gunned the engine, raced down the road, zig-zagged around cars, ran a red light, and screeched to a stop in front of the police station. He jumped from the driver's seat and yanked open the passenger door. "Get out! You don't owe me nothin'."

Agnes lunged from the back seat onto the sidewalk.

The cab driver slammed the door, jumped back into the taxi and sped off. Apparently, he'd watched too many James Cagney movies recently.

Agnes hurried up the marble steps, past the USA and New Mexico flags fluttering in the breeze beside the front door. It looked as if all police stations were designed by the same architect, but not quite. This one boasted a coffee shop just beyond the elevators.

The tantalizing aroma of coffee teased her taste buds. *No time for that now.*

Agnes brushed past a tall potted plant. Overhead, a whirling ceiling fan made a brave but futile effort to cool the large room. A whoosh of air lifted a strand of hair from her brow. She ran her finger down the glass on a framed *Information* sign.

Homicide Division—Second floor

Missing Persons—Third floor

A bronze bust of Socrates scowled at her from a carved wooden desk beside the elevator. Agnes punched the elevator button. *Come on, come on!* When the elevator failed to appear within a minute, she raced up the curved staircase to the second floor, marched down the carpeted hallway, checking the signs outside each door.

Here it is. Homicide Division. Chief Homer P. Pettibone.

Agnes threw open the door and rushed into the office. Uniformed officers stopped clacking on their typewriters. Others pulled their feet off their desks and stared at her. Another stood, slugged down a gulp of some undistinguishable liquid and grimaced. It was likely something that passed for coffee. He strode toward the front desk. None of the officers appeared overly busy or particularly frazzled.

Murder must be on the decline in Albuquerque. Well, she'd have all of them dancing on their toes in short order, once they learned the nature of Geraldine's demise and the name and description of her killer.

She shook away the notion that Irving might have followed her across town and be waiting right outside the door. On second thought, if he followed her, no doubt he knew why she'd come to the police station. Wouldn't he hightail it out of town on the next Greyhound? *Of course, he would! Well, that settles that!* Who would have thought it was so easy to get rid of the threat, not only to Colonel Farthingworth's package, but to her own life?

Now, a quick report and she'd be on her way back to the train and headed to Washington D.C. without a care in the world.

She fluffed her hair, her fingers resting momentarily on Douglas's silver chopsticks. Instantly reassured by the coolness of the silver, she stepped up to the counter and set her handbag at her feet.

At the click of the door, racket in the room had halted as eight pairs of eyes ceased their duties and stared. *Humph! You'd think they'd never seen a respectable woman in their office before.*

"I've come to report a murder." Her voice sounded unnaturally loud in the silent room. She cleared her throat, then squared her shoulders and folded her arms across her chest.

Startled officers shot glances at each other. Eyebrows raised and then eight heads swiveled back towards Agnes. The officer at the counter picked up his pen. "What's your name, and who's dead?"

"I'm Agnes Odboddy from Newbury, California." She leaned forward and lowered her voice, "I'm carrying important secret documents to the President of the United States and I've come to report a murder on the train."

A guffaw came from the back of the room. "Now, get all the information right, Sargent. Wouldn't want to let a killer get off Scot free."

The other officers turned away, shrugged and resumed their previous work, typing, writing or grimacing as they sipped from the dregs of their mugs. The officer at the front desk stared at Agnes, the start of a smile now curving his smug lips. "A murder you say. How dreadful."

He's mocking me?

The Sargent licked his thumb and pulled a piece of paper off a stack. Perhaps he intended to take a report after all. Instead, he began to draw tiny boxes on the paper. "And, who might the dead un' be?"

Well, of all the nerve. "Well, *um...* I don't exactly know her last name. Scruggs, I think. Her first name is Geraldine and...and the killer's name is Irving. I'm not sure of his last name either, but it must be Scruggs, too. He told everyone they were married, for appearance's sake, but they weren't really." Perspiration dotted her upper lip. Was he buying this story?

"*Uh-huh.* Go on, what happened next?"

Agnes took a deep breath and sighed. "About three o'clock this morning, I saw him throw her fur cape off the train and this morning she's nowhere to be found. He claims she got off during the night at a water stop. Now, how preposterous is that? Don't you see? The only explanation is that he threw her body off the train just before he pitched off her fur coat."

Now that she said it out loud, the whole story did sound rather ridiculous. Warmth crept from her chin into her cheeks and inched across her forehead. No telling what the officer was thinking. "I'm telling the God's truth. It's just like I said."

"Of course it is, Mrs. Olbiddy and—"

"Odboddy! Mrs. Odboddy, from California. Don't try to humor me with—"

"Oh, I wouldn't think of it, Mrs.…*umm*… We'll look into the matter straight away. Now, why don't you run along and let us investigate your…*umm*…murder." His lips twitched again as he glanced toward his partner. He folded the paper on the desk and turned away. "Good day."

"You don't believe me!" Agnes straightened her shoulders and clutched her purse to her chest. "Well, I never! If you want murderers running around Albuquerque, I guess that's your choice, but certainly not mine. I'll just have to take care of Irving myself." She reached into her purse, expecting to feel her pistol inside. Instead, she touched Colonel Farthingworth's package. *Horse feathers!* She'd forgotten that she left her gun in the suitcase before coming into town, thinking it wasn't a good idea to carry it into a police station. Old age and decrepitude was definitely taking its toll.

She pulled her hand from her purse and wiped her sweaty palm across her skirt. *Probably a good thing. If they saw the gun, it could have made matters worse. I'd probably end up in the clink.* Agnes stepped away from the counter. "I see you're all real busy fighting jaywalkers and folks spitting gum on the sidewalk, so I'll just be on my way." She turned on her heel, yanked open the door and stomped into the hall. Her hand trembled as she pulled the door shut, her thoughts racing, heart pounding against her chest. She flopped onto a bench right outside the door.

Now, what should I do? They obviously thought she was crazy. She leaned toward the door and strained her ears. They were probably having a good cackle at her expense right this minute. She glanced at the clock over the District Attorney's door across the hall. 11:15 A.M. Forty-five minutes to get back across town to the train. There wasn't anything more she could do here since they wouldn't listen, and she didn't have time to convince them.

The hands on the clock clicked from minute to minute. By the time her heartbeat slowed, she had a plan. 11:22 A.M. She'd take a taxi back to the train and consult with Katherine. They'd decide what to do about Irving. Perhaps they could report the murder to the conductor. Maybe he'd convince the railroad to search along the track until they found poor Geraldine's body.

She took the elevator back to the first floor, pushed open the main door to the street and stopped in her tracks. *Oh, my stars!*

Across the street, Irving leaned against a power pole lighting a cigarette, looking for all the world like he was waiting for a taxi.

Agnes's heart plunged. She backed up into the vestibule. He must have followed her taxi, after all! Coming to the police station didn't scare him off. She'd seen too much. He was playing with her, like a cat with a mouse, terrorizing her. At the right moment, he'd do her in.

Should she go back upstairs to the Homicide Division? They hadn't believed her before. Why should they believe her now? It was best to find her way back to the train where she would be surrounded by people. She'd be safe with Katherine by her side.

Racing back through the vestibule, she plunged into the coffee shop, her hand to her heart. "Is there a back door in this building?" She glanced over her shoulder. No sign of him.

The lady behind the counter paused, coffeepot in hand. "Are you in trouble? I can call a cop. They're right upstairs."

"*Huh!* Not much good, that bunch. But, thanks anyway. Is there another way out?"

"There's a back door over there." She pointed down the hall.

Agnes rushed down the corridor and shoved open the door leading to the narrow alley.

Clunk! The door slammed behind her. Garbage cans stood outside the back doors of various businesses. A thin grey cat slunk away as she approached. A couple of police cars parked along the building suggested the alley should be a safe place, but if Irving came around the corner and caught her here, it could be a different story.

Now, which way to a taxi and the train? It seemed more traffic noise came from the left.

She turned toward the sound of a busy intersection, hoping to hail a cab on the corner. Then it was only ten blocks back to the train station and safety!

Agnes hurried down the alley. No sooner had she gone fifty yards when a man turned the corner and started down the alley toward her. *Irving?* Her heart did a twist as she turned and dashed back to the door leading into the coffee shop. She'd have to go back to the Homicide Division. Maybe the cops would believe her. Maybe not. It was her only choice.

She grappled at the door handle. Her hand slipped. She grabbed and yanked again. No use. The door was locked.

Chapter Twenty-One

With two starched shirts you get eggrolls.

A pall fell across the alley as the sun skittered behind a cloud. Agnes glanced over her shoulder and shivered as a rat scurried from behind a garbage can across the alley. Irving was even closer now, hurrying toward her. He was a brave one, she'd give him that. To contemplate murder right on the back stoop of the police department was the height of brazen defiance. He was truly the instrument of the Devil.

Irving raised his hand and called out to her. "Mrs. Odboddy! Wait!"

Agnes clutched her purse to her chest and ran down the alley. The chilling footsteps close behind put wings to her feet.

At the corner, she looked both directions. Which way? Or did it matter with a killer at her heels? She ran left, up one street. Right, down another. Her chest burned with each breath. A stitch in her side screamed. And still Irving followed, yelling her name. She kept her gaze straight ahead, not daring to look back.

She couldn't go on much longer. Her head throbbed with each heartbeat. He was closing the distance between them. There! The back door of Ching Chow's Chinese Laundry and Chop Suey. *With two starched shirts you get eggrolls?* She grabbed the handle. Maybe she could lose Irving inside. Locked! Footsteps pounded closer! She couldn't keep running. Where could she hide? She squeezed behind some garbage bins and crouched. *Why didn't I take the gun from my suitcase?*

The only semblance of a weapon at hand was one of her sterling silver chopsticks. She pulled one from her hair. It was long and sharp, and if she had to die behind a garbage bin, it wouldn't be before she left a few holes in her killer. If luck was with her and he hadn't seen her duck down, he might run right on by.

She held her breath as his footsteps thudded closer.

He shouted, "Wait, Mrs. Odboddy. Why are you running away? You're running out of time!" His voice was drowned out by traffic as he turned at the corner.

Wasn't that the understatement of the year? Running out of time, indeed! How long did she dare stay there? Not long. Irving would retrace his footsteps when he couldn't locate her on the street. If he found her huddled there...her life wouldn't be worth a crumbled fortune cookie.

Agnes shoved the chopstick back into her hair, heaved her bulk out from behind the bins and hurried back down the alley to the corner.

Longview Boulevard was a fairly busy street with a smattering of vehicles and a traffic light at the intersection. She was safe for the moment, as long as Irving kept heading the opposite way, but she had to find a taxi, and fast.

Traffic chugged past, but no taxis. A wooden bench and a newspaper stand stood beside a bus stop sign. Maybe the bus went to the train station. But, how would one know? There was no bus schedule posted nearby.

As she anxiously perused the street, a man in worn clothing approached, his hat slung low over his eyes, his elbows protruded from his threadbare jacket.

Despite her own predicament, Agnes's heart went out to him. *So sad. Probably a veteran, maybe mentally ill.* So many people were homeless these days, their lives destroyed by the horrors of war.

She stepped away. Best not to get involved. She had her own problems right now. She gazed up and down the street. Where was a confounded taxi when you desperately needed one?

The man moved closer. He stopped beside her and reached out his hand. "You got any spare change for a cup of coffee, lady?" A crooked smile creased his bearded cheeks.

Agnes jerked her head back as the scent of body odor mixed with the taint of alcohol wafting from his coat assaulted her nose. She reached to open her purse. Maybe he'd go away if she gave him a quarter. He'd probably buy booze instead of coffee, but that was on him. Her generosity might buy her some credit in Heaven. At a time like this, she needed all the credit she could get, especially with a killer apt to come around the corner any second.

As she drew out her wallet, the man pulled a pipe wrench from behind his back. In one swift move, he drew it back and struck it across Agnes's head. She jerked back. Flashes of light momentarily blinded her. The light pole and the park bench tumbled and spun. Sounds of traffic dimmed. Falling...falling... through a dark tunnel...*Katherine!* Her purse was jerked from her arm and everything went black.

Agnes slid out from a dark place of peace and rest to the sense of pain throbbing across the top of her head. Blinding lights flashed as she zoomed past stars and clouds, and then landed with a thump. She opened her eyes. Honking! Voices! People...hurrying by, headed somewhere, but all too busy to aid an old lady crumpled on the sidewalk.

She reached out her hand. Why wouldn't they stop? Did they think she was a bag lady, maybe drunk, and unwilling to stop lest they have to deal with her? Did they feel no guilt for passing her by? She stirred as a woman approached. "Help me," she whispered. The woman hurried on.

"Hey, lady!" A man's voice sounded far away, then nearer. "You okay?"

She ran her hand across her face, blinked, and looked up.

A young colored man crouched over her and shook her shoulder. Short dark stubble covered his chin. A frayed shirt collar peeked out from a worn jacket. Faded marks on his sleeve revealed remnants of threads where military insignia had once been attached.

Agnes cringed and put her hand to her mouth. "Don't hurt me! What do you want?" She caught her breath. Wait. He wasn't the ragged man who attacked her.

The young man released her shoulder and knelt on his haunches. A smile played across his face, showing strong white teeth. "You're okay now, aren't you? Shall I help you up?"

Agnes rubbed the lump on her head, sending throbs of pain at the touch of her fingers. "What…what happened?" She felt for the chopsticks and ran her hand over them. Good. They were still there.

Agnes glanced toward the street where cars had stopped for the red light. The drivers kept their eyes straight ahead, looking neither left nor right, making sure they couldn't see her.

Several people veered to the side to step around her and then moved on. Guess they didn't give a fig that an old woman was knocked down and robbed. Could she really blame them? Hadn't she planned to ignore the ragged man when he first approached her? If he hadn't spoken to her, would she have tried to help him? A sobering thought, to be sure.

She glanced around, suddenly aware of her belongings. "Oh!" The contents of her purse lay spilled across the concrete. *My package! Where is my package?* She rose to her knees and scrambled around, gathered items and stuffing them back into her purse. The roughness of the concrete sidewalk scratched her knees. Her head spun. *Did he take my package?*

In desperation, she scanned the space around the bus stop sign and the bench. Her chest felt hallow as the loss swept over her. After all she'd gone through with Irving, was it possible she'd lose the package to a common street thief? *Oh, woe is me! I've failed!*

Her gaze came to rest on the area within the four legs of the newspaper rack. There lay her package, even more tattered than when she removed it from the chicken yard. She pointed.

"My package!" *Praise the Lord!*

The young man retrieved it and handed it to her. "Here it is. Something important?"

Agnes clutched it to her chest. "Thank God. I was afraid that was why he...*umm*...never mind." She opened her purse again and looked inside. "My wallet's gone. No surprise."

"The important thing is that you're safe. Here, let me help you to the bench." The young man lifted her to her feet. He held her steady as she stumbled forward and flopped onto the wooden bench. "What's your name, lady? Are you okay?"

Agnes swiped her hair off her face. "Thanks. I...I," she said, feeling the back of her head again. "I'll live...just a little dizzy." She eyed the blood on her fingers. "My name's Agnes."

The man touched her cheek and turned her head toward him. "The bump probably looks worse than it is. Here. Let's clean you up a bit. I don't think you need stitches." He pulled a handkerchief from his pocket and dabbed at her head.

"You're a doctor?" Agnes peered with new admiration at the young man. Did the military have colored physicians now? Maybe what Katherine said about desegregating the military was true.

The young man smiled. "Not exactly. I was a corpsman's assistant in the Army until I got a bullet in my leg and they gave me my walking papers..." He chuckled. "So to speak. No pun intended." He patted his shoulder where his military insignia had been. "Left me with a limp, and I can't run worth a plug nickel, but I get by." The state of his clothing and scruffy exterior suggested that *getting by* was about all he was doing. *Maybe he's one of the homeless who wander the streets mugging old ladies. Shame, Agnes. The man has been more than kind. The least you can do is appreciate...*

Agnes's eyes flew open. "Oh! What time is it?" Her hand trembled.

"Must be close to noon." He glanced at his arm. "Don't have a watch any more. I had to pawn it. Had a toothache and the dentist insisted on cash."

Agnes put her hand on his arm as she struggled to her feet. She wavered for a moment and then her head cleared. "I have to get back to the train station. My train leaves at noon. I don't suppose you have a car." Her cheeks warmed as she realized the absurdity of her request. What a stupid thing to say. "I'm sorry. I haven't even thanked you for helping me. Or asked your name."

"I'm Charles Blackwell. You don't have to thank me. I'm happy to help."

"Agnes Odboddy." She put out her hand. She wished she had some money to give him, but right now, she was in the same financial situation as he. "Can you direct me to the train station? Maybe if I hurry, there's still time." She pulled on his shirtsleeve. A pain shot through the goose egg on the back of her head.

The young man stood and took her arm. "This way." He led her to the corner, hustled her across the street and headed west. The clock on the bank at the corner struck the hour. Twelve bongs…

In the distance, the faint sound of a train whistle cut through the air. Her train, leaving the station…and they were blocks away and on foot.

Chapter Twenty-Two

You want me to sit on the handlebars? I can't do that!

Katherine glanced at the clock on the train station platform. 10:45 A.M. *I've missed her!*

The passengers had scuttled like Egyptian locusts before Moses's staff, leaving the station bare. A lone man nodded a greeting as he scurried toward the curb, perhaps to make a quick trip into town for a last minute purchase before the connecting train departed for points east.

Katherine sighed. *Grandmother is probably already at the police station reporting her murder.*

She had had no choice but to stay with Madeline with Nanny missing. It was doubtful she could have dissuaded Grandmother from such a ludicrous plan, anyway. She had an uncanny knack for making a scene whenever she got a crazy notion in her head. Her tendency to see conspiracies at every turn was getting tiresome.

Imagine, accusing Irving of murder. Sure, his wife didn't seem to be on the train, and maybe she left under suspicious circumstances, but that didn't mean Irving killed her and tossed her body off the train. Grandmother's wild imagination turned whatever she saw during the night into another giant conspiracy. Even accusing him of planning to steal Colonel Farthingworth's package was hard to believe.

Truly, Irving's behavior was suspicious. He appeared around every corner, but considering the confinement of the train, couldn't you say that everyone was following them, even Nanny, for goodness sake?

Katherine returned to the observation car, settled in a comfy sofa and opened her novel. Before long, she checked her watch. 11:20 A.M. My! How time flies when you've got your nose in a good book. Just enough time to run out and mail her postcard to Donald. No point in trying to call him. He'd be on duty at the hospital now. Maybe she'd have time to take a little walk and stretch her legs before the train left. Grandmother should be back any minute. She was cutting it pretty close, going into town with such a small amount of time between trains.

A flutter skittered through her stomach. What if Grandmother missed the train? *Don't even think that!* Grandmother might be eccentric, but she had a good head on her shoulders. She'd check the time and return long before noon. Wait! Grandma lost her watch! She might have a problem keeping track of the time. *Oh, now, I wish I'd gone into town with her.* Too late. What's done is done.

Katherine mailed her card and then walked briskly around the train platform until her cheeks warmed from the exercise and sunshine. The sound of guitars down the street drew her attention. A woman dressed in a Mexican dress rolled a cart loaded with local fruit and strolled beside a man strumming a guitar. Katherine walked toward the musicians. Several women clustered around the fruit cart and purchased apples and oranges.

Such fresh fruit was in short supply or nearly nonexistent in Newbury markets since the beginning of the war. *Where do you suppose this vendor got her merchandise?* Perhaps the fields around Albuquerque yielded enough produce to sell here at the station. Katherine lingered beside the cart and enjoyed the music.

Returning to the train station platform, she stopped to listen as Jackson gave directions to a returning passenger. "Your connecting train to Washington is on yonder track, just beyond the ticket booth."

Katherine's gaze moved in the direction where he pointed.

"We'll be serving lunch to the folks what hasn't eaten in town." He grinned and waved. "Howdy, Miss Katherine."

Taxis and buses pulled up to the curb and passengers straggled back into the waiting area laden with bags and parcels purchased from shops in the surrounding blocks.

11:45 A.M. Where is grandmother?

Another taxi pulled up to the curb. Katherine scanned the street as a lady wearing spiked heels and a fox fur stole stepped out and sauntered toward the station. *Could that be...?* No, it wasn't Geraldine. Surely Grandmother would be along in the next taxi. A flood of concern rushed through Katherine's chest.

11:53A.M. Katherine wrung her hands. What if something happened to her? Could she have had an accident? Had they held her at the station for some reason? Maybe they thought she was a nut case they needed to question further about the alleged murder? *What shall I do if she isn't back in time?* Should she get back on the train or stay in Albuquerque and search for her? Katherine's stomach twisted.

Was it possible that Grandmother had returned while she was mailing the postcard or taking a walk? *I stopped around the corner for a couple of minutes to listen to the music.* That must be it. Grandmother was probably already on the train and she'd missed her!

But, what if something unexpected had delayed Grandma? She'd be stuck in Albuquerque with very little money, no clothes, and...

Katherine unsnapped her purse and reached inside. *Just as I thought! I have both tickets!* Perspiration trickled between her breasts. She jerked when the train whistle blew, announcing its imminent departure. She searched the faces of the people shoving toward the train, grabbing the handrails and climbing the steps.

"All aboard!" Jackson waved to the crowd and beckoned toward the door.

The last few passengers, including Irving, leaped up the steps onto the platform and entered the train. If Irving had gone into town, maybe he'd seen Grandmother.

Jackson stepped off the bottom step and shouted. "All aboard, Miss Katherine. We're leaving!"

The train inched forward. A blast from the whistle ripped through the station, and steam *swooshed* from the engine several cars ahead.

She had to decide. Go, or stay? *If Grandma's already on aboard and I get off, I'll be left behind.* Katherine ran and seized the handrail.

The porter grabbed her arm and pulled her onto the bottom step as the train started to move. Another screech from the whistle cut through the air.

Katherine turned and leaned against the platform rail guards as the station edged past. They picked up speed past rows of engines, flatcars, and warehouses. Within minutes, buildings were fewer and farther apart, with the open plains stretching ahead as far as the eye could see.

If Grandmother hadn't returned, every minute that passed put more distance between them. Katherine clasped her hands. "Oh, Lord, please let her be on board." She wiped her eyes, opened the door into the observation car and stepped inside. She hoped against hope that she would find her grandmother calmly chatting with another passenger, drinking a dollar cup of coffee, and spouting one of the wild adventures she was so fond of sharing with anyone who would listen.

Twelve bongs. Agnes glanced up at the clock on the bank at the corner. Her stomach lurched. Twelve o'clock! "We'll never make it," she wheezed as Charles hustled her down the street. "That's the train whistle. I'm too late."

"Maybe not! Sometimes, the first whistle blows several minutes before it leaves. We might still have a couple of minutes."

Agnes shook her head. "We're blocks away." Tears pricked her eyes." *Katherine will be frantic when she discovers I'm not on the train.*

Charles stopped beside a bicycle rack and jerked one from the stand. "I have an idea. Here, get up on the handlebars and we'll be at the train station in two shakes of a puppy dog's tail."

Agnes gasped, "You've got to be out of your mind. You want me to sit on the handlebars? I'm old. I can't do that."

"Do you want to get to the station before the train leaves or not? It's your only chance. Make up your mind. Time's a'wastin'." He held up a finger, then two, then three.

"I can ride a bike. Why don't I take it?" She reached for the handlebars.

"You'd be stealing the bike and you'd have to leave it at the station. I can return it before the owner even knows it's gone. What do you say, Mrs. Odboddy?"

Agnes hefted her skirt and backed over the front tire. "You'll have to help me a bit. It's too high."

"Get off a minute." He wheeled the bike to a cement planter. "Step up on that. From that height, you should be able to climb on."

Agnes complied, and with only a little bit of help from Charles, she balanced her rump on the handlebars. "Oh! This is never going to work." She clutched at the handlebars beside her hips and spread her legs, lest her skirt get caught in the spokes.

Charles pushed off and waggling the bicycle back and forth for balance, stabilized it and wheeled off down the street.

Agnes held on for dear life and screamed as the air rushed past her head.

With Charles steering, the bicycle deftly wove in and out between the cars, raced through a red light, and sped toward the train station.

Agnes shrieked at every turn. *This will be the death of me yet!*

A driver in a 1930 Model A Ford raised his fist and honked. A child on the sidewalk pointed and laughed. *Ohh! Hang on for dear life!*

"*Oww!*" Hairpins flew like miniature missiles from the back of Agnes's head, stabbing Charles's neck and shoulders. "We must be quite a sight, Mrs. Odboddy," he yelled. "Imagine how funny we look… A black man driving a bicycle with a white woman perched on the front handlebars. *Whoo hoo!*"

The train whistle blasted again and was inching down the track, just as Charles rounded the last corner and skidded to a stop at the edge of the platform.

Agnes lurched off the front of the bicycle. Following the blow to her head and the wild ride, she found it difficult to walk in a straight line. She staggered forward toward the train.

Charles dropped the bicycle, rushed to her side and grabbed her arm in time to keep her from falling. "We're too late, Mrs. Odboddy. Come and sit down. I'm sorry." He helped her to a bench just as the caboose disappeared down the track.

The only sound on the platform was a slight gurgle in Agnes's chest. She closed her eyes and tried to catch her breath. *Too late! Now, what shall I do?*

"Well, we tried, Mrs. Odboddy." Charles patted her arm. He ducked his head. In the distance, a faint whistle cut through the air.

Agnes dabbed her sleeve across her eyes and smoothed her flyaway hair behind her ears, stabbing wayward hairpins back into her bun. She reached for the silver chopsticks and rammed them firmly into place. A wan smile trembled on her lips. "I can't thank you enough, Charles. I know you tried. We gave it our best Christian darnest, didn't we?"

"We surely did, ma'am. Another minute and we'd have made it."

Agnes twisted her handkerchief. Tears blurred her gaze across the deserted platform and down the track where only moments ago the train carried away the one she held most dear.

Charles picked at his fingernail. After a couple of minutes, he lifted his head. "Okay, so you've missed your train. What are you going to do now?"

Agnes shrugged. "I guess I should talk to the station master and tell him what happened. Unfortunately, I have no money to buy another ticket on a later train. I'm not exactly sure what they're going to do with me." She sighed and opened her purse.

Inside, the battered chicken-spotted package with its somewhat tattered string had suffered no further ill effect from her wild ride. She pawed through comb, lip rouge, powder compact, nail file, scissors, little sewing kit, and three cookies wrapped in a linen handkerchief. She found the tiny pencil and tablet she kept on hand to take down the license plate numbers of any known criminals whose faces she had memorized at the post office.

Everything was there except her wallet with identification, passport, money and Social Security card. How should she proceed? With no identification or money, she was a non-person. A few coins lay in the bottom of her purse alongside four crumpled dollar bills, insufficient for another ticket to Washington.

"Oh, my goodness! I just thought of something." She clawed frantically through the items again, her hands shaking. "My passport! Where is my passport?"

Charles raised his eyebrows. "He took your wallet *and* your passport? You weren't planning to travel overseas, were you? Haven't you heard, there's a war on?"

Agnes brought her trembling hand to her face and wiped it over her lips and chin. "I was on my way to Washington with my granddaughter. We were going to travel with…" She hesitated. "We were going to… to…" *Uh-oh. Do I dare share Mrs. Roosevelt's secret trip with Charles?* Had he not proven to be trustworthy over the past half hour, a wounded veteran who helped a stranger, stole a bicycle, and risked his life on a wild ride across town? At this particular moment, who else could she turn to if not this man?

"Charles, I'm going to trust you with the truth. I hope you won't disappoint me. I'm not just an unfortunate old lady who got mugged. Actually, I'm a courier carrying secret documents to President Roosevelt." She opened her purse to show him the tattered package inside. "I'm supposed to meet Mrs. Roosevelt in Washington. I'm going with her on a secret mission to the Pacific Islands. Now, without any money, I don't know how I'll get to Washington in time to meet Mrs. Roosevelt or deliver my package. Will you help me?"

The blank expression on Charles's face took Agnes by surprise. Hadn't she just bared her soul and asked for his help? Surely, he'd believe her and have some suggestion how she could proceed. Was that too much to ask? After all, wasn't she a warrior on the home front, the scourge of the underworld, the… *What was I going to say?*

In spite of the seriousness of the situation, her confession struck her funny bone. How utterly ridiculous her entire story must sound to a total stranger. Imagine finding an old lady bleeding on the street corner without a shred of identification, four dollars to her name and the only evidence of her tale, a chicken-spattered package tied with a dirty string. She giggled. The more she chuckled, the funnier it became. She held her stomach as chuckles bubbled up, overflowed and turned into guffaws.

Now, here she was asking for help to get to Washington. No wonder he looked like he'd just opened the refrigerator and found elves dancing in the vegetable bin.

Agnes chuckled. "I know what you're thinking. That the story I just told you is a crock of doo-doo and I'm a senile old lady, but I'm not. Honest, everything is the God's truth." Agnes smiled. *He probably thinks I'm suffering from delusions due to the bonk on my head.*

"*Umm*… Sure, sure, Mrs. Odboddy. Anything you say. I'll bet you could use a drink of water. Maybe I can find a policeman and he can help—"

"Charles! Listen to me. I'm not hysterical. I know how ridiculous it sounds. That's what struck me as funny, but everything I said is true. When Colonel Farthingworth at the Boyles Springs military base heard about my trip with Mrs. Roosevelt, he asked me to deliver the package to the President."

Should she tell Charles how Irving chased her around Albuquerque trying to kill her? Better not share that part of the story just yet. How much crazy talk could Charles handle before he bolted, thinking she was off her rocker or suffering from spotted jungle fever? Anyway, Irving was likely back on the train headed for Washington, so there wasn't much chance he'd cause her any more problems today.

Charles sat with his head lowered, his eyes closed and his hands folded in his lap. Minutes ticked by.

Agnes sucked in her breath. "Charles?" *Had he fallen asleep?*

Her voice quaked as she shook his arm. For whatever reason, divine intervention had thrown them together. Surely, he was sent to help her, now that she was broke and stranded. She didn't have a shred of a plan how to get back to Katherine, much less how to repay a homeless ex-military corpsman's assistant for helping her thus far. "Charles?"

Charles's head jerked up. "Sorry! I was thinking about what you said. It all sounds pretty far-fetched, but I believe you, Mrs. Odboddy. I don't know why. Something tells me I should run like *hell…icopters*, but crazy as it sounds, something else tells me that you and I were destined to meet like this. I'm probably crazy, but I'll help you see it through. How's that sound?"

"Oh, thank you, Charles." She threw her arms around his neck. "I guess the first thing I should do is talk to the stationmaster and see if they're willing to stake me for another ticket on the next train to Washington."

Charles gurgled and pulled himself from her embrace. "I'm sure they will, once they see your train ticket. You can't be the first person who missed the train."

Agnes reached for her purse and paused, her hand on the latch. She shook her head. "Katherine's got both our tickets."

"What?" Charles sighed. "Of course, she does! So much for that bright idea. Well, go on in and talk to him. I'll see what I can do about some lunch."

"You got money? I have a couple of dollars." She opened her purse and held the crumpled bills toward him.

"We don't need money if we're hungry enough and willing to leave our pride on the curb…so to speak."

Agnes's eyebrows went up. "Oh? Whatever you say." She dropped the money back into her purse. She supposed that if she could trust him to drive her on the handlebars across town and agreed to help her get to Washington, she could trust him to get lunch. "I'll meet you back here in half an hour. Wish me luck."

"You don't need luck, Mrs. Odboddy. You have *right* on your side."

Agnes hurried across the platform toward the ticket window. *In my experience, it's going to take more than luck to help me out of this mess. Having right on my side doesn't pay the bulldog.*

Chapter Twenty-Three

Perhaps she thinks Grandmother is tetched in the head!

W here could she be?" Katherine stood on the steps of the train and wrung her hands as they pulled away from the Albuquerque station. *When I get my hands on her, I'm going to shake the stuffing out of her!* The train lumbered past the empty platform. Cartons and crates of merchandise just offloaded from one of the sidecars slid by. Back at the station, a bicycle careened around the corner and skidded to a stop.

Katherine hurried into the observation car and glanced over the passengers' heads as they chatted in little groups of two and threes.

A gentleman spread a deck of cards across a table, ambled up the aisle and stopped beside each seat, "Wanna play a game of poker?" He got no takers.

The waiter moved from row to row, scribbling in his notebook as he took each passenger's dinner order.

Winnie and her sister sat several rows from the doorway.

Katherine hurried over. "Hello, ladies. Did either of you see my grandmother get back on the train?"

Evelyn laid down her book and looked up. "Hello! Where have you been keeping yourself? Won't you join us? We were just considering ordering a drink. The waiter announced the bar was open and he's taking—"

"Excuse me. My Grandmother? Have you seen her?" Katherine twisted her handkerchief. "She went into town alone and I don't think she got back on the train. I'm worried…" Her hand moved across her forehead. Would Grandmother's antics never stop being so exasperating? *If she missed the gol-darned train…* "I suppose it's possible she's in another car and I didn't see her, but…" She couldn't even consider the consequences. Just thinking about it made her head ache.

"Now, don't jump to conclusions. Maybe you should sit with us for a bit and gather your wits." Evelyn patted Katherine's hand. "I can see that you're upset, dear, but surely your grandmother isn't so careless as to miss the train. She knew we were leaving at noon. It's not like she's senile or…or…is she?"

The color drained from Katherine's cheeks. She ducked her head and then glanced up through her lashes. *Perhaps she thinks Grandmother is as* tetched *in the head as Winnie!* "No. No. Of course not. Grandmother's as sane as any of us. Maybe a bit eccentric. She misplaced her pendant watch last night, so I'm concerned that she might have lost track of time in town and missed the train. I should have gone with her, but I was detained."

"Oh! That reminds me." Evelyn opened her handbag and pulled out Grandmother's watch. "Winnie admired it at the table last evening and Agnes showed it to her. Winnie put it in her pocket and forgot it was there." She patted Winnie's hand. "She does that sometimes. Picks up things and puts them in her pocket. It's not stealing, you understand. It's just that she takes a *funny turn* from time to time. We were going to return it to Agnes first thing this morning, but I haven't seen her. I hope she wasn't too concerned about it. Will you forgive her? Winnie didn't mean any harm." She gazed between Katherine and Winnie with a wobbly smile.

Katherine dropped the watch in her purse. "Of course! Grandmother will be delighted to get it back." She stood. "I really must go and look for her. If she missed the train, I don't know what to do. Thank you for returning the watch." Katherine turned and hurried through the observation car into the dining car brimming over with travelers in each row.

Waiters hastened from table to table, already delivering soup and sandwiches to early returnees from town.

As Katherine studied each face, searching for silver-pronged flaming auburn hair, Irving rose from a nearby table and hurried to her side. "Won't you join me, Miss Odboddy? And, of course, your dear grandmother. I presume she'll be joining you momentarily?" His expression was subdued, unlike the haughty manner he usually exhibited when they exchanged words.

Katherine raised an eyebrow. *What is he up to now? He looks almost concerned. Despite what Grandmother thinks, I'm more inclined to think he's a thief, not a killer.* Whichever the case, wasn't it odd that he should invite her to sit with him now, considering the cold shoulder from Grandmother over the past few days?

Perhaps a little chat *was* a good idea. He might have followed Grandmother into town this morning, and might have some information as to her current whereabouts.

Katherine slid into the chair opposite Irving and laid the napkin across her lap. She flashed him a smile innocent enough to change the verdict of a hangman's jury. "Actually, I'm looking for Grandmother as we speak. I'm a bit worried. I haven't seen her since we got back on the train. Did you go into town? I don't suppose you saw her…there in town…if you went…"

Irving's face turned as white as a bride's hoop skirt. "She didn't make it back to the train?"

Aha! So, he did follow her into town. "I'm not sure. I watched at the station, but I didn't see her return. It's good of you to worry. I wonder…"

"Good grief, young lady. Of course, I'm concerned!" Irving stood and tossed his napkin onto the table. "We must search the train. If she was left behind, we must notify the authorities as quickly as possible!"

Katherine's chest tightened. If Irving was worried about a

casual traveling companion, she had good cause to be even more alarmed. Wasn't it odd that he should be so troubled? Was his dismay for Grandmother's safety or for the package she carried? Maybe Grandmother was right!

Katherine followed Irving to the door. He plucked at the porter's arm. "Excuse me. We have a problem. It appears that Mrs. Odboddy may have missed the train. Can the staff search for her?"

The porter's eyes opened wide. "Our Mrs. Odboddy? Yessuh. Yessuh. I'll notify the head conductor and he'll arrange a search most immediately." He snapped his fingers and the second porter hurried over. He whispered something to the younger man who hastened out of the dining car.

"There now, Miss Katherine." His dusky face broke into a grin with just the hint of concern still gleaming in his dark eyes. "We'll have the entire train searched within fifteen minutes. We has a procedure for just this kind of situation. Now, don't worry. If you'll sit down, I'll bring you some lunch."

"I suppose there's nothing I can do until we know more." Katherine stumbled back to Irving's table and dropped into her chair.

Irving wiped a handkerchief over his face and cleared his throat. His lips trembled as he attempted a smile. "I know you're worried, but it's not the end of the world. If she missed the train, the first thing she'd do is report to the stationmaster. Our conductor can contact him at the next stop and arrange for her to be on the next train headed this way. All she has to do is show her ticket. She'll catch up with us, eventually."

Katherine's cheeks tingled. *Uh-oh!* She opened her purse and drew out the two train tickets. "That might not be so easy. She gave me her ticket this morning for safekeeping. I doubt she has enough money with her to purchase another one."

Irving's face paled and dots of perspiration popped out on his forehead. His Adam's apple bobbed as he swallowed.

Strangely, he looked quite ill for a man who hardly knew Grandmother.

Chapter Twenty-Four

The pompous aa…uh…agent doesn't believe me.

Agnes crossed the deserted Albuquerque train platform. She stepped carefully over the cracks in the uneven wooden decking surrounding the stationmaster's ticket window. *Step on a crack…break your mother's back!* It's not that she was superstitious, just careful. Reverting to a childhood game at a time like this! *Now, why did I think of that?* Was it symbolic of her helplessness?

A dog trotted past, sniffed briefly at the potted trees beside the ticket window, and then lifted his leg before moving on. *You got that right. I feel the same way.*

Inside the ticket window, a man stamped paperwork, scrutinized documents and sorted papers into various stacks.

Agnes stepped up to the glass, rapped, and plastered on her brightest smile.

The ticket agent's head jerked in surprise. He looked up. Hadn't the train departed, not five minutes before? He stood and moved to the counter. "Yes ma'am, can I help you? I'm afraid you've missed the train." He jerked his head toward the track, and then reached back for his cup of coffee. He took a sip, his gaze fixed on something behind her head.

"Yes. I can see that. I have a terrible problem and I desperately need your help."

"Yes ma'am. Just exactly what is the matter? Our company prides itself on providing the most exacting customer service. No matter how large or small your problem, I'm sure we—"

"Yes, yes. Stop prattling and listen to me! When is the next train heading to Washington, D.C.?"

"Our next passenger train leaves tomorrow morning at 10:45 A.M." He picked up a tablet from a stack on his counter and waved it toward the window. "I have the tickets right here."

Agnes shook her head. "Here's the problem. I was traveling with my granddaughter on that train that just left." She fluttered her hand toward the empty track. "I went into town and I was mugged. The thief stole all my money and my passport. I barely escaped with my life. If it hadn't been for the kindness of a stranger, who knows if I'd even be here to tell the tale." She glanced toward the street where Charles leaned over a trash can, pulling out bags and bottles, and set them on the sidewalk. *What on earth is he doing?* Surely that wasn't his idea of *getting lunch.*

Agnes's attention jerked back to the ticket agent. "Never mind all that. Due to a cowardly assault by one of your upstanding citizens, I'm sure…I've missed my train. Now, what shall I do? I'm on an important assignment to Washington." Agnes squared her shoulders and tried to look official. She reached up and straightened her ripped collar.

The ticket agent nodded. A smile teased the corner of his mouth. "You do have a problem. What shall we do? *Ah!* If you'll just show me your ticket, we'll get you on the train tomorrow morning. The only other train leaving today is a mail train…" He checked his watch. "…in about an hour."

The pompous aa…uh…agent doesn't believe me! What nerve! "Well, here's the thing. My granddaughter has both our tickets and she's on the train."

"Then, I'm afraid you'll have to purchase another ticket, ma'am." A smarmy smile tugged the corners of his mouth. "Of course, you'll be reimbursed when you get to Washington and your granddaughter produces your…*ahem*…ticket."

Agnes cringed at his mocking smirk. He'd probably heard a

similar story several times this month already. Of course he'd think she was lying to get a free ride. In spite of her best effort to look dignified and truthful, her cheeks warmed. *I must look as guilty as sin.* "I know what you're thinking. Of all the insulting insinuations! I just told you a thief stole my money. You know I can't purchase a ticket. What do you suggest I do, sir? Sleep on your park bench?"

"I'm afraid there's no way I can help you. Here's a thought. There's a mission six blocks up that way." He pointed to the right. "Why don't you go up there and see if someone will lend you enough money for a ticket. I hear they serve meals and they even provide the homeless a cot for the night—"

"Homeless! I've never been so insulted in all my life!" Agnes huffed and turned on her heel. "This is no way to run a railroad. And, *so much* for your customer service! Indeed." Agnes stomped back to the bench where Charles waited.

"Lunch is served." He grinned and waved his hand over the bags and soda bottles sitting beside him. "I've got French Fry potatoes, cold but still edible. I'll cut off this part of the apple with the bite in it. The other half is perfect." He gripped the apple in one hand and his pocket knife in the other. "And here are several cookies, perfectly clean. I don't suppose you want the soda pop." He waggled the half-empty soda bottle.

"You pulled all this out of the garbage. Do you expect me to eat it? Really, Charles, I don't think so." Agnes crossed her arms, squinched up her nose and plopped her ample rear on the bench. "It'll be a cold day in *you-know-where* before I resort to eating out of a garbage can!"

Charles chopped the apple in half. He tossed the half with the bite into the garbage can and held up the other half. "Look. This half is as good as new. See? Shiny white, and clean."

Agnes shook her head and turned away.

"Suit yourself. When you get hungry enough, even the half with the bite will look good to you. What do you plan to eat?" He opened the bag and bit into one of the cold French Fries.

"I…I don't know what I'm going to eat, or how to contact Katherine, or how I'm getting to Washington." She buried her face in her hands. "Maybe we should walk down to the mission. The agent said they had food and cots for the homeless. I guess that's what I am." She lowered her head. "I just don't know what to do. He said the only train leaving today was the mail train and—"

"There's a mail train? Which track?" Charles stuffed the soda bottles into the largest bag and gathered up the other bags. "Come on. We have to hurry." He started toward the train tracks, and then stopped and turned. "You gonna' sit there all day or do you want to get to Washington?" His head jerked toward the railroad tracks.

Agnes hurried after him. "What do you mean? I told you the train isn't leaving until tomorrow and I don't have any money. Where are you going?"

Charles's face lit up with a mischievous grin. "You'll see. Do you trust me? Will you do exactly as I say?"

"I've already put my life in your hands on the bicycle. I guess I can trust you a little bit further. I don't seem to have a whole lot of alternatives, do I?"

Charles led her back to the railway waiting room. At the entrance, he whispered, "You'd better go in and visit the restroom. Where we're going, there won't be any facilities. Wash out these two soda pop bottles and fill them with water." He handed the bag to Agnes. "I'll meet you out front in a couple minutes." Charles shoved open the door into the men's room and disappeared inside.

Agnes looked around the deserted station. She stared wistfully down the tracks where her train had departed with Katherine, her train ticket and control of her life. Of all the pickles and predicaments she'd encountered over the years, she'd always known just what to do, no matter how crazy it might look to others. But, never had she felt so helpless and out of control as today. Maybe the mission down the street was the best thing.

What *did* Charles have in mind? Putting her life in the hands of a stranger, a Negro man at that, was not the conventional thing a woman of her age would normally consider.

But, when had she ever done anything conventional? Hadn't Charles proved himself several times already? God love him, as misguided as he was. A half-eaten apple, indeed!

Agnes squared her shoulders and shook her head. *I must be getting old. What am I afraid of?* This wasn't any worse than a few other situations she had found herself in recently. For once, she'd allow someone else to take control. Surely, Charles had her best interest at heart.

She washed her hands and dried them on the loop of cotton towel in the dispenser, filled the soda bottles and stuffed the tops with wadded up toilet paper.

With her stockings straightened, her face washed, hair combed, and a fresh coat of lip rouge, she was ready to face whatever Charles had in mind. She jammed her silver chopsticks firmly into her bun. Feeling the reassurance they always inspired, she stepped out the door.

Charles led her beyond the railway station, past a cold and lifeless hunk of blackened steel, where half-naked men shoveled coal into its yawning mouth. They tiptoed past the workers and past the lifeless hulk, soon to be changed into a shrieking beast of burden, plunging down the tracks to some faraway city.

Chapter Twenty-Five

Just what kind of hanky-panky was he intending?

Katherine stirred her coffee and absently gazed at the fields zipping past the window. *Whatever shall I do if she's not found?*

"There you are, Katherine. It's almost 2:00 P.M. I've been looking for you." Irving slid into the adjoining seat.

She glanced up and her stomach lurched. He was alone. Obviously, the search for Grandmother had been in vain. "Nothing? Not a sign of her?"

He shrugged. "The porters searched the entire train. Even those colored soldiers, Samuel and David, helped. There's not a sign of her, Katherine. I'm afraid we have to face it. She missed the train. She's still in Albuquerque."

"Is there any way we can call and see if she returned to the station? Where is she going to sleep tonight?" Katherine bit her lip, fidgeted with her spoon and laid it beside her cup.

Irving shook his head. He took Katherine's hand and squeezed it. "There, now. Don't fret. I'm sure your grandmother will be fine. She's a resourceful woman. She'll figure out something. Unfortunately, until the train stops in Oklahoma City tonight, we can't call back to Albuquerque to see if she returned to the station and what do they plan to do about it. Maybe they can put her on the next train."

"When do we get to Oklahoma City?"

"I'm afraid, not until 3:30 A.M. tonight. It's only a thirty minute stop. Not much time to make many calls."

Tears prickled her eyes. Katherine pulled her hand away from Irving's grip and put her fists to her eyes. She would not cry. She must be strong now, and make the right decisions.

Irving lips tightened in a grimace. "If she hasn't shown up at the train station, we can call the police department and the hospitals." He handed her a slip of paper with scribbled phone numbers.

"In case it becomes necessary to go back and look for her, I'll have the porter put our luggage off in Oklahoma City."

Katherine's head jerked up. "What do you mean? Our luggage?"

"You can't think I would let you face this alone? If you decide you have to go back to Albuquerque in the morning, I'll get you settled in a hotel tonight in Oklahoma City. We'll take the first train back in the morning."

"Now, Irving, don't be ridiculous. Why would you consider such a thing? You're not responsible for me." Katherine pulled her handkerchief from her purse and dabbed her eyes. Hotel room? What kind of *hanky-panky* was he intending? *Stay calm, Katherine. Don't let him know you're onto him.* "Thank you, but I can't possibly keep you from your business in Washington!"

"Oh, pooh! My business isn't urgent. What kind of a gentleman would abandon a lady in trouble in the middle of the night? His boyish grin was *almost* convincing.

Balderdash! Grandmother saw through him all along. He cared more about the package, not Grandmother's safety. Not to mention whatever shenanigans he thought he could get away with in a hotel room.

How unnerving, knowing his ulterior motives, but what choice did she have? How could she arrange for her luggage to be unloaded, make all the calls and decide what to do within thirty minutes? If she did have to go back to search for Grandma, it would be better to have a man along. *I can handle him, at least until we find Grandmother. After that, who knows what might happen?*

"Come now, Katherine. Run and fix your face. You don't want your eyes all puffy with tears. I'll see you later, okay? Let's have dinner together." He stood and smiled down on her.

"All right, but how am I supposed to eat, knowing Grandmother is out there somewhere, maybe hurt, lost, and hungry?"

Irving shrugged and ambled down the aisle toward the dining car. "You'll manage."

Indeed I will, with or without you. Katherine dabbed her eyes and blew her nose. She pulled her novel from her purse and opened it to the book-marked page. She sat hunched in her seat, her head tilted over her novel, the words swimming in front of her eyes. As hard as she tried to concentrate on the Joad family's difficulties finding work in the San Joaquin Valley during the Great Dust Bowl, her thoughts kept returning to Grandmother. Was she lying dead in a ditch? Had she been arrested? Was she huddled on a hard, cold seat at the train station with no ticket, only a few dollars in her purse and no way to get to Washington?

Shivers crept between her shoulder blades as she fingered the slip of paper with the phone numbers printed in Irving's hand. Was Irving a friend or someone to fear? Grandmother certainly thought so. She lifted her purse from the floor into her lap. The gun she had taken from Grandmother's suitcase weighed heavily inside. How she wished she had taken more interest in learning how to shoot the thing! She dropped the paper inside her purse and snapped the latch.

"Wait! Charles! Where are we going? There's nothing out here but railroad tracks and trains." Agnes glanced around the rows of rain-stained boxcars covered with faded lettering and graffiti. *Loose Lips Sink Ships, Victory, Buy US War Bonds*

The bunions on her big toes screamed as she tromped across the uneven gravel between the tracks.

"You said you'd trust me, so hush and come along." Charles tugged on her sleeve.

Agnes stopped and crossed her arms. Okay, trust was one thing, but this was ridiculous. "I'm not going one step further until you tell me what you're planning." She glanced around. Several tracks over, men were operating a forklift to load containers into a boxcar.

"As it happens," Charles said with a nod, "I overheard a conversation in the restroom. He mentioned that the mail train is leaving soon, headed for Little Rock, Arkansas. That's four states closer to Washington. You said the stationmaster mentioned it too."

"So, how does that help? Are we going to stick a stamp on my forehead and mail me there?" She wrinkled her nose and grinned, pleased with her sarcastic response.

"No, we're going to stow aboard the train." Charles grinned from ear to ear, his white teeth gleaming like ivory piano keys.

"You have got…to…be…kidding. Have you, by chance, noticed that I am a somewhat rotund woman of advanced age? Though in the peak of health, I assure you, hopping onto and stowing aboard a mail train is somewhat beyond my comfort zone."

She shook her head to dismiss the sudden memory of the previous summer when she had engaged in a somewhat similar activity that involved her husband's raincoat, a moonless night and the back end of a pick-up truck.

"I'm not kidding," Charles said. "I hadn't exactly planned that we should make a running leap at the boxcar. It's just sitting out there, fully loaded and perfectly still. We'll wait until no one is looking, find one of the open cars and climb inside. We should be quite comfortable. You'll see. I have this all planned out. Trust me."

How many times in her life had she heard those words? And, how many times had she agreed, only to have it end badly? Memories from 1918 when she had traveled into unpronounceable towns on unspeakable missions flitted through her mind, only to be pushed aside. *Some deeds are best forgotten.*

"Besides, I don't see that you have much choice if you want to reconnect with your granddaughter and get to Washington."

"I could try my luck at the mission. They might help me. They might…" The protons, neutrons, and electrons in Agnes's brain collided in an explosion of color as another thought burst like a firecracker on a Fourth of July night sky.

"Did the workman happen to say when the mail train would arrive in Little Rock?" Agnes held her breath as Charles rolled his eyes toward heaven.

"Saints above. Now, she's interested. Not that it makes a hill of beans of difference, but he said it gets to Little Rock at 12:55 P.M. tomorrow."

"Perfect. Let's get going. Katherine's train arrives in Little Rock tomorrow morning at 9:00 A.M. She has a four-hour layover before she changes trains. She doesn't leave Little Rock until 1:15 P.M. It will be close, but if the mail train is on time and arrives before Katherine leaves… Oh, Charles! This might work after all. What a perfect plan!"

"Thought you'd be pleased." He beamed.

Agnes's heart warmed toward this young man. Charles was probably living hand to mouth. He was accustomed to taking his meals from *Le Café Garbage Bin*. He probably slept in doorways with an occasional visit to the mission for a bath, and he probably thought a day and night on a mail train with a charming mature woman was an adventure, something to break the monotony of the streets of Albuquerque.

A smile creased her cheeks. "Indeed, I am pleased. Well, what are we waiting for? An engraved invitation?" She shoved Charles across the tracks. "Which way to the mail train?"

They tip-toed past the ticket booth and ducked behind a boxcar when a railway worker appeared. "Stay here. I'll check it out," Charles whispered. He leaned forward and peered around a giant wheel. "He's gone. Now stay low and keep quiet!" They trudged down the track until Charles located a boxcar with its door ajar. Likely the cars were left unlocked in the event a late batch of merchandise should arrive.

The floor of the chosen boxcar was about shoulder height. Off to the side of the door, a small metal handle protruded above a round step. Charles checked both directions and seeing no workmen in sight, clambered up into the car. "All right, now Mrs. Odboddy, put your foot right there on that step and I'll help you up the rest of the way."

Agnes threw the strap on her purse around her neck, hiked up her skirt, gripped the handle and stepped onto the step.

Charles grabbed her free hand and with a heft on her part and a yank on his part, she tumbled into the car.

"Shoot! There goes another run in my stocking. Well, no matter. It was for a good cause. Now, let's see what we have in here."

Dust and leaves blown in from many different states littered the wooden floor. From the back wall forward, stacks of merchandise filled about a quarter of the car.

"Aren't they apt to come back and find us in here? I'm not keen on being tossed off the train just when we're back on track toward Washington." Agnes ran her hand inside her purse, assuring that the President's package was safe and sound.

Charles nodded toward the rear of the car. "I'll move these boxes around and make us a hidey-hole in the corner, just in case someone makes a last minute check. We can rearrange things later and get more comfortable. Once they close that door, it's going to be dark in here. If they don't padlock it, I'll open it a crack and let in some light once we're on our way."

He lifted a box and set it to the side. "If they lock it, we'll be stuck in the dark until we get to Little Rock. This isn't going to be the most comfortable twenty hours you've ever spent. Are you sure you're up for it? This is your last chance to bail and go to the mission."

Agnes grimaced. "I've been through worse. My friend, Mildred and I were trapped in a bombed-out building in Paris for three days during WWI. At least in here, we know that tomorrow at 1:00 P.M. we'll be in Little Rock. The worse that can happen is we might be arrested when they open the door and find us. I'll take my chances if you're willing."

"That's the spirit, Mrs. Odboddy. I knew you were a brick!"

Clang! Clang!

Agnes jumped at the sound of doors on the boxcars slamming shut further up the track. The floor of the car vibrated as the engine started with a rumble.

Agnes and Charles squatted behind a stack of boxes in the corner. Her heart picked up a pace as the clanks and slams of closing doors came closer. She clutched Charles's arm and ducked her head. Her lips moved in a silent prayer. Surely, after all that had happened, she wouldn't be tossed off the train now, humiliated and verbally abused, if they were lucky, arrested for trespass if they weren't.

The outer door of their boxcar slammed shut. Agnes closed her eyes and waited for the clank of a padlock. Several seconds passed. She lifted her head. "He didn't padlock the door," she whispered.

Charles patted her arm. "As soon as we get started, I'll open the door."

"Are we safe now? Are you sure he won't be back?"

"I doubt it. He's probably gone on down the line, checking the other cars. It won't be long now. Are you pleased, Mrs. Odboddy? Did I do good? Did I?"

What an odd thing for Charles to say. Almost like an insecure kid looking for recognition for a job well done. Was that the key to Charles's problems? Once recovered from his physical injuries, why hadn't he used his medical skills to take his place in society? Why had he drifted into a purposely homeless existence?

His leg wound had healed, but had a damaged spirit left him without the drive and initiative to fit back into society? How many other wounded veterans came back from war, suffering from emotional injuries?

What could the country do to help veterans who returned, physically sound but mentally wounded? Such a condition didn't even have a name, much less a solution.

"Mrs. Odboddy? Are you pleased?" Charles's voice quavered. He sucked in his breath, as though he might cry if she didn't answer in the affirmative.

"Oh, yes, Charles. I'm very pleased. You had a marvelous idea and I can't thank you enough for helping me get back to my granddaughter."

Charles let out his breath and leaned back against the wall and sighed.

Agnes shifted her legs and tried to find a more comfortable position. It would be cold in there tonight and sitting on the floor wouldn't do her lumbago much good. What luck, that the car Charles chose had a couple of packing blankets atop the boxes. She patted her purse. The President's package was safe and she was still on schedule, though side-tracked, to be sure. *Side-tracked! Ha! I made a joke.*

The train jerked forward. Charles stood. "I'll open the door a little and let in some—"

The heavy cargo door slid open. A slash of light washed across the floor and over the stack of boxes, creating a diagonal shadow on the wall behind Agnes's head. She jerked. *Caught, like a rat in a trap!* Just when they thought they were safe. She'd been too confident, too soon. The railroad guard walking the tracks must have been suspicious and come back for a second look.

"Well, hello! How sweet. What have we here?" A man's menacing voice defied the politeness of his words.

Chapter Twenty-Six

They probably don't have gruel and dry bread on the menu.

K atherine stepped through the dining room door and glanced at her watch. *5:00 P.M.* Several passengers were already seated, drinking coffee and scanning the menus. She chose an empty table across from Samuel and David. "Evening. Thanks for helping search for my grandmother this afternoon." A stab of concern touched her chest.

The young men nodded. "Sorry we couldn't do more."

Katherine stared at the empty chair across the table and sighed. Grandmother should be there. The painful uncertainty of her whereabouts felt more than Katherine could endure. She pulled a handkerchief from her purse.

"Hi, Katherine. Did you find your grandma?"

Katherine dabbed her eyes and looked up into Madeline's sweet face. "Not just yet, sweetheart. What are you and Nanny up to?" She reached for Madeline's hand. "Where is she?"

Madeline leaned closer and whispered. "Nanny's mad at Jackson."

Nanny had stopped at the door to speak to Jackson, but Katherine couldn't hear their voices. From the look on Nanny's face and her animated gestures, she was giving him a hard time about something. *They probably don't have gruel and dry bread on the menu.* Her face warmed. *Shame on me.* "I'm sure it's nothing to worry about, dear." *Should I ask them to join me for dinner? Nah!* "Are you and Nanny having dinner in the dining car tonight?"

Madeline shook her head. "Nanny says everything costs too much."

Katherine's heart lurched. So, the witch was putting the child to bed without supper…again. *When we get to Washington, I'm going to track down the Senator and give him a piece of my mind.* She reached into her purse for the banana she bought at the Albuquerque train station. "Here. You take this. I have another one in my berth. *Lie…but God will understand.*

Madeline took the banana, smiled, and then threw her arms around Katherine's neck. "Thank you. I love you so much, Katherine."

Katherine's heart seemed to burst like rockets over the Aleutian Islands. *I never wanted a child more than I do this minute.* More specifically, she wanted *this* child. A child she just met on the train. A child belonging to someone else. Perhaps it was just her biological clock ticking—*Grandmother would say I'm…*

Grandmother! Lost! Left behind in Albuquerque! Grandmother's plight and the sudden obsession for a child overcame Katherine's usual restraint. She pressed her face into Madeline's curls and sobbed as though she had lost her last friend. "I love you so much, too." *Oh, Grandmother, where are you? What shall I do?*

"Don't cry, Katherine. You'll find your grandma, I just know it." Madeline patted her back.

"What are you doing? Let go of Madeline this instant!" *Nanny!* Her voice, shrill like an icy wind off a frozen lake, sent knives through Katherine's chest.

She gulped, released Madeline and jerked back. Her arms felt empty and barren, as though her own child had been ripped from her. She pushed back her chair, her heart pounding and peered into Nanny's face, nearly purple with rage. "I…was just… We were talking and…" The faces around her became hazy through her tears. She clutched the back of the chair to steady herself.

"How dare you take such liberties? She's not your child."

Madeline's face paled. She turned from Katherine to Nanny.

Katherine's fingers tingled as she dashed tears from her cheeks.

The room began to spin and the lights seemed to dim. She collapsed into the chair and laid her head on her arms. Now Nanny's insults and shrieking voice seemed further away. She slipped from the chair, falling, falling…

"Here, now. What's going on here?" Irving's voice echoed through the dim room.

Katherine felt his arms lifting her.

All the pent-up emotions in her heart released. She accepted the shelter of his embrace, wrapped her arms around Irving's neck and knelt her head on his shoulders. Her tears soaked into his jacket as he carried her into the club car and laid her on a sofa.

"Jackson. Run and fetch a cold cloth and a glass of water, please. Miss Katherine isn't well."

For a moment, she felt reassured and safe. Nanny's ugly voice faded away, replaced by the comforting clack of the train's wheels on the tracks. A cold cloth touched her face. She jerked back to the present. *Irving! Jackson!* Others stood nearby, staring. She put up her hand and pushed away the cloth.

"Here, drink this. You'll feel better." Irving shoved a glass of water toward her.

She drank. Clearer now. All the windows and seats, tables and chairs snapped into view. Her cheeks warmed. "I'm sorry. I don't know what got into me." She struggled to sit up. "I'm fine now. Please."

Winnie, Evelyn, and Jackson hovered nearby. She waved them away. Graciously, they turned and left the club car. "I'm so embarrassed."

"Never mind that now. Come. You'll feel better after you've had something to eat." Irving took her hand in a possessive manner and pulled her to her feet.

She tried to free her hand from his grip. At his touch, her secure feeling disappeared like a wisp of smoke over a campfire. *Grandmother thinks he killed his wife.* Perhaps he was just pretending to be her friend so he could steal Grandmother's secret documents.

He gripped her hand tighter, crushing her fingers.

She could not pull away.

"I'm holding on to you this time, whether you like it or not."

A chill passed through her body as Irving opened the door to the dining room. Inside, the passengers turned to stare as they took their seats. Katherine cringed. No longer did the crowd feel like friendly traveling companions. Now, they felt like leering strangers, drawn by the spectacle of her break-down, anticipating what she might do next.

"Well, hello! How sweet. What have we here?"

At the sound of the man's harsh words, Agnes scrambled up from the boxcar floor, her purse containing the precious package clutched to her chest. If they were to be heaved off the train or carted to jail, she must protect the package at all costs.

A man in a grease-stained plaid shirt crawled over the threshold into the car. He shoved his crumpled hat tighter onto his head, stood and brushed dust from his pants. The bristles on his chin hadn't seen a razor for many days. Dirty, straggled hair covered his ears.

Agnes breathed a sigh of relief. This couldn't be a security guard. If he was, the railroad wasn't paying him nearly enough. *Humph! Must be another hobo traveling without a ticket.* This man could still be trouble.

"This car is occupied." Charles's voice sounded strong as he stepped between Agnes and the stranger.

Once again, my hero. God bless you, Charles. "You aren't a railroad man. What do you want with us?" Agnes's voice cracked. She cleared her throat and tossed her head, trying to exude confidence she didn't feel.

"Guess I want the same thing as you. A free ride to Oklahoma City." The man grinned, revealing a missing front tooth. The rest of his teeth looked like he'd never owned a toothbrush. "Guess I'll join your little party. Got a problem with that?" He dropped a knapsack onto the floor.

Agnes glanced at Charles.

He stood, balanced on the balls of his feet, his fists clenched, ready to face whatever the man had in mind. *Thank my lucky stars for Charles.* Sharing the space with another traveler wasn't in their original plan, but faced with physically throwing him out the door or sharing the space—it came down to the lesser of two evils.

Agnes smiled, ignoring her rapidly beating heart. "There's plenty of room for all of us. But first, let's get a few things straight." She held the stranger's gaze. "We have exactly four dollars between us, so don't even think about robbing us. We don't want trouble. You're welcome to stay on that side of the car and we'll stay over here. Is that agreed?"

The scruffy stranger squatted beside the door, still ajar about six inches. He grunted, pulled his hat down over his eyes and dropped his head on his chest.

"I assume that means you agree." Agnes's voice took on an acid tone.

No answer.

Agnes shrugged. She walked back toward the corner Charles had made as comfortable as possible with the traveling blankets he found in the boxcar.

Charles shoved one of the wadded blankets behind her back. "Here, lean against this, Mrs. Odboddy. You'll be more comfortable. You'll want to pull it around you tonight when you sleep. I'll sit up over here and keep an eye on our friend."

"Won't you want to sleep too?"

"I'll catch a nap this afternoon." He dropped his voice to a whisper. "I don't exactly trust our traveling companion. You can stay awake today while I sleep. I'll keep watch tonight until we get to Oklahoma City. Make sure this guy gets off the train. Then we'll have the car to ourselves the rest of the way to Little Rock."

"Oh, Charles, I've already caused you so much trouble. Why are you doing all this for me?"

He chuckled. "I don't know. Just seemed like the right thing to do. Besides, I was getting a little tired of Albuquerque. Little Rock is a great town. I grew up just a few miles north of there. Town where I lived has three saloons and a gas station. When I joined the Army, I swore I'd never go back." He lowered his head. "Can't, for the life of me, remember what made me feel that way. There must have been a reason at the time." He turned his head and stared at the wall.

"You lived near Little Rock? Wait! This is your chance to go home. Are your folks still alive?" Agnes caught her breath. Maybe there was a better future for him, after all. If he reunited with his family, at least he'd have people to help him get back on his feet again. No more sleeping in doorways and eating from trash cans.

"My Pop is still alive. We didn't get along when I was a kid. I don't think he'd be too pleased if I just showed up on his doorstep."

"Oh, that can't be true. I'll bet he'd be thrilled to see you. Your Pop must miss you a lot. How about brothers and sisters? Or a girlfriend?"

"No brothers or sisters. I dated a girl, but when I got overseas, I stopped writing to her. I saw some terrible things, Mrs. Odboddy. All those boys dying around me. Figured my number would come up pretty soon. What kind of guy writes to a girl and then dies on her? She'd just feel bad. I liked her too much. Didn't think it was right to do her that way."

"My granddaughter, Katherine, wouldn't agree. She cherished every letter from her Stephen, even though she lost him at Pearl Harbor. You didn't die. Wouldn't she—"

"Got shot, though, didn't I? Spent three months in rehab. Left me with a limp and I can't run or lift. What kind of life can I offer her? Me, a cripple."

Agnes gave his arm a gentle slap. "You're not a cripple. Stop talking like that. You rode that bike and hauled me on the handlebars. A cripple couldn't have done that."

"There's more than one way to be a cripple. I quit high school to join the Army. Got no education and can't do physical work. When all the boys come home, jobs will be in short supply. I doubt I could even get a job as a door-to-door Fuller Brush man. Just seemed best not to bother folks at home with my troubles, so I bummed around the country until I ended up in Albuquerque."

"And, that's where you picked me up off the street and did all this to help a total stranger. Me, a white woman. I'd say that kind of fellow has a lot going for him, high school diploma or not. You can always finish school through a correspondence course. I've seen the ads in magazines. I'll bet you could find a job that doesn't require heavy lifting. I think your biggest problem is in your head. You've lost your confidence. Aren't there veteran programs to help guys like you, who come back from war with injuries?"

"I guess they give home loans to vets. Don't know about retraining." Charles was silent for a minute. Had a spark of hope ignited? "You really think my Pop would want to see me again? And, my girl?"

Agnes shrugged. "I can't be sure, Charles, but I know if you were my boy, I'd want to see you. Katherine would, too, if you were her fellow. Since you're going to be in Little Rock anyway, why don't you go by your Pop's house and find out? What's the worst that can happen? Maybe your girl found another fellow. So, you move on. Or your Pop doesn't fall all over himself welcoming you home. So what?

"You've already been to hell and back. You've dealt with unimaginable things. You think you can't take a little rejection? On the other hand, what if your girl waited for you? Your Pop might welcome you with open arms. Shouldn't you find out?" Agnes glanced toward the tramp at the door. His head had slumped on his chest. *Asleep. Good. Stay that way.*

Charles's smile trembled. "No one has ever talked to me this way before, Mrs. Odboddy. Being on the road, no one ever said where they came from or where they were going. We just…you know…made small talk. Everyone kept things bottled up inside. Let me think about it. I'm going to get some sleep now. Wake me in a couple of hours."

The train swayed around a corner. Agnes smiled and shivered, as the boxcar jittered and rumbled down the track. "Guess we're really on our way, now." *I can complete my mission, after all, thanks to Charles.*

Agnes leaned her head against the wall. It would be many hours before they reached Little Rock. Her thoughts flitted back to her comfortable life. How blessed to have friends and family and the means to put food on her table. *Even if chicken wings are fourteen cents a pound and ever so scarce.*

Between now and tomorrow afternoon when the train caught up with Katherine, she would have plenty of time to ruminate and be grateful for her blessings. After tomorrow, never again would she have to eat from a garbage bin or sleep on the floor, unlike the tramp nodding in the doorway. What would she have done if Charles hadn't picked her off the sidewalk, brought her to the train and helped her continue her journey?

Though not anxious to sit on a lumpy boxcar floor for the next twenty hours, it would be more than enough time to convince Charles to go home. Her counsel could change his life. In some small way, it might repay him for his kindness.

Would his family welcome him back? Could he make the changes necessary for a more positive life? Could she be sure he would succeed? Of course not. If his family didn't respond well, there were other ways she could repay him. He was a bright young man. Trade schools were a possibility. Maybe he could take one of those correspondence programs that teach how to fix radios, like you see in the Popular Mechanics magazines. Wouldn't it be great if the government ponied up some education funds for the returning veterans?

She pulled a paper and the stub of a pencil from her purse. *Check into government funded schooling for veterans.*

Agnes smiled down at Charles, sound asleep on the blanket. His head had no sooner hit the floor than he was asleep. *Just like a man!* Many a night, she had lain awake well past midnight, her brain hopping from subject to subject and sleep eluding her like a butterfly in a dream garden…dancing just beyond her reach, alighting on a flower and disappearing with a *poof* just when she reached to touch it.

Chapter Twenty-Seven

Was Grandma huddled over a burn barrel, with a can of beans?

"iss Katherine. It's 3:10 A.M. We're pulling into Oklahoma City. You need to get up if you want to get off the train." Irving rapped gently on the wall beside Katherine's berth.

She rubbed sleep from her eyes, threw back the covers, stood, and brushed wrinkles from her clothing. "Of course I do. I need to find Grandmother. Let me run to the washroom. I'll be ready in a few minutes—"

"But, Katherine. I need to tell—"

"My suitcase is there in the aisle. I just need to throw a few things in this overnight bag. Why don't I meet you in the observation car in ten minutes?"

"Wait a minute. I need to update you on a few things. I spoke to—"

"Irving! Please leave, so I can get ready. We'll have time to talk later." Men were so exasperating under the guise of taking charge and trying to be helpful.

"But, Katherine. Listen. I talked to the head porter again late last night. He said if we call the Albuquerque station this time of night, no one will be at there to answer."

Katherine stared across the aisle at the purple striped curtain pulled around the berth. *No way to know if Grandmother had arranged for another train. No way to know...*

"There's another problem. Apparently, there's no train from Oklahoma City back to Albuquerque until day after tomorrow. If you decide to go back, we'll have to stay another day in Oklahoma City."

"You mean we can't call the stationmaster until morning and there's no train back… Someone needs to invent a better system." Katherine scowled and snapped the lid on her overnight case.

"Maybe we should all wear wrist radios like Dick Tracy," Irving chuckled. "Then we could call Agnes tonight and ask her where she is."

If Irving was trying to lighten the mood, it wasn't working.

When Katherine didn't answer, he quickly continued. "The good news is, we arrive in Little Rock at 9:00 A.M. in the morning. The staff will be at the Albuquerque train station by then. The porter said there's another train leaving from Albuquerque to Little Rock in the morning. I'm sure they've already made arrangements for Agnes to be on that one. They pride themselves on excellent service, you know."

"From your lips to God's ears."

"So, if you still want to get off at Oklahoma City and call the police and the hospitals, I'll go with you, but you don't need to take your luggage."

Katherine put a trembling finger to her lips. What to do? If the situation were reversed, what would Grandmother do? *She'd move heaven and earth to find me, that's what she'd do.*

Katherine shook her head. "You don't understand. She doesn't have enough money with her to buy another ticket."

"Really, Katherine, you're just making yourself sick worrying about her. When we call in the morning, we'll guarantee her ticket, or you can wire her the money. It's really no problem. You'll see. Now, do you still want to make those calls to the hospital and police department, or do you want to go back to sleep?" He checked his watch. "It's 3:15 A.M."

"I couldn't sleep, not knowing if she's in a hospital or if she's been arrested."

Irving lifted an eyebrow. "You're kidding. Arrested?"

"Don't laugh. You don't know Grandmother. It wouldn't surprise me if she was sitting in a jail cell right this minute, waiting for someone to bail her out." Katherine wiggled into her jacket. "Disturbing the peace is one of her favorite pastimes." She giggled. "At this point, I'd almost be glad to find her in a jail cell. At least, we'd *find* her!"

At 3:55 A.M., after departing the train and making various calls, Katherine hung up the phone and slid open the telephone booth door. She shivered with disappointment.

"Well? Has anyone seen her? What did the police department say?" Irving's face looked yellow under the glow of the streetlight as he held open the telephone booth door.

Katherine gathered her purse and stepped onto the Oklahoma City train station platform.

"The officer didn't know anything. He checked his records. She's not in jail and no one matching her description was found murdered today. She's not at either of the hospitals, either.

In her mind's eye, Katherine saw Grandmother huddled over a burning barrel, an open can of beans in one hand, and a hobo shack leaning precariously behind her. Homeless and penniless, she could be the victim of *who knows* what kind of depraved creatures wandering the night streets of Albuquerque. She shook her head, dispelling the image. Tears pricked her eyes. Was Grandmother sitting up all night on a cold bench outside the train station, waiting for some way to arrange a ticket to Little Rock? Katherine swallowed hard. She must stay strong. She must not let Irving see her cry.

"See? I told you not to worry." Irving checked his watch. "We'd best get back on board. The train leaves in five minutes. We'll call the station as soon as we get to Little Rock in the morning. Maybe you can even speak to her, if she's still there." He chuckled. "Nothing like a 3:00 A.M. walk to get the juices flowing. Do you want to get a cup of coffee, or would you rather go back to bed for a few hours?"

Katherine swiped the back of her hand across her forehead. "I think I'll go back to my berth, but I doubt I'll do much sleeping. Thank you for your assistance, Irving. You've been more than kind."

Irving took her hand and squeezed it. "Glad to help anyway I can."

He stepped onto the train and opened the door into the observation car.

Katherine turned and looked back. Steam whooshed out from under the wheels and mingled with the yellow fog floating across the platform. Thumps and clangs and shouted orders echoed around the station as workmen hastily loaded the last crates into the boxcars. The whistle blew and Katherine stepped through the door. The train moved slowly forward toward Little Rock.

Chapter Twenty-Eight

The bum hadn't ratted on them.

Twenty-some hours and twelve Charley-horses in her legs later, Agnes stood and limped across the boxcar until she worked the kinks out of her muscles. Six feet to the west and six feet back to the east.

Charles lay napping, his head propped against the far wall, his legs drawn up, almost in a fetal position.

She eyed the hobo in the opposite corner, just visible in the dim stream of light coming in through the sliding door. He had slept almost continuously since they left Albuquerque, only rising once during the early morning hours to lean out the door and... Good grief, why did men think nothing of relieving themselves anytime and anywhere, especially with a lady present?

Hadn't she held her bladder through the long night until she thought she might burst? Even under the cover of darkness and assured that Charles and the bum were sleeping, it was only after extreme discomfort that she finally gave into nature's call. At last, no longer able to stand the pressure, she had gone into a far corner, squatted behind a few boxes and relieved herself. How humiliating! Would this journey never end?

At the first sign of dawn breaking, she and Charles drank from the soda bottles and split the last few crumbs of the food from the train station garbage bins.

"Should we offer our companion some of these French Fries?" A wilted fry hung at half-mast from her fingers.

Charles shook his head. "That's the last one. You'd better eat it. We have nothing else until we get to Little Rock. What time do you suppose it is?"

Agnes shrugged. "Tuesday! The sun's up. That's my best guess. Did you get any sleep?"

"A little. Have we heard from our friend over there?" Charles nodded toward the door where the man hunched, staring at them, his arms crossed.

"Haven't heard a peep." Agnes popped the wilted potato fry into her mouth.

The boxcar rocked and swayed. From time to time, the distant wail of the train whistle indicated their approach to a small town. At one point midmorning, the train slowed and then stopped.

The bum moved away from the door and settled along the wall closer to Agnes. Bells clanged up ahead and gruff voices approached the boxcar.

Agnes crouched beside Charles. Her heart pounded in her chest. Maybe the jig was up! Light rushed into the boxcar as the boxcar door ground across its track. A burly voice shouted. "Hey! You! Come out of there!"

Agnes froze. The small town's railroad guardian had spotted their unwanted guest. All the guard had to do was step inside and move the boxes! She lay on her belly, put her hands over her ears and closed her eyes. *Silly me.* As if that would help if the official came in and moved the boxes.

Any minute now, the drifter would likely squeal and give up their hiding place.

Agnes pulled her purse closer to her side, expecting to be grabbed by the nape of the neck and heaved out of the boxcar.

A minute passed. Then two. *Thump!* Had the guard pulled the bum off the train?

She lifted her head to listen. Her heartbeat throbbed. She opened her eyes. *One...two...three seconds.* The bum hadn't ratted on them! The door ground three-quarters of the way across its track and the light dimmed. Safe!

Charles crouched alongside her. His grin was barely visible in the dim light. Now, if they were truly blessed, they would arrive on time in Little Rock, just minutes before Katherine boarded her connecting train to Washington, D.C. How much more good luck could she expect? It gave one pause.

Chapter Twenty-Nine

He's like a leech in a stagnant pond.

W e're slowing down. I think we've made it!" Charles stood at the door, pointing to the *Little Rock, Arkansas* signs that flashed by. He held out his hand to help Agnes stand. "Are you ready, Mrs. Odboddy?"

"I wish we knew the time." Agnes fingered her lapel where her missing watch had been pinned. "If we figured right, Katherine's train should still be here for a few more minutes. But, what if I'm wrong? How will we find her? Which train are we looking for?"

Charles patted her arm. "There, there! We'll figure it out. Listen!" The train brakes squealed and the whistle blew. The boxcar lurched and then jolted to a stop.

Light filled the boxcar as Charles shoved open the door, revealing another train parked alongside. "Come on. Are you ready?" He jumped onto the platform, turned and extended his hand. "Sit there on the edge and I'll help you down."

Agnes squatted, put her legs over the edge and leaned into Charles's arms. "*Oomph!*"

At the sight of a train agent making his way down the track, Charles whispered, "Quick! This way."

"Hey! You two! Stop. What are you doing there?" A guard in a striped jumpsuit waved and started toward them.

Charles pulled Agnes the opposite direction, helped her over the coupling between two cars as they scrambled toward the station where they mingled with a group of passengers waiting to board the train.

"Oh, my stars!" Agnes gasped for breath and clutched her purse to her chest.

A porter directed them to the platform where the Washington-bound train chugged, ready to depart. Travelers with carry-on luggage clustered around the passenger car doors.

"There she is! *Whoo-hoo!* Katherine! Here I am, over here!" Agnes dashed toward her granddaughter. *What the heck? What is Irving doing there beside her? I'm never going to let her out of my sight again.*

Katherine's head jerked up. Her mouth dropped open! "Grandma?" Tears streamed down her face as she stumbled into Agnes's arms! "I can't believe you're here." She gulped and dashed tears off her cheeks. "How on earth…?" Another hug almost crushed Agnes.

"Here, now. I'll explain everything in good time." Agnes's gaze moved to Irving, hovering nearby. "What are you doing here? How dare you! Haven't you caused enough trouble?" Her mouth crumpled in a scowl. *He's like a leech in a stagnant pond, ready to latch on the minute I get here.*

She pulled Katherine away from Irving and over toward Charles. "You have to meet Charles. He's been my absolute savior. I'd never have made it without him. Charles, this is my granddaughter, Katherine." She beamed at him and then at Katherine.

Katherine put out her hand. "I can't even guess how you managed to get her here, but thank you from the bottom of my heart. I thought I'd lost her for sure. I've been beside myself with worry."

"Only too happy to help, Miss Katherine. Your grandma is a fine lady."

Katherine glanced around the station platform and then checked her watch. "We don't have much time, Grandma. Our train is about to leave. Come over here and sit down for a minute." She gestured toward a bench. "Now, tell me what happened."

Irving moved off to one side, and then leaned against a stack of crates and lit a cigarette.

"Oh, there's not much to tell. I missed the train in Albuquerque. Charles and I hitched a ride on a mail train, and here we are." Agnes squeezed Katherine's hand. She leaned closer and whispered, "What's the idea? Why are you sidling up with that one?" She jerked her head toward Irving. "Have you lost your mind? Don't you know—"

"Grandma, you're wrong about him. Irving stood by me every inch of the way and kept my spirits up when I couldn't find you. I thought I'd go crazy. We've been on the phone ever since we got to Little Rock. I called the Albuquerque police department and every hospital in town. The clerk at the train station remembered talking to you. He was all apologetic when I told him how you missed the train." She glanced back toward Irving. "I guaranteed your ticket on to Washington, in case you went back to the station, but, guess you didn't go back. How did you say you missed the train?"

"Well, after I was mugged in Albuquerque, I only had—" Agnes sent a glare in Irving's general direction.

"Mugged! Oh, my goodness. Then what?"

"If it hadn't been for Charles, I'd have never made it." Agnes gave him a broad smile.

Katherine took Agnes's hand. "Well, believe me, it hasn't exactly been a picnic for me, either. I didn't know if I should go on to Washington, or go back to Albuquerque and try to find you. I thought you might call Mildred to wire you some money for another ticket.

"So I was debating with Irving, the alternatives just now when you showed up." Katherine threw her arms around Agnes's neck and hugged her again.

She glanced at her watch and then turned to Charles. "How can we thank you?" She opened her purse.

Charles shook his head and waved his hand. "No…no…that's not necessary." The train whistle blew. "You ladies better get on board. Your train is about to leave. You don't want to go through all that again, now, do you, Mrs. Odboddy?"

"Wait! How can I leave you like this? How will I know…?" Agnes stood, sucked in a breath. Tears pricked her eyes. She grasped his hand and squeezed it.

"Give me your address, Mrs. Odboddy. Soon as I get settled, I'll write and tell you."

The whistle blew again. Irving ambled to the club car and lingered by the steps, his gaze fastened on Agnes.

Is the old goat afraid he might lose track of me again and not get another crack at my package?

Katherine pulled a business card from her purse and handed it to Charles. "This is where I work. *Curls to Dye For.* Call me when you get settled. I know Grandmother wants to keep in touch with you." She shook his hand and took Agnes's arm. "Grandma? We have to go! Now!"

Agnes hugged Charles again. "Thank you for everything."

Katherine pulled her toward the train as the whistle blew.

Irving swung into the car and put out his hand to help Katherine up the steps.

Agnes stepped up on the landing. As the train pulled forward, she turned to wave. "Charles, take care. Call me!"

"I'm gonna' call my Pop, Mrs. Odboddy, just like you said! Good-bye! Good-bye!" Charles was still waving as the train turned and he disappeared from sight.

Chapter Thirty

They risk their lives for our right to eat strawberries.

Katherine stirred a second spoonful of sugar into her coffee and lifted the cup to her nose. "*Aaahhh!*" The aroma of delicious coffee, thick with cream and sugar wafted upwards. "What I'd give to live like this forever. Imagine! All the coffee we can drink and meat at every meal. I feel downright scandalous." She sighed. "I'm almost sorry to reach Washington tomorrow." She turned to smile at David and Samuel seated at the table across the aisle from her and Grandmother.

Spoons and forks clanked against china, punctuating the contented murmur of passengers consuming chicken, salmon and steak smothered in mushrooms; all in short supply since the United States joined the war. Outside the windows, a brilliant sunset streaked the pink and yellow Arkansas sky, casting shadows across the terrain.

Agnes raised her eyes to gaze at Katherine's pouty face. "So, now what's wrong? You look like you're sucking lemons."

"Where do you suppose they are?" Katherine whispered, glancing around the dining car. "We haven't seen Madeline or Nanny since we left Little Rock. They weren't at lunch either." Katherine slid her plate away and pulled a dish of fresh strawberries closer. "Just look at the size of these berries! Wouldn't Madeline love these?" She sighed and poured cream over the fruit.

"Yes, yes. I see." Agnes leaned closer. She jerked her head back toward Irving. "Of course, Jack the Ripper is right over there, watching me like a spider watches a fly. I tell you, Katherine, I barely escaped with my life in Albuquerque. If he'd found me in that alley, I wouldn't be here to tell about it. He chased me—"

"I know, Grandma. You've told me three times already. It's just hard for me to believe he would do such a thing, considering how concerned he was when you were missing. You know how your imagination tends to run away with you."

Grandmother's notion that Irving had killed Geraldine was bad enough. But, following her around Albuquerque with murder in his heart? Ridiculous! *Should I try to talk her out of it or ignore her ranting and hope she'll forget about it?*

Agnes shook her head. "Never mind that now. I'm safe enough on the train. We can deal with Irving when we get to Washington."

Jackson hurried down the aisle carrying a coffee pot and cups.

Katherine waved him over. "Jackson. A moment. Have you seen Madeline and her nanny? I hope they're not ill."

"No, ma'am. I sure hasn't. I don't allow they came back onto the train at Little Rock. Excuse me, please. Gotta run." He set the coffee pot on the table and hurried on.

"Well, isn't that a caution!" Agnes sliced a bite from the steak on her plate and smeared it around in gravy. "Nanny said she was taking Madeline to her father in Washington. Now, why on earth wouldn't she have taken the connecting train? You don't suppose they missed it?" She turned again to glare over her shoulder at Irving. "I do hope nothing has happened."

Katherine nodded and popped a strawberry dripping with cream into her mouth. "I'm concerned for Madeline, too. The way Nanny neglects her just isn't right."

"Katherine, for all you know, Nanny was spinning a yarn about Madeline's father being a Senator. Or even that she was *going* to Washington, for that matter. She probably said all that to make herself look important. I feel bad for Madeline, too, but what can we do about it now?" Agnes picked up the coffee pot. Here, have some more—"

"Gentlemen," Jackson appeared again in the aisle and stopped beside Samuel and David. "This here is Mr. Josiah Feigleman, the conductor." He stepped back and a tall man with a red handlebar mustache leaned over the soldiers' table.

"If you've finished your dinner, would you colored boys please come with me? We just crossed the Tennessee border, and we're obliged to move you out of the dining car."

Samuel set down his fork and glanced at David. "Told ya'. I'm surprised they let us get through Texas and Oklahoma. Get your stuff." He stood and pulled his satchel from the overhead compartment.

David gazed between Samuel, Jackson and the conductor. He stood, followed his friend's example and pulled his gear down. He glanced toward Agnes and Katherine and touched his forehead. "Ma'am. Miss Katherine. It's been a pleasure traveling with you. Thanks again for your kindness."

Agnes flung down her napkin and lurched from the table. "What kind of nonsense is this? Jackson? Where in blazes are you taking my friends?" She grabbed his arm.

You tell them, Grandma! Katherine slid out of her seat and took her Grandmother's hand. "I agree with Grandma. What's all this about?" Leave it to Grandma to call out an injustice.

Jackson patted Grandma's hand. "It's the law, ma'am. Ever since the border of Texas and through the connecting states, we been in Jim Crow country. Them's segregation states. A Negro can go to jail if he's seen commiseratin' with a white woman, unless he's got a good reason. In Tennessee, coloreds aren't allowed to mingle with white folks in public places, such as restaurants, buses, or even here on the train." He lowered his eyes. A muscle twitched beside his mouth. How hard it must be for a Negro to bring such a dreadful message to the two soldiers.

Grandmother's face paled. "I've heard about these laws, but I didn't believe it would matter on the train. If they had such laws in Texas and Oklahoma, why didn't you mention it before?"

Jackson shrugged, his gaze darting between Katherine and Agnes. "In them states, we can choose not to enforce the law if no one complains, but now we in Tennessee, they more strict. We gotta move these boys now or they could make trouble for the railroad." He glanced nervously at the conductor.

Grandmother snorted, "I've never heard of anything so idiotic. It's disgraceful. They're United States soldiers!"

Katherine's face warmed. Hadn't Charles shared a boxcar with Grandma all the way across Texas and Oklahoma? If they had been caught in those Jim Crow states, things could have been terrible for Charles. He had risked jail by 'commiserating with a white woman for no good reason!'

Agnes knotted her fists. She leaned forward until she was just inches from the conductor's face. "How dare you treat these fine young men like this? Has anyone told you there's a war on? David and Samuel are on their way to train as fighter pilots. They're going to risk their lives for our right to sit here and eat chicken and strawberries!"

"Where ever you're taking these boys, we're going with them." Katherine's gaze swept the travelers in the dining room. "Is anyone else coming with me?" Katherine scanned the dining car. All her traveling companions stared out their windows or lowered their heads, pretending they couldn't see the scene playing out in front of them. Must be the same mindset as the Roman citizens when the Christians were thrown to the lions. Don't get involved. Don't make waves. There were plenty more hungry lions.

Katherine caught Irving's eye. Would he stand up for justice and come with them?

He shrugged and turned away, his cheeks burnished with a red glow.

So that's how it's going to be. Irving is as lily-livered as the rest of them.

"Anyone else coming? No? Okay, then, Katherine and I will go alone." Agnes said. "Give me a minute to get my purse."

The conductor smoothed his mustache. "Sorry, ma'am. I can't let you do that. You don't understand. The law states coloreds must be separate from whites. It don't allow for dispute. If you make a fuss, I'll have to put you under citizens' arrest, and turn you over to the Memphis authorities. They can be most unpleasant with folks who disallow the Jim Crow laws."

David touched Agnes's arm. "Please, Mrs. Odboddy. Don't get into trouble on our account. It's all right. We'll be in Memphis in an hour. We were getting off the train there, anyway. We're taking a bus from Memphis to the Tuskegee Air Base."

"Now, don't you worry about these boys, ma'am," the conductor interrupted. "They'll be most comfortable, I assure you. We'll put them in the back of the club car where we can just pull curtains around their seats. That separates them from the others."

"Curtains, is it? So as not to *offend* the white folks by the sight of two Negro soldiers? Most considerate of you, I must say. It would have been so much easier to throw them off the train and make them walk."

Katherine's loosed Grandmother's hand and sat down. She was right to object to such blatant discrimination, but at this point, how could they risk an encounter with the law? Landing in a Memphis jail hardly seemed the most productive way to accomplish their mission. Just thinking of such a justification of the act made her ashamed. Her cheeks burned.

Chapter Thirty-One

Imagine! The First Lady, serving me tea!

ook! Katherine! There she is." Agnes pulled Katherine to the window and waggled her finger toward the Washington D.C. train station where Mrs. Roosevelt stood beside several men. The train whistle screeched as it pulled into the depot. Agnes raised her voice to be heard over the deafening shriek of brakes as metal grated against metal. "I see they've increased her security since last year in Newbury. Now, she has two bodyguards." She giggled.

Passengers pushed toward the exit while the porters did their best to keep order. Agnes gathered her personal belongings, hugged her purse to her chest and moved into the aisle. She glanced over the top of the passengers heads. Was Irving still lurking around? Having failed in his attempt to get her package along the way or find an opportunity to *do her in*, in Albuquerque, it was possible he might make one final attempt in the bustling and shoving as they exited the train?

Yes, there he was, pushing past Winnie and Evelyn, trying to get close to Agnes.

She had had about as much railway fun as she could stand.

"I'm so glad this trip is almost over. I can't wait for you to get rid of that thing." Katherine nodded toward Agnes's bag. "It's been nothing but trouble since Colonel Farthingworth asked you to deliver it."

Agnes smiled down at Katherine's hand, gripping her arm. *She has no idea what trouble is. She should have been around twenty years ago when I was an undercover agent.* The train lurched to a stop.

The porter slid the door open. Passengers poured onto the platform and then milled hither and yon like scalded ants.

A man in a grey suit stood just to the side of the door. He tipped his hat and moved forward as Agnes stepped from the train to the platform. "Mrs. Agnes Odboddy?"

"Yes." Agnes's stomach seized. Youngish, good looking, smart, tailored suit. Was he an official who heard that she had protested the treatment of the Negro boys on the train yesterday? Or was he one of Mrs. Roosevelt's personal security guards? He didn't look like the agent she met in Newbury last year when the First Lady attended Clyde's funeral. Agnes swallowed a knot in her throat. No need to pursue that line of thought. All's well that ends well. "I'm Mrs. Odboddy."

"I'm Edgar Plumbottom, Mrs. Roosevelt's senior security agent. If you and your granddaughter would step this way, she is waiting over by the ticket gate. The car is here to take you to the hotel."

"Oh, how exciting. We'll need to get our luggage—"

"Don't worry. Agent Brown will take care of that."

"Aren't we going directly to the White House? I was hoping to see the President."

"Not today. Mrs. Roosevelt is delivering a speech tonight at a Red Cross Meeting downtown. She's taken a hotel room directly across from the meeting hall at the Washington Hotel. We've booked you and Miss Katherine a room next to her. We'll all return to the White House tomorrow morning. You have an 11:00 A.M. appointment with President Roosevelt."

Agnes smiled. What luck to arrive on such a day! Attending Mrs. Roosevelt's Red Cross speech, plus staying in the Washington Hotel where celebrities stayed! How thrilling. Their early arrival in Washington allowed for a quick bit of sight-seeing before leaving on the hush-hush Pacific Islands tour.

Though a government goodwill tour, the trip was under the auspices of the Red Cross, and as such, they would wear Red Cross uniforms. In addition to the appearance of good-will, the uniforms limited the need to carry extra luggage. 'We're only allowed forty pounds each,' Mrs. Roosevelt had instructed her by phone when she called to make arrangements. 'The White House will pay for all your traveling expenses and uniforms. You'll need a jacket and several pairs of sturdy shoes. I expect we'll do a good deal of walking.'

Mrs. Roosevelt stepped forward and extended her hand. "I'm so glad to see you ladies again. I hope your trip was pleasant." The feather on her trim hat bobbed as she spoke.

Agnes glanced at Katherine. *Pleasant trip?* Not the description she would have used, but not a topic of discussion while standing on a train platform. She cleared her throat. "Oh, my, indeed. We met some *very* interesting people, to say the least." Agnes glanced around the station. Her gaze fell upon Irving, leaning against a taxi stand, supposedly reading a newspaper.

The big faker! I know what he's up to. Feeling smug and safe with Mrs. Roosevelt's security guards, Agnes nodded to Irving and grinned. *Thought you could outsmart me, didn't you, you old scoundrel. That didn't work out so well, did it?* Wasn't she a true warrior on the home front, and scourge of the underworld? She turned away and tuned in to Katherine's conversation.

"…such an honor to be included. We can't wait to visit the White House."

Mrs. Roosevelt nodded to her handsome young escort. "Edgar, instruct the driver to take us back to the hotel via the Lincoln Monument and past the cherry trees. Let's give these ladies a taste of Washington. We'll have tea at the hotel and have a nice long chat."

Edgar took Mrs. Roosevelt's arm and led her toward the parking lot where the White House car waited, its engine purring in anticipation of the entourage.

Agnes grinned at Katherine, took her arm and followed.

"Do you take milk or lemon, Mrs. Odboddy?" Mrs. Roosevelt tipped the teapot and filled Agnes's cup.

Imagine that. The First Lady, serving her tea in the hotel dining room, resplendent with white linen, thin china tea cups and fresh flowers adorning every table. What an atmosphere of splendor and comfort befitting Mrs. Roosevelt's tea party. Wouldn't Mavis be impressed?

"Here. Let me do that." Katherine took the teapot from Mrs. Roosevelt and filled her cup and then her own. "We should be serving you, Mrs. Roosevelt."

"Nonsense! I'm nothing special. You must think of me as a friend and companion. We're going to spend a lot of time together this next month. We might as well be on a first-name basis, Katherine." Mrs. Roosevelt turned toward Agnes. "Please call me Eleanor. And, may I call you Agnes?"

Agnes's face warmed. *She wants me to call her Eleanor?* "Of course you can call me Agnes, but I just wouldn't feel right addressing you any other way than Mrs. Roosevelt." Agnes's lips trembled. She twisted her hankie.

"As you like. But, please think of me as a friend. Agreed?" She glanced toward her two agents, seated at an adjoining table.

"Yes, ma'am…*umm*…Eleanor." Katherine smiled.

Agnes nibbled a cookie. *Katherine's braver than I am, but young people usually are.*

"I'm so pleased you'll be joining me on the trip. It would be most unpleasant traveling alone with all those men. Any other time, my assistant, Tommy, would accompany me, but her mother is quite ill and Tommy felt she shouldn't leave the country for so long."

"Oh, we're delighted that you asked us." Agnes patted her purse. "I'm looking forward to meeting President Roosevelt. As it happens, I'm carrying a package from Colonel Farthingworth from the Boyles Springs Military Base. It's for the President."

"Oh? Why don't I have one of my men run it over to him tonight?" Mrs. Roosevelt gestured toward Edgar. She picked up a tray of cookies.

"Try one of these Capitol Caramel Cookies. They bake them here specifically for the hotel guests."

"Thank you." Agnes chose a cookie. She laid it on her plate and shoved her trembling hand under the table. "If you don't mind, I'd rather hold on to the package tonight and deliver it myself tomorrow. I was told to put it in the President's hand personally, and I must follow directions. No offense, ma'am, I hope you understand."

Mrs. Roosevelt smiled. "Of course." She set her teacup down and pushed away from the table. "Now, you ladies must excuse me. I have some things to attend to before my speech this evening. Are you doing any sight-seeing? Edgar will drive you wherever you wish to go."

"Katherine and I thought the Smithsonian Institute would be a lovely place to start."

"Indeed. I've been there myself several times. Be sure and check out Charles Lindbergh's airplane in the Aeronautics display." Mrs. Roosevelt stood. "Edgar will call for you at 7:45 P.M. this evening and escort you to the meeting hall. I will likely be busy with dignitaries, so I may not get a chance to speak to you again until breakfast. Shall we say 7:30 A.M., here in the dining hall?"

Agnes and Katherine stood.

Mrs. Roosevelt shook hands with Agnes and then Katherine. "I'm so pleased you'll be joining me. Won't we have fun? Until morning."

Agnes bent her knee and curtsied.

Mrs. Roosevelt covered her smile with her hand. "Ladies." She bobbed her head and hurried from the dining room, her agents trailing behind like puppy dogs.

Agnes's gaze followed Mrs. Roosevelt out the door. "Isn't she just a saint? I think she's about the grandest woman in the world."

"You seem so intimidated by her. You need to get over that, Grandma. The only difference between you two is that she married someone who became President. It could just as easily have been you. She's not royalty."

"You think so? She's just done so many wonderful things."

"You'll get over that feeling soon enough when we're together twenty-four hours a day, washing your dirty stockings in the same sink and swatting the same mosquitoes. Pretty soon, you'll be as comfortable with her as with Mildred."

Agnes giggled. "I suppose you're right. Are you ready? Shall we go back to our room?"

Chapter Thirty-Two

If I was the First Lady, where would I go?

Bam! *Bam!*

Harsh blows landed on the door.

Agnes padded over. "If that's room service, they needn't be so rude." She flung open the door.

"Is Mrs. Roosevelt here?" Edgar pulled off his hat. "She's not in her suite." The lines in his forehead resembled the wind swept Sahara Desert.

"Come on in and sit down. Mrs. Roosevelt told us she had some things to do this afternoon. Why did you think she might be here?"

Edgar shook his head. "I left to check some security issues with management. When I got back to the room, she and Agent Brown were both gone."

"So, she's probably with—"

"That's the problem. Agent Brown just returned…alone!" Edgar flung himself into a sofa chair and ran his hand over his face. "He said Mrs. Roosevelt sent him down to the pharmacy to buy some aspirin tablets. When he came back, she was gone. Said he's looked all over the hotel. She didn't leave a note. That's just not like her. She knows she's not supposed to go anywhere without one of us."

Edgar glanced around the room. "I knew she wasn't over here, but I had to come and check." He jumped up from his chair. "Can I use your phone? I'll have to call headquarters and report her missing." He picked up the phone on the desk.

"Wait a minute, Edgar. Mrs. Roosevelt wouldn't just leave like that without good reason. Did you check in the bathroom?" Agnes shook her head. "Of course, you would have done that first thing. Was her purse in her room?"

Edgar shrugged. "I didn't think to look."

"She's probably gone down to the dining room," Katherine said.

He shook his head again. "Agent Brown already checked there, and at the gift shop, the front desk and at the beauty parlor. No one has seen her. Agent Brown should never have left her alone." Edgar hung his head.

Wasn't he the epitome of misery? If something happened to Mrs. Roosevelt while in his charge, it was guaranteed he'd never work in the security business again. "Maybe she had a *moment* and just needed to find some peace and quiet. Maybe she sent Agent Brown away on purpose so she could escape for a little while." Agnes patted Edgar's arm. "I'm sure she'll turn up any minute. Did you look in the garage?"

"She doesn't have a car key. Agent Brown drives everywhere."

"But maybe she went back to fetch something she left in the car."

"That's a thought. Agent Brown is still downstairs. I'll run down to the garage. Would one of you wait in her room in case she comes back? Here's the key. I'll only be a few minutes." He tossed the key on the coffee table and dashed out the door, coattails flying.

"I'll go, Katherine. You stay here."

Agnes opened the door and nearly collided with the waiter, carrying a tray of tea and snacks.

"Oh! Here you are. Great timing. I'm just on my way out. Go on in. Katherine will take care of you." She nodded to the waiter and glanced toward Mrs. Roosevelt's room. *Why, of all things. Edgar left her room in such a hurry, he left her bedroom door ajar.*

Agnes edged to the doorway and listened. There was someone inside. Mrs. Roosevelt must have returned up the back stairs while Edgar took the elevator.

She chuckled. Like two ships passing in the night. *End of mystery.*

She pushed the door open wider and peeked inside, not wanting to startle Mrs. Roosevelt if she burst in unannounced.

Agnes jerked her head back out of the door. Her pulse quickened. Were her eyes deceiving her or was there a man standing on a chair, reaching around inside Mrs. Roosevelt's chandelier? Surely not! *What on earth is he doing?*

She peeked through the crack in the door again. The hair on the back of her neck stood on end.

The chair was back under the table, and the man had tip-toed into Mrs. Roosevelt's bedroom. A thief? Or a spy, snooping around Mrs. Roosevelt's room.

Scraping noises! Then the sound of shoes scuffing back across the rug toward the door.

Agnes hurried across the hall and lowered her head over a drinking fountain.

Mrs. Roosevelt's door squeaked open.

Agnes turned toward the man. Tall, hat pulled low over his eyes. Thin mustache, clean shaven. "Good morning. Lovely day, isn't it?" She wiped water from her mouth. The innocence of a newborn babe couldn't hold a candle to the grin Agnes directed at the sneaky *son-of-a...a...sea cook.*

The man yanked the First Lady's door shut, snapping the lock. His face flushed. The muscles twitched beside his mustache, panic flashed in his eyes. He touched his hat, mumbled something, ducked his head and scurried toward the staircase.

He was up to no good, that's for sure. Agnes tiptoed over and tried the door handle. Locked! How had that man gotten into Mrs. Roosevelt's room? Edgar wouldn't leave the door open. The intruder must have picked the lock! Her heart pummeled.

She sucked in her breath, used Edgar's key to unlock the door, stepped inside and peeked into the empty hotel room. She blew out her breath to calm her pounding heart. But, she hadn't expected to find Mrs. Roosevelt here. Had the dear lady left of her own free will or been taken by force? *Now, I must use my intuitive powers to discover where she might be.*

Pillows were straight on the divan. Nothing overturned or broken. Mrs. Roosevelt's purse was nowhere to be found. Therefore, she must have left the hotel room willingly. Good.

Now, to find a clue. What might Ellery Queen do in a case like this? Agnes stood in the middle of the suite, closed her eyes, and put out her hands to feel for an aura. She opened her eyes and gazed around the room. There! On the table! A clue. A wrinkled menu from a Chinese restaurant. Maybe Mrs. R. saw the brochure and left to buy egg rolls. Or pot stickers. Or noodles!

Agnes sat on the small sofa near the window and closed her eyes, put her feet on a hassock and leaned her head back. *If I was the First Lady, where would I go?* Try as she might, her thoughts would not stay with Mrs. Roosevelt but drifted to events back on the train. *Madeline. Nanny. Winnie. Irving and Geraldine.* Irving *had* followed her all over the train and into Albuquerque where he nearly frightened her to death outside the police department, in spite of Katherine *pooh-poohing* her story.

Knock, knock, knock!

Agnes jerked upright. Had she dozed off for a minute? She hurried across the room and opened the door.

Edgar stood in the hallway. From the hangdog look on his face, he had not located the missing First Lady.

"No luck?" Agnes motioned him inside, rubbed her eyes and tucked her blouse back into the band of her skirt.

"She wasn't in the garage. How about you? Find anything?" He tossed his jacket onto the sofa.

"I searched the rooms. Mrs. Roosevelt's purse is gone. I think that's a good sign. She must have left under her own steam."

Edgar shook his head. His cheeks were the color of Limburger cheese. His left hand trembled as he wiped his brow. "She's never done anything like this before. I just can't understand it." He glanced at his watch. "It's been thirty minutes. I'll have to notify the White House."

"Wait. I did find a brochure on the coffee table from a Chinese restaurant nearby. Is it possible Mrs. R just went for a little walk? Let's check it out before we—"

The door handle rattled. Did they dare hope? Edgar rushed across the room and yanked open the door. "Mrs...."

Agent Brown stood with his fist in the air, ready to knock again. "It's just me." He raised his eyebrows and glanced inside. "Any news?"

Edgar's shoulders slumped as he sighed and shook his head. "Come on in."

Agent Brown stood at attention just inside the door. Perspiration beaded his forehead. The pallor of his ashen face matched Edgar's.

Edgar checked his watch again. "Mrs. Odboddy suggests we check the Chinese restaurant down the street." His voice lowered. "If we haven't located her in the next fifteen minutes, we'll have to call the White House. They'll probably have a firing squad waiting for us by sundown." Edgar's joke hardly lifted anyone's spirits.

Agent Brown's smile quavered and then turned to a scowl. He grabbed his jacket. "Are you coming with us, Mrs. Odboddy?"

"I think not. I'll wait here a few more minutes in case she comes back. You will let me know as soon as you hear anything, won't you?" She gripped Edgar's arm. "Good luck!" Her words sounded hollow, considering the seriousness of the situation.

Edgar flashed a wan smile as both men stepped into the hall. They stomped toward the stairway, too much in a hurry to wait for the elevator.

Agnes pulled the door shut and sat back down to think. What a foolish act, if Mrs. Roosevelt had carelessly gone off by herself without regard for her security team. *I don't believe for a minute that she would do such a thing.* There must be a reasonable explanation. They just hadn't discovered it yet.

Just then, a breeze from the window fluttered the curtains. The restaurant menu drifted off the coffee table and slid part way under the edge of the sofa. Agnes leaned down to retrieve it. *What's this?* Alongside the menu, just the corner of another paper peeked out. She dropped the restaurant menu and pulled out the pink hotel stationary:

Going to the day spa for a massage. Back at 3:30—Mrs. R

Agnes's gaze swept toward the door. How had they missed this? The breeze must have blown the note off the table.

While Edgar and Agent Brown were tearing the neighborhood apart looking for Mrs. Roosevelt, she was in the day spa all this time! Why hadn't they inquired there?

Agnes hurried to the elevator. Hopefully, she could catch the agents on their way to or from the restaurant before they called the White House in a panic. *And before the firing squad is assembled!* She grinned.

Stepping off the elevator, she spotted the two agents pushing open the glass lobby door. "*Yoo-hoo!* Fellows!"

The dejected look on their faces reminded her of Ling-Ling's expression after being scolded for licking the meringue off a coconut cream pie baked for the potluck at The First Church of the Evening Star and Everlasting Light. Agnes's grin turned into a chuckle as the two men charged across the lobby.

"Come with me, guys. I know where she is." Agnes tugged Edgar and Agent Brown toward the day spa. In the third private room from the rear, they found an unrecognizable Mrs. Roosevelt caked from head to toe, basking in a mud bath.

No small wonder Agent Brown hadn't found her when he inquired at the spa. And, it didn't help that for security reasons, Mrs. Roosevelt had registered under the name, Mrs. Agnes Odboddy!

Chapter Thirty-Three

I must keep better informed of technology.

Gnes unlocked the door and swept into her hotel room to find Katherine sitting on the sofa, reading a magazine. "You won't believe what we've been through looking for Mrs. Roosevelt."

"Did you find her?" Katherine gestured toward the teapot and plate of cookies on the coffee table. "Help yourself."

Agnes nodded. She sat and poured a cup of tea, then leaned back against the sofa and took a sip. "It's cold." She grimaced and reached for a cookie. "Would you believe we found her in the Day Spa? She was there all the time. Edgar about had a stroke running all over the hotel looking for her. She left a note, but it blew under the sofa." Agnes chuckled. "I told those men she wouldn't just run off and get them into trouble like that, but they ran around like Mildred and Mrs. Whistlemeyer."

"You mean the chickens, not your friends."

"Of course. Listen. When I looked into Mrs. Roosevelt's room, I saw the strangest thing. There was a man standing on a chair, sticking something into her chandelier—"

"What kind of *something*?" Katherine laid down the magazine and sat up straight.

"I don't know. I didn't take the time to find out. We were still looking for Mrs. Roosevelt."

"Did you tell Edgar and Agent Brown what you saw?"

"I guess I was so relieved when we found Mrs. Roosevelt, I forgot.

I didn't think it was that important. Why?" Agnes popped the last bite of cookie into her mouth. "Do you think I should have? I don't think he was fixing the light."

"Maybe he was *bugging* her room." Katherine waggled her eyebrows and grinned.

"Bugging? What does that mean?"

"A *bug* is an electronic device that transmits voices. It would allow someone in a nearby room to hear what's said in Mrs. Roosevelt's room. I'm surprised you don't know about such things. I'm sure it's against the law, especially here in Washington, D.C."

Agnes jumped to her feet. Her chest itched. Her hands tingled. "How come you know about such things, Katherine, if I don't?" Wasn't she supposed to be the scourge of the underworld? Why *didn't* she know about such things?

"Remember that Vincent Price movie we went to last month? They bugged the thief's room. That's how they overheard his plans and caught him."

"I must have missed that one. So, this listening device is a real thing? Not just in the movies? You can actually hear what people say in the next room?" How embarrassing to be so poorly informed. Wasn't it her duty to keep up with the doings of thieves and spies and *ne'er-do-wells*? "It's very clever on the part of the listener, isn't it?" Her cheeks warmed. *I must keep better informed of advances in technology.*

Katherine nodded. "In any event, Edgar needs to know that someone got into Mrs. Roosevelt's room and messed around. How do you suppose he got in there in the first place?"

"He must have picked the lock. I doubt he had a key. The door was ajar when I got there. Obviously, Washington is full of Nazi spies. Poor Mrs. Roosevelt could be in danger. I'm going over there right now and tell her about the listening device."

"Is she back from the spa? Maybe you should wait a while."

"At least Edgar could remove the blasted thing." Agnes wrung her hands as she paced the room. How infuriating! That some nasty

Nazi spy should invade Mrs. Roosevelt's privacy! She stared up at the chandelier. "Do you think there's one of those things in here, too?"

Katherine gazed around the room. She put her finger to her lips, stood, and moved books and inspected the artificial plants. She checked inside the table lamp and behind the sofa pillows, and then climbed up on a chair under the ceiling fixture and felt all around the inside of the chandelier. "I can't find anything. Why would they bother to bug our room, anyway?"

"You know, because of Irving, and the *you-know-what* in my *you-know-where*."

"Grandma. Really! I've told you a dozen times that suspecting Irving was absurd."

Katherine was right. They were safe in Washington. Tomorrow they would deliver the package and the following day, begin their trip to the Pacific Islands with the First Lady. They would most likely never see Irving again, but questions still niggled in her mind. Had he followed her into Washington? Was he lurking in the hotel hallways this very minute, hoping to catch her unawares and steal the package?

"If we're going sight-seeing this afternoon, we'd best get going. I'll run over to Mrs. Roosevelt's room and speak to Edgar while you finish dressing."

Chapter Thirty-Four

It's true? I suspected as much.

A dapper, tuxedo-clad gentleman sat at the piano while soft music wafted through the dining room. The gentleman gazed around the room from time to time. Guests turned from their Eggs Benedict, slices of ham, bacon, and bagels at the sound of a particularly pleasing bar of music and cast appreciative glances his direction.

Agnes sat across from Katherine and Mrs. Roosevelt at a small table set with elegant antique china, linen napkins, and shining silverware. A small black vase in the center held a single red rose. Sunlight streaming through the window warmed the rose, releasing its sweet fragrance.

Agnes smeared blackberry jam over her toast and beamed at the piano player. "This is so lovely. We are so honored to join you for breakfast this morning, Mrs. Roosevelt. Your speech last night was absolutely riveting. It's such a pleasure to hear more about your travels and experiences in other countries. I hoped you would talk about our trip to the Pacific Islands, but of course, as it's a secret, I understand you couldn't."

Mrs. Roosevelt glanced at Edgar and Agent Brown, hovering by the front desk, far enough away not to intrude, but close enough to come to her aid, should she need them. She sighed and leaned closer to Agnes. "I'm glad you enjoyed my little talk. Did you find time to visit the Smithsonian Museum yesterday?"

"Oh, my, yes. I can't think of the last time I've walked so far and we still didn't see everything. They threw us out at 6:00 P.M. We had to hurry back to get dressed for your speech." Agnes reached for another slice of toast.

"I'm so pleased you were able to attend." Mrs. Roosevelt dropped her voice even lower, almost to a whisper, barely able to be heard over the strains of Clair de Lune emanating from the piano. "Thank you for telling Edgar about the intrusion to my bedroom yesterday afternoon. He recovered a listening device from the chandelier."

Agnes gasped! Her slice of toast wavered, midway to her mouth. "So, it's true? I suspected as much. You know, in my experience as a former undercover agent, such things are commonplace. I'm surprised, though, that someone would have the nerve to place one in your private residence."

Katherine's coffee cup clinked into the flowered Prince Albert saucer. She raised an eyebrow and stared at Agnes.

The vein beside Mrs. Roosevelt's eye throbbed. She pursed her lips, closed her eyes and took a breath. "What I'm about to tell you must go no further. Do you both promise?"

"Of course, Eleanor, anything you say. You know you can trust us." Katherine sat back, her hands folded in her lap. "Please, if there's anything we can do to help, do tell us."

"It is no secret that J. Edgar Hoover believes I am a Communist supporter. He believes it to be the only reason I champion so many social reforms. He thinks I am attempting to make the United States a Socialist country. He adamantly opposes our goodwill tour, thinking I'm doing it to gain glory for myself. In the past..." Mrs. Roosevelt turned toward Agnes. "My dear, Agnes, I can see that my revelations have shocked you. Indeed, you look quite pale. Do have some more coffee." She picked up the porcelain coffee pot and filled Agnes's cup.

"The idea that our very own FBI leader should believe such things *is* shocking, but I have just begun to tell you—"

"I...I...can't believe it." Tears sprang to Agnes's eyes. "You've helped so many people." Why, the woman almost deserved sainthood. How could the leader of the FBI accuse her like this? "Your programs have supported coal minors, orphans, Negros, college youth, and women's organizations. I can't even count how many other charities!"

Mrs. Roosevelt blushed. "You're too kind. I try to help where I can."

"Do you think Mr. Hoover placed the listening device in your room?" Agnes's cheeks tingled. How terrible Mrs. Roosevelt must feel, knowing that the FBI leader entertained such ugly, hateful ideas.

"Most likely someone in his office installed the device with his blessing. I expect they hoped to overhear me say something they could claim is treasonous. His spies come to all my speeches and take notes that are given to Hoover in a written report. I hear that he keeps an extensive file on all my activities." Tears sparkled in her eyes and threatened to spill over. She dabbed her eyes with an embroidered hankie, squared her shoulders and sat back. "Nevertheless, I shall endure."

"How can you expect us to keep silent about such a vile thing? I don't understand. Why hasn't someone done something to stop him?" Katherine twisted her linen napkin.

Mrs. Roosevelt patted Katherine's hand. "We do live in a free country, thank God. He is the leader of the FBI, and it is within his right to investigate anyone he thinks is…shall we say…an enemy of the country. I can't stop his men from following me and taking notes on my activities, but, this time, I do think he has gone a tad too far. I shall speak to Franklin. Indeed, that is what I shall do. Perhaps he will have a word with Mr. Hoover. Now, ladies, that's quite enough of this depressing subject. Shall we just enjoy our breakfast?"

"Grandma, isn't there anything we can do to help? I can't stand to think of Mr. Hoover spreading such lies about Mrs. Roosevelt." Katherine threw her napkin onto her plate. "I'd like to wring his scrawny neck!"

Eleanor grinned, "Well, dear, if word got out that you felt that way, he'd probably have you tossed in the hoosegow on some trumped-up charge, and we'd never see your pretty face again."

Agnes lowered her head. The clink of sterling silver utensils against antique china plates and the buzz of quiet conversations surrounded her. Her stomach roiled at the injustice directed toward her friend and soon-to-be traveling companion! And, she was powerless to stop it.

The waiter approaching with a coffee pot reminded Agnes of Charles. She had intended to speak to Mrs. Roosevelt about a program to help veterans re-entering society. But, how could she ask Mrs. Roosevelt to champion yet another worthy cause, after hearing how her efforts for the working poor were perceived by Mr. Hoover? No, she'd best hold her tongue. There would be plenty of time over the next month to discuss the situation. Clearly, this was neither the time nor the place.

Chapter Thirty-Five

Vindicated! Exonerated! Exculpated! Absolved.

H*ere we go, ready or not.* Agnes paused beside the elevator door and drew in her breath. Only moments now until her long-awaited interview with the President! Her footsteps were muted by the thick flowered carpet as they approached the Oval Office.

Agnes glanced at the photographs and paintings of previous presidents and White House dignitaries, smiling or glaring down on passing visitors. She returned George Washington's grin, feeling at once calmed by his serene face. Vases of fresh cut flowers adorned little tables outside the various offices. A giant *Ficus Benjamina* plant stood beside the door marked Oval Office.

Agnes gripped her purse. Her heart pitter-patted like raindrops in a tin bucket. Surely the fate of the free world might hang on the delivery of the package. And to think that in spite of all the attempts to thwart her, within minutes she would place it directly into the President's hand. The carpet at the doorway had worn thin from the thousands of visitors, advisors and emissaries, both men and women, foreign and domestic who had passed through this entrance.

The young Marine at the door of the Oval Office nodded to Mrs. Roosevelt. "I'll need to check your bags, ladies." He reached for Agnes's purse. She gasped and clutched it to her bosom. Warmth rushed into her cheeks. "I…*um*…wait! I have…" She had forgotten to remove the stupid gun from her purse! They'd think she was here to assassinate Mr. Roosevelt! *Oh, Lord! Leavenworth, here I come!*

Mrs. Roosevelt put her hand on the soldier's arm. "That won't be necessary, Bates. These ladies are my guests. I assure you, they have no intent to harm my husband!"

Agnes blew out her breath. *Does she read minds, too?*

The soldier nodded. "As you wish, Mrs. Roosevelt." He stepped to the side of the door.

Agnes caught her breath. She wrung her hands. The sound of laughter burst from one of the many offices leading off the corridor.

Mrs. Roosevelt reached for the doorknob and then paused. "Now, Agnes, you mustn't be nervous. Franklin is just like any other man, except he's—"

"Easy for you to say, Mrs. Roosevelt. He's your husband. He's *my* President." Agnes shifted her purse from under one arm to the other and reached for Katherine's hand.

"It's okay, Grandma. Just be respectful and say, *sir*, when you speak to him." Katherine patted Agnes's arm. "You'll be fine."

"Wait, ladies…"

Agnes bent her ear close to Mrs. Roosevelt. Was she about to impart a national secret?

"Before we go in, I must tell you. You may not know this," Mrs. Roosevelt put her hand to her mouth and whispered, "Franklin is in a wheelchair."

Agnes gasped. Her head reeled.

"He contracted polio some years ago and is paralyzed from the waist down. We don't allow photographs of the chair, so many folks aren't even aware of his disability. He works very hard to portray himself as a robust and capable man, which, of course he is. The wheelchair hasn't affected his ability to overcome the Great Depression, or serve as Commander and Chief of the military in this time of war."

Agnes sent a startled glance toward Katherine. "I didn't know that he had a disability. We wouldn't dream of saying anything to embarrass him." She opened her purse, shoved the gun to the side and checked the package; ragged and frayed but, nevertheless, safe and secure.

"All right, if you're ready, we'll go in." Mrs. Roosevelt smiled at the Marine standing at attention. She turned the knob, opened the door and put her head in. "*Yoo-hoo*, Franklin. It's me. I've brought our guests."

Agnes stepped through the door. Her gaze swept the office. *Whoa!* Not at all how she had imagined the Oval Office. Shelves were loaded with dozens of books, pictures of Navy ships on every wall, and landscapes of the President's home town in the Hudson Bay area. A large Jefferson chair sat beside an odd-shaped table piled high with files and papers.

Guess her cluttered bedroom could be forgiven, considering the President's jumbled assortment of books and souvenirs.

Several books and papers nearly buried three chairs facing the desk. A Camel brand cigarette holder, lighters, paperweights, a stuffed elephant and a toy donkey, salt and pepper shakers, Uncle Sam hats and two figurines depicting Benito Mussolini and Adolf Hitler, plus numerous other items blurred into a collage on the President's desk. Behind his chair was a long table covered with stacks of papers and files that defied explanation.

The President nodded, his blue eyes sparkling. He removed the cigarette holder clamped between his teeth and boomed, "Come in, Eleanor. So good of you to visit, ladies!" He jiggled a finger toward the chairs. "Move some of that stuff and take a seat."

Agnes stammered an incomprehensible reply, lifted a stack of files from a chair and set them on the floor.

A black Scottish terrier stepped out from behind the desk, shook vigorously and scratched his left ear.

"This is Fala," Mrs. Roosevelt stroked the dog's head. "He's Franklin's constant companion." Fala flopped down on the carpet beside her chair.

Katherine sat beside Agnes, straightened a wrinkle from her skirt and folded her hands in her lap. "We are so pleased to meet you, Mr. President. Thank you for taking the time to see us." Katherine's head swiveled toward the nautical décor decorating the walls.

"No trouble. No trouble at all." The President slid the papers he'd been reading to the side of his desk, tapped ashes from his cigarette into an ashtray and clamped the holder back between his teeth. "So, what have you gals been up to this morning? Have you had lunch? I could order in some sandwiches."

Wasn't it amazing how he could talk with that thing in his mouth?

"No, Franklin. That won't be necessary. We've already eaten." Mrs. Roosevelt nodded at the clock over the desk. "Besides, it's only 10:00 A.M."

The President craned his neck and glanced up at the clock. "Really? I hadn't noticed. I've been here since 6:00 A.M. So, Mrs. Odboddy, tell me what you think I should do to win this gol-darned war." President Roosevelt's cigarette holder jiggled as his grin widened.

Agnes sucked in her breath. Whatever possessed the President of the United States to ask such a question of a homemaker from a small town in California? Despite her self-proclaimed title of home front warrior, her only recent battle experience was with aphids on her rose bushes and gophers in the victory garden. *Is he mocking me?* Or, had he heard of her vast expertise in dealing with the Germans during WWI while she was an undercover agent?

On the other hand, maybe he asked every Oval Office visitor, whether critic or supporter, their opinion of the war? Reporters said that he valued different points of view. Folks of any persuasion might suggest some new revelation of how to bring the enemy to their Nazi knees. *OK, he asked for it. Here goes.*

"Well, sir, let me tell give you an example that might illustrate my ideas." Agnes tapped her top lip. "If I had a weed in my victory garden that was choking out the vegetables and giving me grief, I'd just yank it out. It seems to me that Mr. Hitler is an evil man, bombing all those countries and killing folks over yonder. So, I'd say he's kind of like that weed in my garden."

Agnes stood, paced the floor with her purse under one arm. She waved her hand as she spoke. "You've got troop ships fighting the Japanese in the Pacific Islands and soldiers fighting the German army in Africa, so I suppose—"

"Grandma, sit down." Katherine hissed, tugging at Agnes's sleeve. "I don't think Mr. Roosevelt really wants to hear about the weeds in your garden."

Agnes face warmed. She sat and twisted her hands in her lap. "I'm sorry, sir. I got carried away." *Now, I've gone and made a fool of myself, again.*

"No, no! That's all right." The President chuckled and waved his cigarette holder. "You're right. Our troops are spread pretty thin. What were you saying about the troops in Africa? Indeed, we've had some terrific battles there. But, every victory is hard won. Across the Pacific, as well. I'm curious where you're going with your *weed theory.* Please continue."

He really wants to know what I think. "Well, as I was saying, sir, Mr. Hitler is like that weed in my victory garden. I'll bet the war would end right quick if something unexpected sent him off to meet his Maker, kind of accidental-like, of course. Like plucking out that weed, it should put a might quick end to the war."

"Grandmother! What are you suggesting? That the United States should assassinate Hitler? What a terrible thing to say." Katherine half-rose from her chair, her cheeks flushed. "The United States would *never* do such a thing." She glanced at the President. "Would they?"

Mr. Roosevelt coughed, his cheeks turning a rosy red hue that matched Katherine's. "Well...um, er..." He cleared his throat. "*Humph*... That's an interesting idea. I don't think... Well, could we actually get away with it? I mean, we would have to...*er, ahem*..." He scooted several items around on his desk, glanced up at the clock and then folded his hands.

He cleared his throat again, his blush fading to his natural color. "Let's move on. I understand you're acquainted with my friend, Colonel Farthingworth. He tells me that you've been of great service to him in the past."

Agnes sat forward on her chair, clutching her purse to her chest. "Yes sir. I've had the pleasure of assisting Colonel Farthingworth. Just last summer—"

"Yes, of course. It's been most interesting. I'm sorry to rush you ladies off, but I really must be getting back to work. Before you go, Agnes, I believe you have something for me?" President Roosevelt leaned forward on his elbows.

Agnes hopped out of the chair, her hand in her purse. "Oh, yes sir, I do. That's what I was just about to say. Colonel Farthingworth asked me to deliver this item directly to you, sir." She grinned, and laid the chicken-speckled parcel on the President's desk.

He reached for the package. "It looks like it's been through the Boar war! What's happened to it?" He ran his fingers over the bedraggled string.

"Well, sir, you wouldn't believe what I've gone through to bring this to you. In fact—"

"Agnes, I'm sure Franklin doesn't have time to hear this right now. We must let him get about his duties." Mrs. Roosevelt stood and picked up her handbag. "We should be on our way."

The President pawed through the jumble on his desk until he found scissors. He snipped the string and tossed it to the side. The paper fell away, revealing…a cigar box.

The ladies rose and moved toward the door. Agnes stopped at the door to admire a photograph, just as Mr. Roosevelt opened the lid. "Ah, my favorite Cuban cigars! Wasn't that thoughtful?"

Agnes whipped her head around and stared. "Cigars?" She hurried back to the desk. "Did you say cigars? That's what was in the box?" Chill bumps raced up and down her arms. *Cigars!*

To think what she had gone through to get this blasted box from Newbury to Washington! Nanny—snooping in her berth. Getting mugged in Albuquerque. Fending off Irving every step of the way. Riding the rails with Charles. Hadn't she risked her life to protect the package, believing it carried information that might end the war?

"Why, my dear Mrs. Odboddy, whatever is the matter? You're as white as a sheet. Please be seated. You look downright ill. Shall I send for a doctor? Eleanor! Come back in here and tend to your friend."

Agnes put her tingling fingers to her cheeks. *Am I about to faint?* She flopped into the chair and dropped her purse to the floor. "Sir, I thought... I mean, the package... Colonel Farthingworth led me to believe that it was—"

"Was what? Just what did you think it was?" Mr. Roosevelt tossed his head back and laughed. "Oh, I get it. I'll bet you thought you were bringing me some important documents related to the war." He chuckled. "Well, there, there. Don't fret. We all make mistakes." He picked up a cigar and twirled it in his fingers. "See? Cuban cigars. They're for my birthday." He closed the cigar box and set it to the side of his desk and reached for the phone.

Katherine and Mrs. Roosevelt hurried to Agnes's side. "Grandma? Are you okay? You look ill. What's wrong?" She knelt by Agnes's chair. "Grandma?"

Agnes shook her head. "It was a box of cigars. All this time we thought... And, it was just cigars." She clutched Katherine's arm and stood. A wave of dizziness washed over her.

"Cigars? My stars!" Katherine walked with Agnes toward the hall. "Thank you, sir. Good day. Thank you for seeing us." She pulled the door shut and nodded to the young Marine guard outside the door.

Agnes's thoughts a-jumble, barely aware of the hand leading her, she staggered down the hall beside Katherine. *This is what I need, all right. Someone to lead me. I'm just a foolish old woman, given to delusions of grandeur.* She needed a *keeper*, the way she went off half-cocked with notions that mostly led to her humiliation. But, nothing she'd ever done compared to her delusion about the President's *secret documents*!

All this time, thinking she was carrying documents that might change the course of the war. Ridiculous! Hadn't Irving thought the same? His outrageous efforts to steal her package had fed her illusion that she was on a secret mission for the President. And, all the time, she was carrying cigars.

What a fool I am. What a prize fool. And what a joke on Irving! She caught her foot on the rug, stumbled, and clutched at Katherine's arm to steady herself. Her head swam. Nausea swept through her stomach.

They had almost reached Mrs. Roosevelt at the end of the hall when Agnes stopped. Her muddled thoughts cleared and her balance steadied. "Oh, dear me, Katherine. We left his office in such a hurry, I left my purse by the chair. Wait here. I'll just be a moment." She retraced her steps back to the Oval Office, smiled at the Marine and reached for the doorknob.

"Hold it, ma'am. You can't go in there." The young man shook his head and stepped in front of her. "I can't let anyone in without orders." His hand moved to the pistol strapped on his hip.

Was he really intending to shoot her? She glared into his youthful face. "Young man, if you'll recall, I had permission fifteen minutes ago when I stepped into the office, and I just stepped out the door not twenty seconds ago. President Roosevelt, himself, invited me here." She gestured toward the door. "I'll just be a second. I left my purse inside."

"Sorry, ma'am. Orders. No one goes in without permission. You went in with Mrs. Roosevelt before, which was fine, but I can't let you go in alone."

Mrs. Roosevelt approached. "What's wrong? Of course she can go back in. She left her bag inside."

Katherine moved alongside Agnes, a questioning expression on her pale face.

"Yes ma'am. If you say so, ma'am." The guard twisted the doorknob and stepped back. "Mrs. Roosevelt and guests, again," he announced as he shoved open the door.

Agnes strode into the office. She hurried across the room toward the President, her gaze sweeping the office, momentarily resting on her purse and then up to the pile of cigars on his desk. "I'm sorry to bust in again like this, but I forgot my…"

Mr. Roosevelt sat, half-turned toward the window, holding the empty cigar box. His head jerked up at the sound of Agnes's voice. "What?"

A piece of paper floated out of the box onto the desk. Agnes gasped. "Is that a map?" A second map and a letter fluttered onto the floor. War plans, secret communications, hidden beneath the cigars! Why had he deceived her? Something smelled, and it wasn't Cuban cigars!

"Eleanor? Mrs. Odboddy?" The President whipped the offensive papers under a book and folded his hands. "*Umm*…I thought you ladies were gone…*umm*… Did you forget something?" His cheeks flared with color. "Oh, hang it all, Eleanor. Close that door. All of you! Come over here and take a seat."

Agnes sat, picked up her purse and placed it in her lap. "Sir? You had something you wanted to share?" A smug smile tugged at her cheeks. *Vindicated! Exonerated! Exculpated! Absolved!*

Maybe she wasn't such a foolish old woman, after all. The box *did* contain secret documents. No small wonder Irving tried so hard to get his hands on it. Probably some great invasion plan General McArthur and Colonel Farthingworth had cooked up.

Agnes turned off her mental back-patting and tuned in to the President.

"…so now that you know that the box held more than cigars, I have to swear you all to secrecy. What I have here in my hand—" he pulled the papers from under the book—"could considerably shorten the war. Not a word of it can reach the outside world, for the sake of national security." He turned to Agnes.

"That's why we asked for your help, Agnes. The papers *had* to get through to me. We couldn't risk the enemy getting hold of the information. It wasn't even safe sending it through normal security channels, for fear of spies within our own ranks. There are spies everywhere, you know."

Agnes smirked and nodded. "Oh, I assure you. I know."

"We felt a woman like you would draw less attention than sending them by a military courier. We probably should have told you what you were carrying, but we thought you'd act more natural if you didn't know." Mr. Roosevelt folded his hands and leaned forward.

"Unfortunately, Colonel Farthingworth's aid overheard him giving you the package. We arrested him shortly after you left Newbury on the bus. It was too late to warn you. We weren't sure if the scoundrel had alerted the enemy about your assignment. I'm sure you were quite safe along the way. I do hope you aren't angry, Agnes." He clenched his cigarette holder tightly in his teeth and grinned.

Agnes crossed her arms and tossed back her shoulders. "Angry? Why should I be angry? I've had my house burglarized, been chased across nine states by a Nazi spy, and spent two days in a boxcar to get this package to you."

Mr. Roosevelt's eyes flew open. "My dear! Surely not." He picked up the detailed map and pressed it against his chest. His face went a little pale. Was he thinking how often the papers might have fallen into the wrong hands? "But, you prevailed and brought it to me, somewhat the worse for wear, I must admit, but nevertheless…it's safe, even covered with mud and chicken *caa-caa*. No harm, no foul…" His hand went to the tattered brown paper "You won't hold it against me for getting you involved, right?"

"As a red-blooded American citizen, I was willing to risk life and limb for my country. It was the least I could do." *Is that really true? Now that I know they purposely put me in danger and didn't even warn me of the risk?*

"Grandmother? Perhaps we should let President Roosevelt get on with his business. Now that he has this information, I'm sure he needs to deal with it. He does have a war to win, after all."

"Indeed, ladies. I'm just sorry there's no way we can adequately reward you for your magnanimous service, but I'm sure you understand, Agnes. There can't be a whisper of what you've done, or even the hint of a reward. If the enemy even thought there was something afoot, it could jeopardize the operation."

"I understand. I'm getting quite used to being involved in circumstances the government withholds from the public. No doubt it's for our own good." Agnes bit her lip. Harsh sarcasm, but apparently, it went right over his noble, self-righteous head.

"Then, I'll bid you farewell and Godspeed. I hear you're joining Eleanor on her little vacation." He started sliding things around his desk. "You'll pull that door shut on your way out, right?" He reached down to scratch Fala's ears.

"Yes sir, thank you, sir." Agnes stood. "Come, Katherine. We're no longer needed here."

Katherine nodded and stood.

Mrs. Roosevelt started to speak and then shook her head. She turned on her heel and stomped out the door, muttering, "…little vacation…indeed."

Chapter Thirty-Six

You never know who might be a Nazi spy.

Agnes's head felt as if it was spinning. Without a word of fore-warning of the danger, and because she was an eccentric, foolish old woman, the President used her and endangered her life. *Okay! I volunteered for the assignment, but did Mr. Roosevelt give a rat's behind about my safety? He knew Nazi spies had discovered my mission.* Somehow, the idea gave her pause.

"Grandmother, let's find a place to sit down. You look like you're about to faint."

Agnes opened her mouth in a rebuke and then closed it. Katherine was right. Her head might spin off her neck at any moment. She *had* volunteered, but suddenly, everything felt topsy-turvy. Enough that *she* was in danger, but what about Katherine? *What if Mrs. Roosevelt's invitation was just a ruse to get me to carry the package to Washington?* If that was true, how was she to leave with Mrs. Roosevelt in the morning and act as though things were all right between them?

It was no wonder she couldn't catch her breath. Agnes clutched Katherine's arm and pointed toward a carved bench, just outside the French doors. "Can we go into the Rose Garden and sit for a minute?"

Mrs. Roosevelt pushed open the French doors and stepped into the sunshine. "Here, Agnes. Have a seat. You look like you could use a little rest."

The scent of roses wafted on the breeze. A sparrow chirped and jumped from limb to limb in a nearby shrub, as though God was in his Heaven and all was right with the world…but, in Agnes's head, it wasn't!

Agnes sat. She glanced at Mrs. Roosevelt, pulling off her gloves and gazing around the garden, as though nothing untoward had just happened in the President's office. *She doesn't give a fig for how foolish I feel. Does she even know how they used me and endangered my life? Or care?*

Agnes pulled her hankie from her purse and wiped her forehead. Had Mrs. Roosevelt known about the deceitful assignment? What better person to carry the secret documents than the daffy old woman Mrs. Roosevelt met last summer while attending her cousin's funeral?

Her head whirled with questions, suspicions of Mrs. Roosevelt, feelings of being duped and used, not necessarily in that order. How does one acknowledge that a hero may have feet of clay? How could she spend the next month with Mrs. Roosevelt, thinking she was involved in the plan? *Maybe I should bow out of the trip while I still have the chance.*

"Are you sure you're all right, Grandma? You look so pale and you haven't said a word since we left the Oval Office. What's wrong? You were right about the secret documents all along. You should be proud of yourself." Katherine patted Agnes's arm.

Bile rose in Agnes's throat. Should she confront the President's wife about her role in the plan? Colonel F's request came on the heels of her invitation. Had the President suggest that she invite Agnes or was it a genuine invitation from Mrs. Roosevelt?

The more she thought about it, the more it seemed likely. "Mrs. Roosevelt, if you'll excuse me, I need to lie down." Agnes put her hand to her head. "Can someone please drive me back to the hotel? I feel quite ill."

"Of course. You don't look at all well. I hope it's not the flu." Mrs. Roosevelt wrung her hands. "Our plane leaves at 4:30 in the morning." She stood and nodded to Edgar. "Please bring the car around and drive the ladies back to the hotel. I have some last minute business here in the

White House before I leave tomorrow. You can return for me in about an hour."

Within minutes, Edgar had the car in a nearby driveway.

Mrs. Roosevelt walked Agnes to the car. "I'll call later, Agnes, and see how you are. Oh, dear, at this late date, I do hope you'll be able to make the trip. It would be such a shame if you weren't able to accompany me." She slammed the car door.

As Edgar drove slowly away from the White House, Agnes peered out the back window.

Mrs. Roosevelt had already returned down the path toward the building. When she reached the French doors, she paused to speak to a man in a dark pin-striped suit, like the one Irving wore on the train. She turned and pointed back toward Agnes's car.

The man nodded, opened the door, and followed the First Lady inside.

If she didn't know better, Agnes would have sworn that it *was* Irving…but that wasn't possible, was it?

Agnes scarcely listened on the way back to the hotel, as Katherine and Edgar jabbered about the Lincoln Memorial, the Smithsonian Institute, and the Washington Monument.

"Nice, dear," Agnes mumbled and closed her eyes. The thought of the President's deception and his wife's possible culpability clashed through her mind.

Shortly, the car jerked to a stop. Agnes opened her eyes at the hotel archway. Had she actually dozed off? *Huh! Guess that's one way to relieve worry.*

"Here you are, ladies. Home again, home again, jiggity jig." Edgar chuckled and tipped his hat.

"Thanks Edgar. See you later." Katherine called as they stepped out of the car, nodded to the doorman and entered the lobby. She paused in front of the gift shop. "Do you mind if we stop here for a minute, Grandma, or would you rather I walk up to the room with you? I want to buy a post card and send it to Dr. Don before we leave Washington. I called him long distance last night. He apologized for not seeing us off at the bus station and said he'd make it up to me when we got home." She grinned and winked.

About time Katherine starts paying a little more attention to her beau. "That's fine. Take your time. I wouldn't mind some time alone. I have some things on my mind to sort out." She put her hand to her forehead, waved, and turned toward the elevator door.

"Are you sure you're all right, Grandma? You've hardly said a word all the way back." Katherine called to Agnes's retreating figure.

Agnes returned a weak smile and nodded. "I'm fine. We'll talk about it later."

The elevator slid open. "Floor, ma'am?" The attendant held the door as Agnes stepped inside. She glanced at the gaudy interior design. Ornate carvings framed the elevator door. Mirrored interior walls displayed etched designs in each corner. The gaunt face of a female singer covered a small poster on the back wall.

"Fifth floor, please. Our room is right next to Mrs. Roosevelt's." Her chest seized as she shared the information. She probably shouldn't have announced that the First Lady was in the hotel. More likely, the elevator man already knew, so no harm done. Admiration for Mrs. Roosevelt collided with suspicion that she may have played a role in Agnes bringing the package to Washington.

"She's a lovely woman." The elevator man smiled. "Have you ever met her?"

"We're joining her on her trip to…" Agnes stopped just short of revealing her goodwill tour. *Yikes! Shut your mouth, Agnes. You never know who might be a Nazi spy.* That information was top secret.

"Fifth floor." The elevator door slid open into a hallway with maroon-colored floral carpeting. "Have a nice day."

Framed photographs of Washington landmarks lined the wall

across from the elevator. Agnes turned down the padded hallway and paused in front of each photograph. *I should have paid more attention to the monuments as we drove across town. It's likely I won't be back in Washington D.C. for a while.* She took three deep breaths and relaxed. She'd been so busy wallowing in indignation she'd hardly noticed the famous Washington sites.

She stopped beside the photograph of the Lincoln Memorial and then moved on to a picture of cherry trees lining the boulevard in front of the Smithsonian Institute. The last picture was taken outside the Washington Hotel where limousines lined up under the portico. She leaned closer and eyed the picture. Was that J. Edgar Hoover stepping out of his limousine? How interesting. Mrs. Roosevelt said he was behind the listening device they'd found in her room. The old scoundrel! Hard to believe someone so high up in office could be capable of such dirty tricks.

Mrs. Roosevelt has always been my hero. She'd accomplished too many fine things to ever be a party to anything dishonest. Agnes's suspicions of the First Lady melted. On the other hand, she wouldn't put it past the President to take advantage of Mrs. Roosevelt's plans to obtain Agnes's cooperation. Imagine, using his wife's goodwill tour to accomplish his own goal.

Agnes shook her head. Tears pricked her eyes. *I've misjudged Mrs. Roosevelt. She would never betray me that way. Shame on me for even thinking she might.*

Agnes's spirits lifted as she hurried down the hallway toward her room. *I'm going to put this all behind me and relax in a nice hot bubble bath!* She reached her room, shoved the key in her door and twisted the handle. Before she could open the door…

Click.

Something cold and hard pressed against the back of her neck. "Don't even think of doing something funny." Agnes felt the messenger's whispered breath against her left ear.

What…?

"Don't turn around. Just reach in your purse real slow and give me the package."

Agnes blinked. A cold chill started in her knees and plunged through her body. A woman's voice! Where had she heard it before? On the train? Or, here in the hotel? Her knees felt almost too weak to support her body. It took all her willpower not to turn her head.

Disjointed thoughts raced through her mind at the speed of electrical current through a telegraph wire. *She thinks I still have the package. Should I try to disarm her?* Most people wouldn't think of that, but she wasn't *most people*. She was Agnes Agatha Odboddy, warrior on the home front, scourge of the underworld. She had a gun in her purse, but could she sneak it out and use it before the woman shot her dead?

Her thoughts raced on in a split second. Katherine would be along any minute. Poor Katherine would find Agnes's life's blood oozing into that nice thick flowered carpet. What a shame to ruin such beautiful carpet. Not likely the decorating team could match the print and replace just the area she'd bleed all over. They'd have to re-carpet the whole hallway. Maybe they'd try to *remove* the blood. Was it cold water and salt that removes blood? Or was it soda? She'd read something about it somewhere in a woman's housekeeping magazine, and…

What am I thinking? What should I do? Quit dithering. Humor her, Agnes.

"Okay, okay, don't shoot. I'll give you the package." Agnes stepped to the side, reached into her purse as if to retrieve the package. She grabbed her gun and crumpled to the floor, rolled as she cocked the hammer, and turned to face the traitor.

Expecting to see some dark foreign woman with a wart on her nose and tobacco-stained buck teeth peering from an evil sneer, Agnes stared into the thief's face. *What the heck? Nanny? Our nanny from the train? Madeline's nanny?*

Agnes hesitated a moment too long.

Nanny pounced. Her fingers grasped for the gun.

Agnes fired. A deafening report reverberated through the hallway. The bullet missed Nanny and ripped into the photograph of Hoover, striking his forehead. Glass sprayed outward, sending shards across the rug.

Nanny grabbed Agnes's wrist and twisted. A sharp pain shot up her arm as the gun tumbled to the floor. Nanny kicked it away.

How did that happen? That's not what I'd planned. How could namby-pamby Nanny disarm her? *Me! The scourge of the underworld?* Agnes stared into her attacker's cold, cruel eyes, her stomach feeling like Mt. Vesuvius about to erupt.

Nanny stood over Agnes, a pistol aimed at her head. "Give me that blasted package or so help me, I'll put a bullet through your brains."

Agnes's heart pounded. *Nanny!* How we misjudged her! Hadn't she played the helpless little waif, kiting free meals and sympathy from her fellow passengers, pretending to be little Madeline's poor, confused caregiver?

Images flashed through Agnes's head. Back on the train, Nanny had fainted in the club car and clutched at Agnes's purse. That was no accident! And, when she climbed into Agnes's bunk? Not sleepwalking at all. Again, another failed attempt to steal the package!

Now, the clever traitor stood like a demon from Hell, tossing Agnes around like a ragdoll, intent on stealing General McArthur's secret invasion plans. Agnes grinned. *Too late, old girl.* The President already had the documents. But, how would Nanny react when she learned she had missed her chance?

Agnes lay on the floor, her purse clutched to her bosom. She scanned the hallway. Her gun lay three feet away, too far to reach. Her stomach clinched. Nausea swept through her belly. *Now what do I do? I'm not going to lie here and die like a rat.*

Agnes reached up, as though raising her hand in defeat. "Don't shoot. I don't want to die. I'll give you the package." *Keep her talking. It might throw her off guard.*

Nanny's gun hand dropped a few inches. She smiled. Probably

thought she would soon have her prize. She hadn't counted on Agnes
Agatha Odboddy!

Ha! Agnes reached behind her head, pulled one of the sharp
sterling silver chopsticks from her bun and plunged it into Nanny's
calf. *Gotcha!*

Nanny howled, dropped her pistol and reached down to clutch her
bleeding leg.

Agnes yanked Nanny's ankle, throwing her off balance, as she
grabbed the pistol with her other hand.

Nanny crumpled to the floor, then struggled to her knees, flailing
for the gun. Being quicker and stronger, she jerked it from Agnes's
hand. Nanny aimed the gun at her chest and sneered.

Agnes heard the hammer click. *Time to meet my Maker!* She closed
her eyes. *Oh, Lord, take this poor sinner…*

The elevator door swooshed open and a gunshot exploded, echoing
through the empty hallway. Agnes's ears rang. *Funny! Is this what dead
feels like? I don't feel any different.* She ran her hands over her chest
and face, then peeked open one eye.

A man hovered over Nanny, his gun pointed down at her. *Irving?*
The elevator door slid closed with a snap. *Irving? An accomplice, come
to finish the job?*

Nanny grimaced, holding her blood-smeared hand. Her gun lay
against the far wall.

Irving moved toward Agnes. "You okay, Mrs. Odboddy? So, it
was Nanny all the time. Well, well! Can't say I'm surprised. I should
have suspected as much." He nodded toward the woman on the floor.
"Don't worry, Mrs. Odboddy. I'll take care of this traitor."

Agnes's mouth dropped open. "Irving? What…what?" She stared
at the gun aimed at Nanny. "It wasn't you trying to steal my package?
Then, why were you following us on the train?" How could she have
been so wrong about so many people within the span of one hour?
Mrs. Roosevelt, then Nanny, and now….Irving? Her people skills were
desperately in need of an adjustment.

The elevator door slid open again and Katherine stepped out. Her eyebrows shot up as she gazed at the scene. Nanny lay on the floor, blood oozing between her fingers. Agnes still sat on the floor, while Irving stood over her with a gun. The color drained from Katherine's face. "Grandma? Irving?" She rushed toward him, her purse raised over her head.

"Wait! He's not the thief." Agnes pointed to Nanny. "She's been after the package all this time. Irving just saved my life."

Katherine turned to Irving. "You weren't the one?" Her cheeks flamed.

"Don't be ridiculous. Of course not." Irving grinned and waved his gun at Nanny. "Fact is, once we realized someone might be on your trail, the FBI assigned me to watch your back and make sure the package got through safely." He glanced between Agnes and Katherine.

Agnes gasped. "And, all that time, we thought it was you." He might have been watching her back to protect the package, but...? "What about Geraldine? Didn't you kill your wife? I saw you throw her cape off the train. How do you explain that?"

Irving chuckled. "Geraldine was supposed to be my cover so we could pass as honeymooners. Sadly, she's a surly sort and we quarreled. I thought I was playing a part, being romantic, but maybe I overdid it. She took offense. She got off the train at one of the stops during the night and caught the next train back to "Frisco". Said she was going to report me for making improper advances. I was mad, so I tossed her cape off the train. I thought you might have seen that. Wondered what you must have thought." Irving chuckled.

"So, how long have you been following us?" Agnes asked.

He grinned. "Actually, I started watching your house that day right after Colonel Farthingworth saw Chief Waddlemucker's police report of the attempted burglary. He thought there was a leak in his office and sure enough, he was right. We figured they were after the documents and might follow you onto the train. I thought you might remember me from the day I followed you around Newbury.

"I've been two steps behind you pretty much ever since, Agnes. The Colonel and the President wanted to make sure their favorite asset got safely to Washington. You threw a fly in the ointment when you missed the train in Albuquerque. Wasn't I frantic for the next couple of days? Thought my FBI career was over. Katherine and I tried our best to track you down, but you managed to get back on your own."

Agnes's face warmed. "Thanks to Charles." And once again, she had misjudged the President, thinking he wasn't concerned for her safety. At least it was nice to know, even if it made her *snit* this morning even that much more foolish. "But, Irving, why are you here now? We already delivered the package to the President."

Nanny groaned, "Now she tells me."

"Mrs. Roosevelt figured you were upset when you left the Rose Garden. She sent me to explain things. To let you know that we didn't put you out there without back up. Guess it's a good thing I turned up when I did. Oh, and by the way... My real name isn't Irving. It's Vincent. Irving is my under cover *alias*." A grin lit up his face.

Of all things! All this time he's been guarding us. Agnes turned toward the cowering woman on the floor holding her bleeding ankle.

Hatred smoldered in Nanny's eyes.

"And, then, there's this one." Agnes swiped her bloody chopstick across Nanny's skirt, leaving reddish-brown streaks. "You don't mind, do you? They'll give you a clean prison dress when you get to Leavenworth." She poked the chopstick back into her tumble-down bun, now hanging sideways.

Mrs. Roosevelt's door opened and Edgar stepped into the hallway. His eyes widened. He rushed to Agnes. "What's all the commotion? We thought we heard something. Thought it was a car backfire. Are you all right?"

"Irving. This is Edgar, Mrs. Roosevelt's bodyguard." Agnes accepted his hand and he helped her stand.

Irving nodded. "I think we have this under control. This is Miss Nanny What's-Her-Name, from the train. Seems she was trying to get hold of Mrs. Odboddy's package she carried to the President." Irving waved his gun toward Nanny.

Agnes added, "She had us all convinced she was just an abused, pathetic woman taking care of a sweet little girl. She's obviously a Nazi spy. And, to think I bought her lunch!"

Nanny glared at Agnes. "I'd have succeeded, too, if you hadn't stabbed me with your hatpin." She clutched her bleeding ankle.

Agnes snickered. "You're a pretty pitiful spy. You didn't even realize that I already delivered the package to the President this morning! By the way, it's a chopstick, not a hatpin."

Katherine pulled a scarf from her purse and wrapped it around Nanny's leg. "Here. This should stop the bleeding. Tell me what happened, Irving?"

"Agnes stabbed her with a hair thing." Irving nodded to Agnes, readjusting the chopstick in her bun. "I just finished the job."

"I should let Mrs. Roosevelt know what's going on out here." Edgar re-entered Mrs. Roosevelt's hotel room.

"We misjudged Irving, dear," Agnes said, brushing the wrinkles from her skirt. "Miss Twitch-It, was the real thief. Remember the night she climbed into my berth? I thought she was sleepwalking. She was after the package even then."

"Are you sure about all this? Is there any proof–?"

"*Huh!* If you'd been here five minutes ago when she held a gun to my head, you wouldn't need any more proof than that."

Mrs. Roosevelt opened her door and she and Agent Brown stepped into the hall. "Is everyone all right out here? Edgar tells us that you've caught a spy. Where did all the blood come from?"

Edgar followed her out the door. "I told you, ma'am, you don't need to get involved. Everything's under control. You shouldn't be here. Agent Brown, take her back inside."

"She's bleeding all over the rug, Edgar. What did you do? Shoot her?" Mrs. Roosevelt leaned toward Nanny.

Edgar sighed and rolled his eyes. "No. I did not shoot her. I believe she accidentally stumbled into Mrs. Odboddy's hairpin thing during a scuffle." He glanced toward Agnes and winked. "Let's just leave it at that."

Agnes threw back her shoulders, standing tall as a warrior on the home front should. She didn't need recognition or glory. It was reward enough, just serving her country.

Several guests approached from down the hall and gawked at the man holding a gun and the woman on the floor. Others promptly turned and hurried in the other direction.

Katherine propelled Mrs. Roosevelt back into her room, leaving the door ajar. "Come with me, *umm*...Eleanor. We'll call the police. Irving and Edgar can take care of this distraction." She picked up the phone and dialed the front desk. "This is Katherine Odboddy, calling from Mrs. Roosevelt's room. Please contact the local police and have them send a car over. There's been a shooting.

"No. Mrs. Roosevelt was not involved and there's no need to contact the newspapers. I'll notify the White House. Just send the police." She hung up the phone.

Mrs. Roosevelt went to the door. "Edgar, bring that young woman into my room. We can at least make her comfortable until the police arrive."

Edgar held up his hand. "I don't think so, ma'am. She can't be in your room. She's a foreign agent and just made an attempt on Mrs. Odboddy's life. There's no telling what she might do."

Katherine moved alongside Mrs. Roosevelt. "Here's a better idea. Take her into our room. We'll wait for the police there. There are bound to be newspaper reporters hanging around when the police show up. Mrs. Roosevelt's good name should not be mentioned."

Agnes rubbed her backside. "Excellent plan, Katherine. I'll call Room Service and have them send up some tea. I must admit, the episode has left me a bit shaken. Not to mention, a tad bruised where I fell on my bum."

"Okay, you. Get up from there." Irving dragged Nanny off the floor. She hopped into Agnes's room, muttering obscenities under her breath, still clutching her leg where blood trickled into her stockings and shoe.

Irving deposited her on the Agnes's couch.

"I'll get a towel for under her leg." Katherine scurried into the bathroom.

"Hold it," Agnes said. "Before *Mata Hari* gets any medical help from anyone, she needs to tell us where she left Madeline." She turned to Nanny. "Or, have you already delivered her to the Senator?"

Nanny sneered. "You stupid old cow. There isn't any senator. I made up that story so you wouldn't ask questions."

Katherine gasped. "You lied about her father being a senator? But, you took her to her father, didn't you?"

"She doesn't have a father…or a mother. I'm her legal guardian. She's my niece." Nanny's eyes lit up. "Maybe you should reconsider before you arrest me, *huh*? You wouldn't want to leave a little kid with nobody to take care of her, would you?" Her mouth twisted into a sneer.

Katherine and Agnes exchanged glances. The evil woman in league with Hitler was willing to commit murder to get the secret documents and could care less how her reprehensible deeds might affect the child in her care. If Nanny was charged and convicted, what would happen to Madeline?

A purpose swelled up in Agnes's chest as Madeline's sweet face crossed her mind. *Does God place opportunities in our path, or do we just see what we want to see and act according to our own wishes?* She glanced at Katherine, one eyebrow raised.

"Are you thinking what I'm thinking?" Katherine whispered.

"I have a feeling we might be on the same track," Agnes whispered back. "We have to give it some thought, though. Don't forget Mrs. Roosevelt's good will tour. We'll be gone for a month or so."

Katherine glared at Nanny and shook her arm. "Where is Madeline? Did you even consider what might happen to her if you got caught?"

"I didn't plan to get caught. I figured to catch the old lady alone and get the package and no one would be the wiser."

"Tell us where she is." Katherine gave Nanny's arm another shake.

"She's at a motel on the outskirts of town. What's it worth to you to know the address?" Nanny's face twisted in a grimace.

"Irving. Go outside and wait for the police. Katherine and I have a few things we want to discuss with Miss Twitch-It, and we don't need any witnesses." A chill crept into Agnes's cheeks.

Irving nodded and headed for the door. "If you're sure you can handle her. Don't do anything I wouldn't do, hear?" He wiggled his eyebrows, and opened the door into the hall.

"Now, my dear," Agnes grabbed Nanny's collar and brought it snug around her neck. "We're going to have a little chat." She tightened the collar.

Nanny reared back and gasped for air. "You can't do this. You're hurting me," she gurgled.

"Am I? Unfortunately, I have a tremor in this darned hand. Sometimes it just gets out of control. Now tell me, dear. Where is Madeline?" Agnes gave Nanny's collar a quick tug.

Nanny raised her hand and grasped Agnes's wrists.

Agnes tightened her collar.

"I'll tell," Nanny gasped. "Let me go."

Agnes loosened her grip. "Talk. Or, so help me…"

Nanny coughed and rubbed her neck. "I left her at—"

The door plunged open and two uniformed policeman rushed in with Irving. "Here's your suspect. She'll need some medical attention, but, I think you'll find her just full of information. The FBI will want to talk to her too, after she's processed for assaulting Mrs. Odboddy." Irving grabbed Nanny's arm and yanked the struggling woman off the sofa.

One of the officers pulled her arms behind her back and snapped handcuffs on her wrists. "Come along, sister."

Nanny limped toward the door. Seeing the blood dripping down her leg and her difficulty walking, the officer took her arm. "Maybe we should call an ambulance."

"I can walk. Just get me out of here." Nanny turned toward Agnes with a triumphant smirk. "This isn't over! I'll get you yet, you old hag! You'll see!"

"Wait, Officer!" Agnes hopped up from the sofa. "She's traveling with a child. She was just about to tell us where she left the girl. Where is she, Nanny?"

"Wouldn't you just like to know?" Nanny jerked her head toward the hallway, put her nose in the air and limped out the door.

"Wait!" Katherine's face paled. "She didn't tell us—"

"I'll go with them and see that she's properly booked, Mrs. Odboddy." Irving followed the second officer through the door. "I think you'll be fine without me now. I'll give you a call as soon as we've taken her statement. Don't worry. We'll find out where she left Madeline." He pulled the door closed behind him.

Chapter Thirty-Seven

What kind of malarkey is that girl thinking?

Agnes pinched a cinnamon toothpick between her teeth and tucked the monogrammed paper placemat from the nearby Chinese restaurant into her purse. "I love wonton soup, and that's the best I've tasted in a while, Katherine." She threw her purse onto the sofa and plopped down with a sigh. "Do you think Nanny will talk? Surely, she wouldn't abandon Madeline in a motel room without anyone to take care of her."

Katherine shrugged. "I'll call Room Service and have some tea and more of those delicious caramel cookies sent upstairs." She dialed the phone and gazed through the window while the phone rang. "Give Madeline some credit, Grandma. I don't think she'd wait too long before … Hello? Room Service? Would you please send up a pot of tea and a plate of cookies to room 501? Thanks."

"I know you're right, but, what if she can't contact anyone?" Agnes wrung her hands. "Maybe Nanny locked her in the bathroom."

"Oh, Grandma, now, you're being melodramatic. Why imagine the worst? After the police get through with her, surely she'll talk. Now that she's in custody, she's not so cold-blooded as to leave an innocent child to fend for herself. Irving will let us know as soon as they have any news."

Agnes sighed. "More likely, Nanny will use Madeline as a bargaining chip for a lesser charge. As if theft and attempted murder isn't enough, now she can add child abandonment to her offenses."

"Even if Nanny doesn't talk, I wouldn't be surprised if Madeline left the motel room. She'd be hungry and go looking for help before long." She sat down beside Agnes.

Agnes stood, crossed the room and stopped in front of the window. Traffic inched along the boulevard below. Across the street, a flag fluttered in the breeze. "If she has no other relatives, I expect she'll end up a ward of court—"

"Over my cold, dead body!" Katherine shoved herself off the sofa, her shoulders back. "Grandma, we have to do something. Do you think they'd let us take her? What's involved to become a foster parent?"

"Now, Katherine, I'm too old to raise a child. They'd never let me have her, and—"

"Well, I'm not."

Agnes turned from the window and stared at Katherine. "That wouldn't work. You don't have a home to bring her to. Our house only has two bedrooms. For that matter, she may have another relative or close friend that might take her in."

"If Nanny is associated with foreign agents, I can't think any court in the land would let one of *her associates* take her. She'd be better off with me."

"Now, Katherine. Be reasonable. You're a single woman. The courts won't let you—"

"Then I'll just have to get married. It's not as if I don't have any prospects, you know. Dr. Don has—"

"You never told me he proposed." Agnes leaned toward Katherine.

"Oh, he hasn't exactly proposed, but he would if I gave him the slightest hint that I'd accept. I've always said I wouldn't marry until after the war, but…I don't know. Maybe I would reconsider, if it meant I could keep Madeline."

Agnes crossed to the sofa, sat down, and put her hand on Katherine's arm. "You're not making good sense. That's not why you should enter into marriage. There's a big difference between getting married and having a baby and taking in a half-grown child, especially one from such a background. Madeline will come with an entire truckload of issues that you wouldn't even guess until it's too late."

Wouldn't you know it? Once again, Katherine's heart was getting in the way of her head. "This is just like you. Do you remember the time you brought home a baby squirrel and convinced me we should nurse it back to health? We had to feed it with an eye dropper. We kept it in a cardboard box in the kitchen for two and a half weeks."

"Yes. When it started to eat on its own, it bit my finger."

"And, we had to turn it loose in the park near an oak tree where it could make friends with the other squirrels."

Katherine turned down her lower lip in a pout. "So? She's not a squirrel. She's a child. That's got nothing to do with Madeline."

Agnes shook her head. "Doesn't it? Baby squirrels are one thing, but now you want to adopt a child you've barely spoken to a dozen times.

"What makes you think Dr. Don would agree to take in a ward of the court? I don't think you've completely thought this through." Most likely, Katherine was running on pure female hormones. She was over twenty-five, after all.

"When I tell him about Madeline, I'm sure he'll want her, too. He loves children."

"That may be, but, he might be inclined to want his own child, not an abused child."

Katherine turned away. "You don't know him like I do, Grandmother. You'll see. He'd do anything to make me happy."

"The question is, would it make him happy?"

Katherine didn't answer. Tears puddled in her eyes, spilled over and trickled down her cheeks. She hurried into the bathroom followed by sounds of sniffing and nose blowing. Several minutes later, she returned to the living room, tissue in hand, wiping her eyes. She lay on the sofa and pulled a pillow under her head.

"Now, Katherine, be reasonable. This is no time to make rash decisions, like getting married and taking on a ten-year-old child.

Really, there's no need to fuss about it today. We'll be with Mrs. Roosevelt somewhere in the Pacific Islands for the next month. We can think about it while we're gone and revisit the situation when we return. Everything will work out for the best. You'll see." Agnes patted Katherine's hand.

Agnes stood and headed for the bedroom. "We should see to our packing. Edgar will expect us to be ready when he comes in the morning. 4:30 A.M. comes awfully early."

Katherine dabbed her eyes. "I'm not so sure I want to go with Mrs. Roosevelt tomorrow. How can I go off and leave Madeline alone with all this unsettled?"

Agnes gasped. *What kind of malarkey is that girl thinking now?* She hurried back to the sofa.

Katherine sat, her arms crossed in defiance, glaring at her.

"That's just crazy, Katherine. You can't change your mind now, after Mrs. Roosevelt put out money for your train fare and hotel. We're supposed to leave in…" She glanced at her watch. "…less than ten hours. How can you even consider such a thing? "

"I can't help how I feel," Katherine whispered.

Agnes's head whipped toward the door at the sound of pounding. "Must be Room Service. My, that was quick, but they sure are insistent, aren't they?" She opened the door. "Yes?"

Two Washington police officers leaned forward. "Are you Agnes Agatha Odboddy?" One of the officers flashed a badge in her face.

"Yes. What's wrong?' A stitch of panic zigged through her chest. Had something happened to Madeline? Had Nanny escaped? Was the hotel on fire?

"We have a warrant for your arrest, Mrs. Odboddy. Get your coat. You're coming with us!"

Chapter Thirty-Eight

Where is a blasted policeman when you need one?

Agnes stared at her blackened fingertips. Over the innumerous hours since she was yanked from her hotel room, she'd been searched…oh, the indignity of it, even with a female officer… photographed with a placard strapped to her chest…most unbecomingly no doubt…and booked on charges somewhat unclear to her. A plainclothes detective finally showed her into an interrogation room.

"Sit down." The detective tossed down a file and sat across the table from her.

Agnes's head whirled. "What on earth do you think I've done? No one will tell me anything. I have rights, you know. I don't have time for this."

The detective laughed. "What's your hurry? You got some place you're supposed to be?" He chuckled.

"As a matter of fact, I'm supposed to be at the Washington National Airport in—" she scanned the clock over the mirrored wall. *3:25 A.M.* "…less than two hours. I'm going with…"

Should she tell the detective about her trip with Mrs. Roosevelt, or was it still considered top secret? Surely, by now, Katherine had notified Mrs. Roosevelt and any minute, she'd be sprung from the pokey.

But, would they get her out of jail in time? The military plane wouldn't wait. If Mrs. Roosevelt wanted to continue her tour, she would have to be on that flight whether Agnes was with her or not. What about Katherine? *Would she go or stay? I don't think she'd go and leave me in jail.*

The detective picked up the file, opened it and thumbed through the papers. He scratched his nose and read. "Let me see...*ah*...here it is. Interesting... It says here, your arrest was ordered by J. Edgar Hoover, himself. You're being charged with espionage for malicious destruction of government property in a time of war and endangering security along the California coastline." He glanced at Agnes and scowled. "Good heavens. In a time of war, too!"

He held up a clipping from the Newbury Times. "And here's collaborating proof. An article telling all about how you accepted responsibility for burning down a watch tower last summer while you were on duty. *Huh!* Don't know why they didn't arrest you back then. Oh, well! *Tch Tch.*" The detective tapped the file on the desk. "Espionage! Who would have thought? A nice old lady like you. Anything you want to add?"

Heat rose from Agnes's neck into her cheeks. "You don't understand. I did admit it at the time because... Well, I was vindicated later. It was supposed to look like I did it because..." She opened her purse and pulled out the old follow-up newspaper clipping explaining the truth behind the watchtower fire. What luck that she had tucked it into the sleeve in her purse. "Read this and then tell me if you think these charges are legitimate." She handed the detective the crumpled clipping.

She closed her eyes. *It doesn't make sense.* Why had they trumped up these charges now? Agnes looked toward the mirror. Who was back there watching? Like a flashbulb going off in a darkened room, she knew the answer! She glared at the mirrored wall.

Hoover would have known exactly why the government asked her to take responsibility for the watch tower fiasco last summer. Mrs. Roosevelt said he was adamantly opposed to her goodwill tour. He also would know that once Colonel Farthingworth was contacted in the morning, the bogus charges against Agnes would be dropped, but by then, the military transportation would be long gone. Maybe he thought Mrs. Roosevelt would cancel her extensive trip overseas if she didn't have a female companion. Maybe arresting Agnes was his way to throw a fly in the ointment of Mrs. Roosevelt's plans. What a devious, corrupt old scoundrel.

She shook her finger at the mirror. "You won't get away with this, you bully! I see you back there, Mr. Hoover. You don't scare me! Why didn't you show this flatfoot both of the newspaper articles?"

Agnes's heart sank. There wasn't much chance of getting the charges dropped in time to accompany Mrs. Roosevelt, now. Agnes glared again at the mirrored wall. "OK, bullet-head, you win this round."

The detective's gaze moved from the newspaper clipping to the mirror. "I see…" His cheeks turned rosy red. He ducked his head to peer intently at his wrist watch.

Agnes's thoughts flitted from Hoover to Nanny. Dealing with Nanny and Madeline was another kettle of fish. "Has the Mata Hari down the hall told you where she left her niece?"

"What? Who? What has she got to do with your charges?" He glanced back at the file. "Oh, I see. You're from the same town as that other woman they brought in. You're probably part of the same espionage cell. Maybe I should lock you and your buddy together." He jerked his head toward the holding cells. "I suppose you want a lawyer?"

"Not particularly. I expect my friends will be here soon to straighten all this out. You know as well as I do what's going on here." She glared at the mirror again and shouted. "If you're back there, Mr. Hoover, you know this is a crock of hogwash!" She turned back to the detective. "Let me talk to the other prisoner. I might get her to spill something about the child's location."

The detective scratched his head. "Well, I suppose I could put you in the cell next to her. We would like to find the missing child. We got an all-points-bulletin out, looking for her."

"Has she said anything at all about Madeline?"

"She won't admit to a thing. Just keeps yelling about how she's going to *take care* of the old biddy she blames for getting caught."

Agnes grinned. "That would be me. I'm the old biddy."

The detective chuckled. "I see. In that case, let's go. If you think you can get some information out of her, we'll give it a try."

The detective stood and opened the door. He walked beside Agnes as they traversed the cinder block corridor. The walls were covered with posters of wanted criminal. Agnes paused and studied their faces in case any of them should show up in Newbury.

Next came the posters with patriotic scenes advocating the purchase of war bonds, recommending the collection of papers and cans, and more brightly colored propaganda prints claiming, *Keep Calm and Carry On,* and *Uncle Sam Needs You.*

At the next corner, the detective guided her toward the cell block. The smell of urine and vomit permeated the air. Agnes drew in a quick breath and put her hand over her mouth.

"Sorry, Mrs. Odboddy. We had a couple drunks in here last night and the janitor called in sick today. It won't smell so bad where we're headed."

At the last cell block, the detective unlocked the door. "Here you go, right next to our other guest from California."

Nanny hunched on a cot in the next cell. She lifted her head as Agnes's cell door clanged shut. Nanny stood and limped up to the dividing bars between them. "What's the neighborhood coming to, when they'll let the likes of you move in?" She snorted and turned her back.

"Nothing to worry about, Nanny. A slight misunderstanding that I'm sure will be corrected long before you'll ever see the light of day. Why don't you help yourself and tell us where you left Madeline? It's just going to go harder on you if she comes to harm. Don't you care what happens to her? She's your niece."

"Not that it's any of your business, but she knows I might be a while. She's used to being alone. She'll be all right. My lawyer will have me out of here before she gets very hungry."

"That's where you're wrong, lady," the detective spoke up. "We've got you on attempted murder and evading arrest, just to name a few. We could add endangering a child if you don't tell us where you left Madeline. Oh, yes, I forgot to mention those pesky espionage charges, thanks to the testimony of your pal, Buzz, the kid in Colonel Farthingworth's office back in Newbury."

The color drained from Nanny's face. "You've got Buzz? I never did trust that little weasel." She pounded the bar with her fist. "What's he saying about me? It's all lies!"

Agnes snorted. "Lies? Of course you'd say that."

The detective locked Agnes's cell door and put the key in his pocket. "Buzz is just an innocent kid. We figure you took up with him when he got assigned to Colonel Farthingworth's office. He admits telling you about the Colonel's conversation with Mrs. Odboddy, which he shouldn't have done. You must have figured the package contained important papers. You used the child as your cover story to take the train and try to steal the package."

Nanny put up her nose. "Lies! All lies."

The detective continued. "The FBI is onto you. They'll be along soon to collect you. They know you're part of an underground cell in Newbury, trying to undermine the war effort. It won't be long and your whole gang will be in custody."

"Ha! You, and what army?" Nanny sneered.

Agnes moved toward her cell door and called to the detective. "If they knew about Nanny's plans to steal the package, why didn't the FBI arrest her on the train before we got to Washington?"

"They tried. She gave them the slip in Albuquerque. Apparently she and the kid left the train. How she got from there to Washington is a mystery." He grinned at Nanny. "Care to enlighten us?"

Nanny smirked. "Because a Third Reich agent is trained in hand to hand combat as well as how to evade capture. I suspected they were onto me when I saw the coppers question Katherine and Madeline at Albuquerque. So we got off the train and I stole a car. We drove from there to Washington. You'd never have caught me if—"

Wouldn't you know, the FBI couldn't track down a Nazi spy but they sure threw me in the hoosegow quick enough. Agnes looked up at the sound of voices coming down the hall.

"Grandmother! Are you all right?" Katherine's voice echoed against the cinder block walls. She rushed up to the cell, gripping Madeline's hand.

"You found her! What happened?" Agnes reached through the bars and touched the *lost sheep's* arm. Are you okay, sweetheart?"

Madeline started to answer but seeing Nanny in the next cell, she cringed and moved behind Katherine.

"There, there, don't worry. I shouldn't have brought her back here, Grandma. We'll wait up front. Irving is arranging your bail. I just wanted you to know we were here."

"It feels like I've been here forever. What took you so long?"

"I've done my best. These things take time. As soon as the officers left the hotel with you, I contacted Irving and he alerted the White House. Mrs. Roosevelt found a judge and talked him into giving us a release warrant. It wasn't easy, since Hoover authorized your arrest." She glanced at her watch and frowned. "It's almost 3:30 A.M. I'm afraid it's too late to make the plane now. Mrs. Roosevelt will have to make the trip without us. I'm sorry, Grandma."

"I'd pretty much given up on that now. Tell me how you found Madeline."

"She went to the motel manager. He called the police and they sent a patrol car to pick her up. They were bringing her into the station just now when Irving and I got here. She saw me and came running. Since she knew me, they let her come with me. " She glanced down at the child's sweet face.

Madeline's lips trembled and tears puddled in her eyes. "You won't let them take me away, will you, Katherine?"

Katherine knelt and hugged Madeline. "Don't worry, honey. Grandma and are going to bring you home with us." She looked up at

Agnes. "Irving convinced the police it was in Madeline's best interest to return to her school and friends in Newbury. They've placed her in our temporary custody pending a hearing in Newbury next week."

"Let go of Madeline this instant!" Nanny shrieked and reached her fingers through the bars, her face screwed up with rage. "You're not taking Madeline home with you now or ever. I'll see you dead before I let you have her."

"Really, Nanny!" Agnes said. "There's no need for such dramatics. The child needs a responsible adult to care for her and you said she had no parents. I'd think you'd be glad that—"

Nanny cursed and kicked the bars. "Never! You can't have her." She grabbed the thin pillow, yanked it off the cot and ripped it apart at the seams. She screamed obscenities and threw fistfuls of cotton batting at the bars, stamped her feet and then flung her body at the cell door. "You'll be sorry you ever set foot on that train! I know people who can make you disappear! You won't live a week if you take that child back to Newbury." Nanny tore at her hair, screeching, and then dropped to the floor. Her whole body shook with convulsions and then she lay still. Blood trickled from her lips.

Agnes stood frozen, watching in horror as Nanny twitched and jerked. Had she bit her tongue? Was she dying?

"Get the child away from here, now!" The detective shoved Katherine toward the front office. He raced to a wall phone and punched a button. "Send a medical team down here. Number 428 is having a stroke!"

He hung up the phone, rushed to Nanny's cell and unlocked the door. As he knelt over her inert body and started CPR, she suddenly reached up, wrapped her arm around his neck and squeezed. He clutched at her arm, kicked his legs and gurgled. She squeezed tighter.

The air in the cell block seemed to chill as Agnes stood aghast, unable to lift a finger to help the struggling officer in the next cell. "Stop! Nanny! You're killing him! Help! Someone! Get in here!" Agnes backed away from the cell door. If Nanny killed the man, would she take his keys and come after Agnes next? Or would she head for the lobby and go after Katherine?

Within seconds, the officer's thrashing ceased as Nanny squeezed the breath from him. Time stood still as Nanny gave the detective's neck a final squeeze and dropped him to the floor where he lay motionless. Was he dead, or hopefully, just unconscious?

Nanny dashed from her cell. She paused in front of Agnes's door, her face ashen and her hair hanging in wet tendrils around her face. Shaking with fury, she wiped the blood from her mouth and pointed a bony finger at Agnes. Her words clung in the air like bats in a wet cave. "I don't have time right now, sister, but mark my words…if you take Madeline, one day I'm coming for you. We have a score to settle."

Agnes screamed, "Unlock this door, you maniac! No time like the present!" She clutched the bars and shook them, as though her fury could break through the steel and let her at the crazed woman. Perspiration beaded on the back of her neck, like drops of cold water trailing down an icy glass. "Someone! Help!" She screamed. *Where is a blasted policeman when you need one?*

Nanny turned and raced down the corridor toward the back of the police station. The outside door crashed open and then slammed shut.

The woman was insane and now she had escaped and was out in the street! But, how far could she get in a strange city with no money and no resources?

Shouts echoed down the hall as three uniformed officers dashed up, weapons drawn. A man in a white jacket came from the opposite direction, tore into Nanny's cell and knelt over the incapacitated detective. His fingers searched for a pulse. "He's still alive, but just barely! You!" He pointed to the closest officer. "Help me get him to the infirmary."

Jumbled shouts echoed through the corridor as the officers scattered, each to his assigned mission, in search of the escaped prisoner. Two officers opened doors and scanned the empty cells. "Which way did she go?"

Agnes pointed and one officer plunged down the hall toward the outer door. He was so close behind her, how could she possibly get away?

"What happened here?"

Agnes's gaze moved from the pursuing officer at the back door to the commanding figure standing in front of her cell, his face pale and drawn.

Irving!

"What kind of police department is this?" Heads turned toward Irving's thundering voice. "You've just let a Nazi agent slip through your fingers." He glanced at Agnes and raised an eyebrow. "Mrs. Odboddy? What happened?"

"She went bonkers when we said Madeline was going home with us. Then she seemed to have a convulsion and...I guess she was playing possum...but it worked. The detective went in to help and she overpowered him. Then she took off out the back door."

"Where does she think she can go with the police six steps behind her?"

"Other than giving a synopsis of my impending murder next time we meet, she didn't leave any details. When are you getting me out of here, Irving? The hospitality around here is wearing terribly thin."

"Working on it, Agnes." He nodded to the guard with the key. "Open this door. This lady is ready to leave."

Agnes gazed down the empty corridor where last she'd seen Katherine and Madeline. *At least they were safe in the outer office. My girls! Bless their hearts.*

Maybe they'd add another bedroom to the back of the house for Madeline, or maybe Dr. Don would jump at the chance to marry Katherine, even with a ready-made family. In any event, Agnes would not spend three seconds worrying about the possibility of Nanny or her friends causing trouble. The Washington police and the FBI were hot on her trail. Surely, within hours, or days at the most, they would apprehend Nanny and check her into Leavenworth for an extended stay. Her threats would become an unpleasant memory. *Admittedly, the sooner Katherine and I get out of Washington with Madeline, the better I'll feel.*

Wait! Wasn't it odd that in spite of their lack of adequate housing or a married couple to foster Madeline, the FBI had so readily agreed to release her into their custody? Even on the heels of Nanny's murderous attack and her threats back at the hotel? *Is it another hastily contrived plan to use me as bait?* Was there more to this than she had figured? Perhaps it was the FBI who contrived the plan for her to carry the President's package, hoping to draw out the Newbury spy ring connected with Colonel Farthingworth's office. It hadn't worked out quite as they had planned, had it? But, if Nanny should come after them now, because of Madeline, it would give the FBI another crack at breaking the Newbury espionage ring.

Agnes shook her head. *There I go again, letting my imagination run away with me. I've watched way too many Ellery Queen movies. The FBI wouldn't put my life at risk, not to mention Katherine's and Madeline's, just to catch a Nazi spy ring. They wouldn't do that... would they...?*

About The Author

Elaine Faber is a member of Sisters in Crime, Inspire Christian Writers, and Cat Writers Association. She lives in Northern California with her husband and three housecats. She volunteers at the American Cancer Society Discovery Shop in Elk Grove, CA.

Elaine has written poetry and short stories since childhood. She has completed six novels. Multiple short stories are published in magazines, on-line weekly magazines and in thirteen short story collections (anthologies). She writes cozy mysteries and humorous mysteries.

Black Cat Mysteries: The three Black Cat Mysteries noted below, feature Thumper, (Black Cat). With the aid of his ancestors' memories, he helps solve mysteries and crimes.

Mrs. Odboddy Mystery/Adventures: Elderly, eccentric Mrs. Odboddy fights WWII from the home front. She believes war-time conspiracies and spies abound in her home town, and as a self-appointed hometown warrior, she must root out and expose malcontents, dissidents and Nazi spies.

(Books) Amazon in print and e-book ($3.99)

Black Cat's Legacy ~ http://tinyurl.com/lrvevgm
Black Cat and the Lethal Lawyer ~ http://tinyurl.com/q3qrgyu
Black Cat and the Accidental Angel ~ http://tinyurl.com/07scsm2
Mrs. Odboddy – Hometown Patriot ~ http://tinyurl.com/hdbvzsv
Mrs. Odboddy – Undercover Courier
Mrs. Odboddy – And Then There Was a Tiger ~ (Coming Soon)

Elaine's Website ~ http://www.mindcandymysteries.com

Email your questions or comments to:
Elaine.Faber@mindcandymysteries.com.

Amazon reviews are welcomed.

Also by Elaine Faber

Mrs. Odboddy: Hometown Patriot

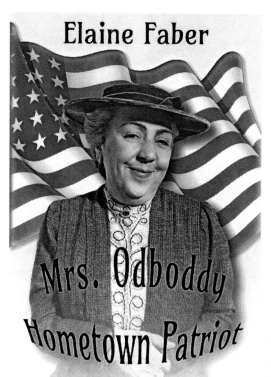

Elaine Faber

Mrs. Odboddy Hometown Patriot

A WWII tale of chicks and chicanery, suspicion and spies.

Since the onset of WWII, Agnes Agatha Odboddy, hometown patriot and self-appointed scourge of the underworld, suspects conspiracies around every corner…stolen ration books, German spies running amuck, and a possible Japanese invasion off the California coast. This seventy-year-old, model citizen would set the world aright if she could get Chief Waddlemucker to pay attention to the town's nefarious deeds on any given Meatless Monday.

Mrs. Odboddy vows to bring the villains, both foreign and domestic, to justice, all while keeping chickens in her bathroom, working at the Ration Stamp Office, and knitting argyles for the boys on the front lines.

Imagine the chaos when Agnes's long-lost WWI lover returns, hoping to find a million dollars in missing Hawaiian money and rekindle their ancient romance. In the thrilling conclusion, Agnes's predictions become all too real when Mrs. Roosevelt unexpectedly comes to town to attend a funeral and Agnes must prove that she is, indeed, a warrior on the home front.

Black Cat's Legacy

Elaine Faber

Black Cat's Legacy

A tale of intrigue and murder with a touch of whimsy.

Thumper, the resident Fern Lake black cat, knows where the bodies are buried and it's up to Kimberlee to decode the clues.

Kimberlee's arrival at the Fern Lake lodge triggers the Black Cat's Legacy. With the aid of his ancestors' memories, it's Thumper's duty to guide Kimberlee to clues that can help solve her father's cold case murder. She joins forces with a local homicide detective and an author, also researching the murder for his next thriller novel. As the investigation ensues, Kimberlee learns more than she wants to know about her father. The murder suspects multiply, some dead and some still very much alive, but someone at the lodge will stop at nothing to hide the Fern Lake mysteries.

Black Cat and the Lethal Lawyer

With the promise to name a beneficiary to her multi-million dollar horse ranch, Kimberlee's grandmother entices her and her family to Texas. But things are not as they appear and Thumper, the black cat with superior intellect, uncovers the appalling reason for the invitation. Kimberlee and Brett discover a fake Children's Benefit Program and the possible false identity of the stable master. To make matters worse, Thumper overhears a murder plot, and he and his newly found soul-mate,

Noe-Noe, must do battle with a killer to save Grandmother's life.

The further Kimberlee and her family delve into things, the deeper they are thrust into a web of embezzlement, greed, vicious lies and murder. With the aid of his ancestors' memories, Thumper unravels some dark mysteries. Is it best to reveal the past or should some secrets never be told?

Elaine Faber

Black Cat
and the
Lethal Lawyer

A tale of betrayal and greed with a splash of fantasy.

Black Cat and the Accidental Angel

Elaine Faber

Black Cat
and the
Accidental Angel

A tale of memories lost and love found with a touch of the divine.

When the family SUV flips and Kimberlee is rushed to the hospital, Black Cat (Thumper) and his soulmate are left behind. Black Cat loses all memory of his former life and the identity of the lovely feline companion by his side. "Call me Angel. I'm here to take care of you." Her words set them on a long journey toward home, and life brings them face to face with episodes of joy and sorrow.

The two cats are taken in by John and his young daughter, Cindy, facing foreclosure of the family vineyard and emu farm. In addition, someone is playing increasingly dangerous pranks that threaten Cindy's safety. Angel makes it her mission to help their new family. She puts her life at risk to protect the child, and Black Cat learns there are more important things than knowing your real name.

Elaine Faber's e-books are available on Amazon for $3.99. Print books. $16.00.

Coming Soon:
Mrs. Odboddy: And Then There Was a Tiger

OH, RATS TUESDAY—

W hat in tarnation is all that mess on the front porch?" Agnes flipped the key on her 1930 Model A Ford, pulled the hand brake, and opened the door. She jammed her silver chopsticks more firmly into the back of her hennaed hair and stepped out of the car.

Shreds of brown paper skittered across the lawn. Upon further scrutiny, clumps of string lay amidst more shredded paper on the porch. The tattered remnants of a shoe box leaned against the pillar beside the front step. Agnes leaned down and picked up the shreds of paper, cardboard and string. Her frown deepened. "What on earth…"

Agnes stared at the big bold letters scribbled across the middle of the brown wrapping paper. *Agnes Agatha Odboddy.* She turned the shoe box right side up. Her nose wrinkled as an unpleasant odor drifted up from inside.

She marched up the steps with the box and stopped short. "Jumping Jehoshaphat! Did Katherine neglect to lock the front door when she left this morning with Maddie?"

Her stomach churned as she pushed open the front door, peeked inside, and sucked in her breath. Pillows–askew on the sofa. Coffee table magazines lay scattered across the rug. Shards of her grandmother's Depression glass vase were strewn on the hearth. One of the living room drapes hung at a cock-eyed angle.

"Oh, my stars! We've been burgled!" She rushed through the living room and into the kitchen. A similar sight met her gaze. Breakfast coffee puddled in the middle of the table. A shattered cup in the sink. A kitchen chair, sideways on the linoleum floor!

Crash!

Agnes turned at a skittering sound coming from the back bedroom! Her fingers tingled. *Someone's still here, probably ransacking my jewelry box.* Should she call the police or run back out the front door? *Agnes Odboddy? Run from trouble? Not on your tintype!* She grabbed a rolling pin from the drawer, the weapon of choice for a woman of her advanced age. As the self-appointed scourge of the underworld, she'd sneak up on the thief, crack him over the head and bring him to his cowardly knees. Before she had taken three steps toward the scuffle, a small, brown critter with a spindly tail barreled down the hall. Agnes jumped back and screamed.

Right behind the intruder, Ling-Ling, her cross-eyed Siamese cat, tore into the living room, a feline pest eradicator in camo-gray. The furry culprit scrambled up the flowered drapes to the top of the curtain rod.

Merciful Heavens! A measly rodent! Agnes sent the rolling pin flying. It hit the wall and clattered to the floor, barely missing the front window.

Rowwwh! Ling-Ling shrieked and leaped toward the drapes, knocking the end table lamp to the floor. *Thud!* The fringed shade spun off the lamp and rolled toward the front door.

"Ling-Ling! Bad girl! No! No…!" Agnes shook her finger. "What am I saying? Go get her, girl. Kill the sucker!"

Ling-Ling clawed her way up the curtain. Down came the rod with a crash as the rat raced out the front door, the cat three leaps behind.

Agnes stepped out onto the porch and put her hand to her eyes in time to see the pair racing up the street toward The First Church of the Evening Star and Everlasting Light. She checked her watch. *Yep, folks should just about be arriving for the afternoon prayer meeting. That'll give them something to talk about.* She smiled and stepped back into the house to assess the damage.

Her heart thumped as she stared at the destruction. How exactly did this happen?

What unknown scoundrel hated her enough to leave a rat-filled box on the porch? She shuddered. *Best not dwell on that question. The list is way too long.*

Ling-Ling must have come upon the package and smelled the rodent. Agnes could almost see her determined, Siamese killing machine, biting, scratching and kicking the box until she had shredded a hole big enough for the rat to escape. She shuddered at the thought.

Roddy Rodent must have dashed through the open door into the house. *Am I getting senile? Did I leave the front door wide open when I left this morning?*

Ling-Ling would have chased the rat with a vengeance and murder in her blue crossed eyes. Perhaps misguided conceit and a too many naps in a sun puddle had tainted her calculations. The result was a successful escape on the part of the rat and a living room and kitchen that looked like a hand grenade had exploded in there. No telling how the bedrooms would have suffered if Agnes hadn't returned just at that moment.

What if Ling-Ling hadn't taken matters into her own paws when she came upon the box? *I would have cut the string and opened the box addressed to me.* Would the terrified rat have leaped out into her face? Was that the sender's intention?

CPSIA information can be obtained
at www.ICGtesting.com
Printed in the USA
FSOW01n0014050217
30339FS

9 781940 781167